T0283720

'A staggering re-creation of an Australian history too few of us know, and a heart-bruising testament of resilience and love. You'll be gripped – and moved – from the first page.' BENJAMIN LAW

'Riwoe's novel explores race, language, privilege, class, exile and identity, while the storytelling is done with lyric sensitivity and feminist sharpness ... reading the book feels transcendental.' JESSIE TU, *WOMEN'S AGENDA*

'This book is a triumph. An eloquent and moving reminder of a half-forgotten history, the casual cruelties of colonisation and exile, the tenderness of connection. Beautifully observed.' KRISTINA OLSSON

'In *Stone Sky Gold Mountain*, Mirandi Riwoe has resurrected a lost world and woven a tale unlike any I have read before. I recognise this place – the smells, the flora, the fauna – but it has been crafted anew, in rich and glorious detail. Just as she did in *The Fish Girl*, Riwoe forces us to change our long-held focus, and the result is one of revelation. Every Australian, indeed everyone, should read this groundbreaking book.' MELANIE CHENG

'Beautiful and true. Broke open an all-too-forgotten history of Australia I needed to know about. Then it broke open my heart.' TRENT DALTON

Mirandi Riwoe is the author of the novella *The Fish Girl* and *Stone Sky Gold Mountain*, which won the 2020 Queensland Literary Award – Fiction Book Award and the inaugural ARA Historical Novel Prize, and was shortlisted for the 2021 Stella Prize and longlisted for the 2021 Miles Franklin Literary Award. Her work has appeared in *Best Australian Stories, Meanjin, Review of Australian Fiction, Griffith Review* and *Best Summer Stories*. Mirandi has a PhD in Creative Writing and Literary Studies and lives in Brisbane.

The
Burnished
Sun

Mirandi Riwoe

First published 2022 by University of Queensland Press
PO Box 6042, St Lucia, Queensland 4067 Australia

University of Queensland Press (UQP) acknowledges the Traditional Owners and their
custodianship of the lands on which UQP operates. We pay our respects to their Ancestors
and their descendants, who continue cultural and spiritual connections to Country.
We recognise their valuable contributions to Australian and global society.

uqp.com.au
reception@uqp.com.au

Grateful acknowledgement is made for permission to quote the extracts on
pages 197, 219, 247 and 261. © Somerset Maugham Estate.

Cover design by Alissa Dinallo
Cover painting *Post-Gauguin* by W. H. Chong
Author photograph by Red Boots Photographic
Typeset in 12/17 pt Bembo Std by Post Pre-press Group, Brisbane
Printed in Australia by McPherson's Printing Group

 University of Queensland Press is supported by the
Queensland Government through Arts Queensland.

  University of Queensland Press is assisted by the
Australian Government through the Australia Council,
its arts funding and advisory body.

A catalogue record for this book is available from the National Library of Australia.

ISBN 978 0 7022 6567 9 (pbk)
ISBN 978 0 7022 6676 8 (epdf)
ISBN 978 0 7022 6677 5 (epub)
ISBN 978 0 7022 6678 2 (kindle)

University of Queensland Press uses papers that are natural, renewable and recyclable products
made from wood grown in well-managed forests and other controlled sources. The logging and
manufacturing processes conform to the environmental regulations of the country of origin.

For Laura

Mislike me not for my complexion,
The shadow'd livery of the burnish'd sun.

The Prince of Morocco
The Merchant of Venice, Act 2, Scene 1
William Shakespeare

Contents

Annah the Javanese

One

ANNAH PINCHES HER COLD FINGERS together as the carriage trundles across the bridge. She shivers, gazing out on the wet night. Light, from cafés and bobbing boats, dapples the Seine, the silhouette of tall buildings a stain against the grey sky. The flare of the moon shimmers across the drift of black water, taking her back to another place, where the warm sea licks the sandy coastline. Squeezing her eyes shut, she wishes to be cradled in the ocean's embrace again. Concentrates on remembering the hot grit of sand between her toes, the salt air taut across her skin. Anything to settle the panic that rises through her body.

'Not far to go now,' Monsieur Vollard murmurs next to her.

Annah tries to make out Madame Pack, seated across from her. But the woman is swathed in shadow and veils of lace. Annah can't quite believe Madame Pack is giving her away. That she will no longer be in the woman's service. But the linen pillowcase is bundled in her lap, filled with her belongings – one comb and an old shawl of Madame Pack's – belying her hopes.

The carriage continues along roads that become increasingly unfamiliar. By the light of the street lamps, Annah takes in the sales booths that line the gutters: dog clippers, travelling dentists, crepe makers. A bicycle slicks past, its thin wheels leaving a snail trail in the drenched road.

When the horses slow and Vollard says, 'Here we are,' Annah's composure dissolves altogether.

She grips the ledge beneath the window until she can feel her fingernails buckle. 'Please, no.' Her lips are numb.

'Come, Annah. It will be all right. My friend is a very fine fellow.'

He opens the door and turns to help her alight, but she resists, cowering into the furthest corner, kicking her small boots at him. His arm circles her waist and he hauls her from the carriage.

Annah tries to snatch at Madame Pack's hand. 'Don't leave me.'

Madame Pack leans back and tugs the black glove from her hand, finger by finger, as though it is now contaminated. Her jet beads glimmer by the light of the street lamp, her kohl-rimmed eyes look away.

'*Pardon*, Madame. I am sorry. *Maaf*,' Annah begs, desperately trying each form of the word that she knows.

Vollard holds the girl by the shoulders so that she can't give chase as the horses pull the coach onto the road, disappearing into the night. Annah wants to wail, double over and roar with fear, but a boy, smut smeared across his face, stops to stare. Two gentlemen, dressed in evening greatcoats and glistening silk top hats, frown at her, look enquiringly at Vollard.

'This way, my dear,' he says, propelling her towards a building dark with grime. Long timber shutters close in the windows of the first floor and the number six is inked onto the wall.

When Vollard knocks, a woman opens the door, her pale

features skewed by the light of a flickering candle. Vollard
explains their presence and she nods, stepping back for them to
pass through. Annah pauses when they step over the threshold,
held at bay by the damp pong of cabbage and mould. So different
from the scent of peonies and spice at Madame Pack's. Too similar
to the room Annah was locked in before that.

'Come, my dear,' says Vollard. 'Everything will be fine.'

As they climb the stairs, the woman returns to her rooms,
closing herself and her candle away. Annah trips on a step, her
eyes unable to adjust to the sudden gloom. It's as though they
wade through pitch and Vollard only releases his grip on her arm
when they reach the landing.

A man wrenches open a door. He's as tall as a bear, a dark
silhouette against the red glow of the room. He holds his hands
out and pulls Vollard into a short, hearty embrace.

'Vollard, you scoundrel. Come in. What have you here?'

'I've brought you that girl I told you about. From Nina Pack.'

The room is dimly lit by one lamp, its scarlet shade frilled
and flimsy like the flounce of a lady's hemline. The man stoops
to light three candles on a saucer, and by the flare of the match
Annah sees that his largish nose is ruddy, covered in a web of
veins. He wears a fez low over his hair, the lamplight lending the
dark wool a rouge tinge. A kerchief with crimson pinstripes peeps
from his shirt pocket.

'No beer? Not a scrap of food for this poor, starving artist?'
The man's laugh is a bark. 'Not to worry. Maurice brought me a
bottle of claret last night. We will finish it off.'

Vollard gestures for Annah to step forward. 'This is Annah.
I thought she might model for you.' He tugs her bag from her
grasp and places it on a chair.

The tall man stands in front of her, rests one arm across his waist, brings the other upwards so his chin rests on his hand as he contemplates her. Her heart shudders against her ribs, making her feel queasy. She stares into the shadows beyond the candles. Tries not to feel his eyes creep across her skin. She should be used to this sort of scrutiny by now. She has learned to pretend she doesn't notice. Doesn't care.

'Quite lovely. She's Malay, did you say?'

'Something like that, I should think. Nina told a fat banker friend of hers that she wanted a Negro girl, and not three months later a policeman brought this girl to her. Found her wandering about Gare de Lyon, with a sign hanging around her neck giving directions to Nina's address. And her French is quite good,' says Vollard. 'Nina did warn me that she might be a trifle stubborn, though.'

'Fascinating. And where are you from, Annah? Before you were with Madame Pack?'

Annah thinks of the grey room on Rue de Clichy, where she spent so many months. But she knows he doesn't mean that. He wants to know where she was born, from where she has travelled. Annah repeats what she was schooled to say to Madame Pack's guests. '*Envoi de Java.*' What was written on the sign that hung about her neck.

'Ah. How exotic. That is almost perfect. I think she'll do quite nicely, Vollard.' The tall man puts his hand out for her to shake. 'You can call me Paul.'

Her eyes flick to his, back to the shadows.

'His name is Paul, Annah. Be a good girl, now. Say Paul,' says Vollard.

'Pol.'

'Paul,' he repeats, pulling a chair out from the table.

She pronounces his name once more but doesn't try too hard.

The tall man shrugs. 'It is of no consequence, Vollard. Pol it will be.' He takes a seat by the other. 'And she will bed here?'

'That would be best. I have nowhere else for her to go.'

Pol pours two glasses of wine. He complains of the rent he must pay for the apartment, of the poor furnishings the owner has supplied him with. He takes to his feet and fetches some cheese from a cabinet, slides it onto a plate next to a hunk of bread.

'Nina said Annah's not so good at housekeeping, I'm afraid. But try what you can with her, Paul.'

'Well, I won't starve her, but I can't afford to pay her. I am still waiting on Theo to give me money for the paintings he has from me. I cannot even afford any studio space. I must work here for the moment,' he says, the sweep of his arm taking in an easel and canvases. 'How am I to feed myself, warm these rooms, if I have not even a few francs?'

It is indeed very cold in the apartment. The chill from the timber floor seems to seep through the thin soles of Annah's shoes, spreading across her feet, snaking up her shins. She shuffles from one foot to the other. The grate is black, barren, one charred piece of wood lying in the ash. She doesn't know what that man Pol might be saving it for, but she wishes he'd light it.

Pol refills their glasses, then leads Vollard across the room to look at three paintings stacked against the far wall. Pol's voice is loud, demanding of attention, and Vollard nods, murmurs in agreement when he can. They have forgotten her. A draught rattles the shutters, tickles the hair at the nape of her neck, and she decides she might retire to the sofa at the end of the room, curl in on herself before her flesh turns to marble.

Just as she slips off her shoes to huddle her feet beneath her skirt, the men return to the table. Pol scrapes mould from the corner of the cheese. He tears off a piece of bread and shoves it in his mouth. Vollard finds an earthenware cup in which he pours some of the claret. He walks across the room, hands it to her, and he's barely turned away before she gulps it down, familiar with – desperate for – the mellowing warmth that follows.

Her eyes dart around the room, so dreary compared to Madame Pack's. The ceilings of the apartment are high, and almost every inch of wainscoting is covered with pictures – a gilt-framed portrait of a simpering lady, her bosom as pale and plump as a lychee; a large landscape featuring a grove of trees; two rows of miniatures neatly framed in lacquered timber. The rest of the paintings are obscured by the shadows that lie beyond the lamplight's glow.

The cabinets are plain, made from dark timber, nothing like the elegant pieces to be found in Madame Pack's drawing room. The side table next to her is covered in a confusing array of objects – a statue of a nude lady, a baby's shoe, an orange, something that looks like a cake knife, a shard of porcelain. All the chairs in the room are mismatched; Annah can see where straw escapes beneath the seat of one. Is this now to be her home? For how long?

She watches Pol. His cheeks are flushed, the red wine wets his lips, and his mouth is as dark as chicken liver gleaming past his brush moustache. Annah pulls her feet in closer, their chill almost painful where they rest against her thighs. She kneads them with her hands through the fabric of her dress. Her breathing is short and pressure builds in her head, tightens a band about her temples. She wants to press her hands to her skull, rock and keen like the older women do in her village when they mourn a dead relative. Except Annah is the one who is dead. She is the one who is lost.

She knows why she's been banished to this man's rooms. Madame Pack told Vollard that this is Annah's punishment for smashing Madame's pretty vase after she was slapped for being too slow fetching Madame's shawl, and also for when Annah hurled a teacup at cook's head when the old crone wouldn't give her any supper. But Annah thinks that perhaps Madame has really sent her away because she caught her special friend Octave with his arm about Annah's waist late one night on his way to Madame's boudoir.

Vollard throws back the rest of his wine. Soon he will be gone. He was always so kind to her when he visited Madame Pack that Annah was relieved when he came to fetch her away. But it seems it was only so he could leave her here, with this stranger – this bear of a man who crackles and spits like a forest fire, aflame with talk of his work, increasingly ablaze with each drink.

Annah's hand trembles as she fidgets with the bric-à-brac on the side table next to her. She is alone, waning from the world she knows. She misses emerald mountains, yellow butterflies, the seashells of her island. Does her aunt wonder about her as she bags cloves for the pallid merchants? Are her cousins awaiting her return?

Annah's fingertip traces the sharp point of the porcelain shard. She cups the fragment in her palm, clenches her fist tight. Squeezes until the pain burns, is a shrill high note, welcome because it cuts out, smothers, all other feeling. Her heartbeat slows, the men's voices fade. When her fingers unfurl, the shard lies in her hand intact, but it's left its imprint – a long crease, a smudge of ruched skin and blood. She stares at the small wound, concentrates on the hot sting of it, wills all the pain in her body to gather there. She drops the porcelain to the table and lifts the nude statue, so dusty it feels as though the lady's pale, cool skin has been coated in powder. She glances from it to the men at the table. Her tongue clamped between her lips, she wonders if she flings the statue through the window, or she kicks in one of those canvases, or even knocks over the candles so that the room becomes engulfed in flames, maybe Vollard will take her back with him.

Her fingers curl more tightly about the statue's body.

But perhaps Vollard will be disgusted with her. He might leave her on the street; return her to Gare de Lyon to wander by herself, a new sign about her neck. Or he might take her to another stranger – somebody worse than this man. Annah eyes Pol. He has returned to his cabinet and brought out a half bottle of something – whisky perhaps, or rum. He seems cheerful enough. She thinks that perhaps she can bear him, that she will have to bear him. Her grip on the statue loosens.

When Vollard does eventually stand to take his leave, Annah refuses to look his way, or say goodbye. As the door closes on him, her chest aches; she has to bite her tongue to stop from crying out. She remains tucked in the corner of the sofa. Only her dark eyes move, watching Pol dunk glasses in a basin and shelve the whisky bottle.

When he approaches, she draws back into herself, wishing she were one of those little crabs that can disappear into their spiralling shell, but all he does is place a candle on the side table next to her, drop a blanket into her lap. He douses the lamp and takes one of the remaining candles with him into the other room.

She listens to the splash of water, the rustle of clothing, the bed's creak. Only when she hears his heavy, even breathing does she straighten out her cramped legs. Shuffling down onto her back, she realises the sofa is a few inches too short for her, so she turns onto her side. But she can't relax. Her muscles remain tense, her bladder is full. She stares out the window through the space left by three broken shutters. She takes in the rickety roof tiles of the house across the road and the skeletal branches of the lone elm tree shuddering against the wind. When she angles her head further left, she can see the full moon, darkly hidden behind blood-red mist.

Two

Light glints across her skin, metallic almost. It doesn't have the warmth of the orange sun that flows through the open doorways in the village *manise* that is so far from this place – so far that its light is starting to fade for Annah. But she has seen that radiance here, too, in this *ville lumière*, on those rare hot days, dazzling days that make the people wilt, hide behind baking walls. That's when she likes to walk the boulevards, surrender her face to the bright sky, feel the heat burnish the dark skin of her cheeks, her forehead, the tips of her ears.

Five nights Annah has spent on the sofa, hunched on her side. Three of those evenings Pol stayed up painting until the candles guttered: a portrait of himself for which he dons a wide-brimmed hat and peers into a spotty mirror on the wall. When she peeked at it that first morning, he muttered, 'I have to paint myself. This is what I am reduced to, girl.' Those nights she fell asleep listening to him hum as his paintbrush swished across canvas. During the day she watches him sketch or play the harmonium in the corner of the room, or she sits by the window and looks down on the street. She avoids catching his beetle gaze when he stares at her for minutes at a time. Each morning he has her sweep the floors, and it seems that every two hours he demands another cup of watery chocolate. The smell of acrid oils, burning wax, tobacco smoke that puffs from his short pipe have grown on her.

On the third day he had sent her out twice – once to buy apples from the market, another to buy bread. It felt strange being outside again. Her head whirled when she stepped into the cool air. As she picked her way across the muddy cobblestones, she felt light, as though suddenly untethered, a feathery dandelion drifting on the breeze, lifted into the air, mingling with the leaves of the yew trees. It was an unsettling feeling, though. She paused, peered up at the strip of slate sky enclosed on each side by brick buildings, filthy terraces and chimneys caked in a film of soot. A pedlar shouted at her to move on, pushing past with a barrow of turnips and carrots. And in that moment she thought of how she could slip away, run. Pol would never find her. But then what would she do? She had no friends and, when she glanced down at the four sous in the palm of her hand, she realised she would need more money.

Annah's brought back to the present by the sound of the fishmonger's call from below. She wraps the blanket about her shoulders and crosses to the windows. Pushing the shutters wide, her blood quickens as she gazes upon Rue Vercingétorix. Pedestrians amble down the middle of the road, paying little heed to the horse and carriage approaching. A group of five men, bowler hats balanced neatly on their heads, lounge in chairs outside the café, and a pedlar peers deep into his wicker basket of cabbages. One woman, neatly buttoned up in a dark bodice, walks her black dog. Another dog, smaller, with a sandy coat, pisses against the tobacconist's doorjamb, and the storekeeper across the way pulls his cabinet of goods out onto the pavement with the help of his skinny assistant. The cold air is still and the pungent, syrupy odours of human offal – refuse, excretions, dung – battle the comforting aroma from the *boulangerie* on the next corner.

'Here, Annah, I have found you a new gown,' says Pol, flinging a mass of black cambric over the back of a chair. He points at her dress. 'Throw out that terrible cheesecloth thing.'

He's been much more cheerful since the man with the nice face and the sympathetic eyebrows brought him a clinking purse of money the day before. Pol immediately bought more whisky and salted meat to put in his cabinet and a large jar of vegetables, *vert* and pickled, which he shared with Annah in front of the hearth where, for once, a lively fire burned.

Annah picks up the gown from the chair. She carries it to the window and sees that the fabric is not black at all, but a deep blue, as dark as the velvety night sky that surrounds the moon.

Pol settles into an armchair. She holds the gown to her chest and, as she walks into the other room, he snorts, says something she can't quite understand.

She strips out of her plain dress and drapes it over Pol's unmade bed. Inspecting the gown, Annah wonders how many other owners it has clothed – one or two at the most, she thinks, her eyes taking in its smooth nap. With her thumbnail, she scrapes away a chalky stain upon the wide lapel. A bit of the stitching has come undone about the waistband, but that she can fix if she can get hold of a needle and thread – tending to Madame Pack's fine apparel was the only chore Annah had really enjoyed at the other house. As she steps into the gown and pulls it up over her body,

13

a puff of mustiness and stale perfume reaches her nostrils. She's had worse, though – like the dress she wore before she met Madame that was stiff beneath the armpits from someone else's sweat.

When she returns to the living room, Pol's removing all the sombre portraits that litter the walls. He climbs onto a chair, directs her to take the dusty frames from him and stack them by the entrance. She moves slowly, wishes he'd asked for her help in this before she donned her new gown. When they have cleared the wainscoting, Annah soaks her dirty hands in a pail of water while Pol slaps long strokes of yellow paint across the walls. They are interrupted by a rap at the door. Annah opens it, and a man clambers through, lugging a large cage that he knocks against the doorjamb, chipping the wood. He wears a velvet coat, and a green parrot is perched atop his shoulder. Dashes of white bird droppings splotch his back.

'Ah, good man,' Pol cries.

Between the two of them, they carry the cage into the corner of the room nearest to the windows. Just as Annah draws close, bends to take a look, a small creature, covered in ginger fur, slams its body against the front of the cage. It clings to the bars with its little fingers, chatters in a high pitch.

The man in the velvet coat hands her a leather leash, tells Pol to feed fruit to the animal.

'A present for you, Annah,' says Pol. 'A monkey.'

Annah frowns. Already, she can smell the *monyet*'s stinky hide. It probably bites. It will make them ill. She will certainly have nothing to do with it.

Later, when Annah returns from the market with a bag of meat scraps, Pol has finished coating the walls and it is as though they

14

must now live within the bright yolk of an egg.

Steadying the single pot over the fire, she waits for it to become hot, and watches as Pol hangs his self-portrait near the doorway to the bedroom. She empties the raw meat into the pot's black depths. The puce cuts of meat turn brown, the honeycombed tripe coils against the heat. She adds water, stirs the muck with a battered ladle.

Pol drags the chair near, steps up onto it to hammer a nail into the wall above the mantelpiece. He squats to lift a painting of a woman seated in a rocking chair. As he attaches it to the wall, Annah steps back, enraptured by the languid lines of the woman, her black hair, her cinnamon skin, which is the same shade as Annah's own. The woman's dress is as red as a nutmeg's lacy mace. Her bare foot reaches from beneath its folds.

The walls of Madame Pack's drawing room were covered with gilt-framed portraits of women, some richly decorated in silks and bows, others with only a coy strip of muslin to hide alabaster skin, offering a glimpse of pink nipple, flushed cheek. But to Annah there is something far more beautiful about this painting here in front of her. Something that feels almost familiar. A sudden sense of aloneness takes her by surprise. She breathes in, breathes in.

'You paint this?' she asks Pol, who's wiping his brow with a filthy handkerchief.

He nods. 'And many more.' He stands with his hands on hips, head thrust back as he gazes at the painting. 'These paintings will be the making of me, Annah. My time will finally come.'

'I like it.'

'I will be a great artist,' he says, nodding, as though he's telling her a secret. His voice is grave. 'I know it.' They admire the painting while the stew bubbles. The monkey scrambles from one side of its cage to the other. 'Here, Annah, help me hang this one now.'

They hang three more paintings: a long, narrow canvas of foliage and terrain, painted the vibrant colours of a fruit-dove's plumage; a group of dark people, dressed in bright robes, seated in the orange dirt beneath a tree; a woman, perhaps the same woman as the one wearing the red dress, with her bare legs stretched out across an expanse of apricot sand, two purple mountains looming behind her. Annah runs her finger gently across the fronds of a golden palm tree. She had almost forgotten the sight of these trees, once so plentiful they were easily overlooked.

She points at the painting of the crowd seated on the ground, says, 'Where?'

'Tahiti, Annah. Have you heard of it?'

She shakes her head. Wonders if it is close to where she is from. Stepping near, she studies the bank of pink flowers behind the woman and the fruit in the bowl by her side. She's sure the orange fruit is a *mangga*, and her stomach constricts for its sweetness. And the dark-green fruit that lies at the back of the wooden bowl is perhaps an unripe papaya. How she misses such things.

Her eyes turn to the people, seeking similarities between these flat figures and her own people, besides the dark skin, the long black hair.

'Annah!' Pol spits meat back into the ladle. He scowls at her. 'This is inedible.'

She stares at him. Looks down at the watery lumps of meat.

What does he expect when she has no spices, no peppery vegetables to flavour the food?

~

That night Vollard returns, another man in tow, who he introduces as Alfons. Pol shakes the newcomer's hand, his voice booming out a welcome, but behind his smile he's watchful, his tall frame drawn broad, defensive, as the men circle the room gazing up at the paintings.

Annah and Pol have arranged the chairs and sofa around a table on which is an assortment of cheese, bread and fruit that Annah fetched from the market after Pol tasted her stew, declaring it too dastardly to serve to his guests.

'You must have an exhibition, Paul,' says Vollard.

The man, Alfons, agrees. 'I have never seen anything quite like it. Superb.'

'It's the primitive aesthetic I am so much in search of, you see. It's the only way I can work now. And the pure colours! Everything must be sacrificed to it!'

By the time they join Annah at the table, Pol is relaxed, softened by his guests' kind words and the wine they have brought.

Annah picks up a slice of pear, slides it into her mouth.

'Annah, bring out your monkey. Show these gentlemen your new pet.'

She slowly bites down on the pear, and a sour note quivers at the back of her jaw.

'Annah, fetch the monkey!' Pol raps his knuckles against the tabletop twice. Murmurs something to Vollard.

The cage is tucked away behind Pol's easel and its barn stench becomes stronger as she slowly approaches. She crouches down, peers into the cage's gloom. The lump of meat she squeezed through the bars earlier in the day still lies on the floor where it fell among the monkey's pellet-like scats and the damp, shredded newspaper. The monkey is hunched by the bars, its wide eyes upon her. Annah is repulsed by how much the *monyet* resembles a little boy. She wrinkles her nose and folds her arms.

'Don't be foolish, girl,' says Pol, pushing past her. He yanks open the side door of the cage and, reaching in, grabs the monkey about its waist. With deft, sure fingers he attaches the collar and leash about its neck. He tries to shove the creature into Annah's arms, which are still crossed, so that the monkey's stubby fingers and toes must grip the folds of her bodice. Her heartbeat leaps with fright when it bares its little, sharp teeth at her. She bares her teeth back. Pol returns to the others. They talk of his work, clink their glasses of wine, laugh, clip the breadboard with the knife, but she stands frozen, unsure of what the *monyet* will do should she move. Its fur is pungent with the odour of sweet urine and something like straw. Its eyes are fathomless, as dark and shiny as a longan pip.

Slowly, she uncoils one arm, takes hold of the leash and crosses the room to lower herself carefully onto the sofa next to Pol. With a friendly dip of the head, Alfons passes her a wine. As she takes a long sip, she examines him over the cup's rim. He has a bushy head of brown hair, one shade darker than his beard, and his moustache tufts upwards at the edges, giving his face a cheerful countenance.

The monkey reaches its thin hand up to Annah's face, its cold fingers dabbing her skin. She leans away, but it clings even tighter about her neck and she lets out a short grunt of disgust. Alfons reaches over and lifts the monkey from her breast, lets it snuggle into the crook of his arm.

'It is only cold, you see.' His right hand strokes the monkey's back. 'What is its name?' he asks her, but his accent is different from Pol's – more guttural, clipped. She narrows her eyes, trying to decipher his words.

'What have you named the monkey, Annah?' Pol repeats.

'*Monyet.*' What a strange question. Why would she be so ridiculous as to name a wild animal as though it were a person?

'*Monyet,*' Alfons repeats, delighted.

'Alfons,' Pol interrupts, 'you were saying that you have seen some of Vincent's work from our time in Arles.'

'I have.'

'And what did you think?'

'I can't be sure what I thought, to tell you the truth.'

Pol nods. 'He still had a thing or two to learn after all, and I was the older man. I read a review just recently, you know, that said, *Gauguin's drawing somewhat recalls that of Van Gogh,* and I had to smile.' But he doesn't smile.

'Vollard says you were there, Paul, when he ...?' says Alfons.

Annah brings the cup to her lips, takes three gulps.

'Yes. It all started out quite well ...'

She stares down at the wine, watches the candlelight's halo ripple across its ruby surface.

'... rough and noisy fellow. Silent in the end, of course.'

The alcohol seeps its way into Annah's blood, loosens her thoughts as it always does. As Pol's voice rumbles over her, as she sits among the three men, she thinks of another – René. His hair so fair, and skin as pale as the flesh of a breadfruit. And still young, almost as young as she. Her eyes flick over Vollard's fingers that are hairy near the knuckles and the greying hair that peeps from beneath Pol's fez. Her gaze drops to her wine again, and she thinks of René's soft hand cupping her face that first time, the sweep of his thumb across her cheek as his lips pressed hers. She closes her eyes and she can almost feel his fingers upon the line of her jaw, curving behind her ear; a whisper, yet searing too.

'I owe something to Vincent, you know, for in the consciousness of being of use to him ...'

Annah tips the last drop of wine onto her tongue, and Alfons takes the cup from her, refills it. Immediately, she takes another sip.

'... confirmed my own ideas about painting ...'

Thankfully, her thoughts begin to blur. The men grow distant, muffled, as though she is submerged in the ocean, dark water filling her ears, stinging her eyes, holding her suspended. Not for the first time, she wonders: if she is to will it hard enough, allow her mind to waver between this world and the next, René will appear in the doorway for some wondrous reason – perhaps he too has become an artist, or perhaps he is friends with one of these men. Perhaps it is simply that he has come in search of her. Annah brings the cup to her lips and finishes the wine, hoping, as she always does, for its magical promise to come true.

'And, of course, in the difficult moments, it is good to remember there are those who are unhappier than oneself.' Pol rests his hand on Annah's thigh. 'But enough of poor Vincent. You must tell me of your studio, Alfons. Perhaps there is room there for some of my pieces.'

Later that evening, when their guests have left, Annah leaves off being Pol's *hamba* and becomes his *maîtresse* instead. He has her straddle him that first time. The wine has left her numb yet supple and, as she sways above him, she wishes his hips were narrower so she could enfold him as neatly as she did her René.

Three

'Annah, I think it is time I painted you,' Pol says as he sorts through a tin box of painting equipment. He holds up two thick paintbrushes, inspects their tips against one another.

A tremor of delight curls through Annah's body. She scans the many paintings that have lately arrived from Tahiti in a padded wooden crate: a clamour of colour and shapes splashed across the yellow walls. Of brown people, cobalt sea, viridian grass. Of sienna heat and blue air. All that she misses of her own home. 'Like this?' she asks, pointing to the languid woman in the red dress.

He glances up from where he melts wax into a small pot of paint. 'No, of course not,' he says. 'There is nothing new in a portrait of yet another gowned mademoiselle. I am thinking of something more like that one.' He nods towards the painting of the nude woman seated next to the bowl of fruit.

'I wear my dress.'

'No, Annah, you will not wear your dress. And you must hurry, before we lose all the light.' He arranges an armchair in front of his easel. When he sees she hasn't moved he tuts. '*Merde*, Annah. You are more difficult than that monkey.' She tries to tug away from his grasp, but his voice becomes wheedling as he unbuttons her gown. 'Alfons visits us tonight, with many of our friends. Wouldn't you like to be famous?' He gestures towards all the canvases that decorate the walls. 'Your portrait will hang in a rich man's house one day. Or perhaps a gallery. You would like that, wouldn't you, Annah? Everyone will know you, forever, long after you have left this world. They will know of who you are and how you lived with me, a very great artist.'

Forever.

21

Annah pauses. Allows Pol to finish undressing her.

As he arranges her in the chair – hands draped over its arms, feet crossed on a footstool – she thinks of the hours she lies awake sometimes, listening to Pol's snores, a clot of dread in her stomach, perspiration cool on her brow. Anxious that she will never return to her island, will forget the sting of *colo-colo* on her tongue, won't ever be among her like again. Who is to remember her? Her aunt will die soon enough, her cousins will marry and have children. There will be little room left for them to wonder about her. René – and it scorches her to think on it – has probably already put her from his mind. She will fade from all memory like the fan of colour disappears from a sun-bleached shell.

'You must concentrate, Annah,' says Pol, pushing her knee towards the other, leaving a cerulean streak across her skin. 'I must get your composition just right before we lose daylight.' He steps back, his eyes skimming her face, her torso, her legs. Standing behind his canvas, he makes brushstrokes long and sweeping. Every few seconds he glances at her, at the three sketches he's drawn in charcoal, then returns to his work.

By the time he tosses his brush atop his palette, announcing he's finished for the day, her toes are almost numb with the cold, and thin, blue veins spider her chilled thighs. She waits until she hears the splash of piss against the chamber-pot in the next room before she tiptoes over to the easel, but she's perplexed by what she finds. Broad swirls, as bright as the kingfisher's lazuli breast, are streaked across the canvas. The paint so thin in some areas Annah can see the weave of the canvas. Other sections are dark, layered with thick strokes of umber.

It is only when she steps back that she discerns her own likeness, in the tilt of the head, the curve of the legs. She is a shadow, a bruise, a wraith without substance. Her breaths squeeze tight. She wonders if Pol doesn't see her, doesn't need to or, worse, he recognises a lack in her, a hollowness.

'Close your mouth, Annah,' Pol says, re-entering the living area. 'It is not finished yet. And help me clear this mess away; our guests are to arrive soon.'

She watches as he drags the easel to the side of the room and pulls all the chairs into a circle. He pours himself half a tumbler of whisky, and she holds her hand out, wants to sip some too, knows how its flame will dull the edges. He shakes his head, says, 'Maybe later. At least light the fire, girl. Make yourself useful.' But she pretends she doesn't hear and picks up her dress.

'No, Annah, tonight I want you to wear the *pareo*.'

She looks across at the length of fabric that partially covers the round table. It resembles a *sarung*, its pattern not unlike that of batik, but it feels rough against her skin. It is similar to what the women are seated upon in some of the paintings, but instead of deep-sea blue, the design on this *pareo* holds the colours of tree bark and coconut husks.

As she winds it around her body, Pol dons a waistcoat with a green and yellow embroidered trim about the collar. He drapes a long cloak with large mother-of-pearl buttons across his shoulders, and on his head he wears his fez. Over his long fingers he draws gloves as white as sea froth. Annah stands by the fire to warm her bare arms while Pol rummages through a box and exclaims with delight when he draws out what looks like a long wooden club. He taps it against the timber floor.

'Look, Annah, it's a walking stick. I carved it myself. See, here are my initials, and this here —' his tapered finger points at a milky glimmer set in the wood '— is a real pearl.'

~

The brass bell clangs and, as instructed, Annah greets the newcomers with a small bow, a lily cupped between her prayer hands. Pol's paintings are ablaze by the light of so many candles and lamps, reminding Annah of the blinding kaleidoscope of coloured glass in the chapel she had visited one prayer day with Madame Pack. Pol has placed clusters of statues about the room – carvings from the South Seas, he informs two of his guests. Mostly the carvings are stubby little creatures of blonde timber, with blank eyes, scrolled nostrils and swollen bellies, but one makes her smile – a dark wooden figure, with two heads and a little *kontol* poking from between its legs.

The men hush for a few moments so that one of them – a slim youth with a rash of blistering spots on his face – can recite from a small leather-bound book. While he reads, Annah tosses back the rest of Pol's whisky that he's left on the mantelpiece. The liquor washes down to her empty stomach, leaving her feeling a little sickened, but it doesn't stop her eyes from searching the room for more wine or spirits to swallow. A man who Annah at first mistook for Alfons – he has similar features and bushy, brown hair, but she remembers now that his name is Molard – takes to playing the harmonium, drumming out a tune. The din is terrible. The men shout above each other, even more so than the farmers at market in the morning.

Somebody – she thinks perhaps the man from a place called Ireland, who is also a painter like Pol – has left his glass of wine on the table next to the platters of liverwurst and roasted fowl. Annah drains the glass. She refills it from one of the several bottles of wine that stand sentinel at the end of the table, brought along by Pol's guests, accepted by him as though they were offerings.

The bell clangs again and, snatching up the lily, Annah opens the door to Alfons, who lugs a box that rattles with bottles of beer. With a joyful cry, the man from Ireland grabs one as Alfons passes. He takes a swig and, smacking his lips, notices the shivering *monyet* crouched beneath the easel. He approaches it, hand outstretched, his shoes treading *monyet* droppings into the floorboards. The monkey dashes towards its cage, tangling its leash about the easel's legs. With soothing clucks, the man squats and unravels the leash, but the ungrateful monkey persists in evading his advances and lopes across the floor, hides under the armchair.

Alfons places a cup of beer into Annah's hands. It's bitter and stings her nose, but she learns soon enough that it adds to the welcome fog in her head, slows down her thoughts, just as wine does. She rocks onto the balls of her feet, amused as she watches the *monyet* creep from beneath the armchair, swing his way to the tabletop, reach his blunt little fingers towards a wrinkled date. Pol gives him a hard rap across the top of his skull, and the *monyet* squeals, leaps to the floor and scoots up the inside of Annah's *pareo*. Some of the men laugh as she slaps at the lump in her skirt, where the *monyet* swings against her shins, but the silly creature won't come out. She shuffles to the armchair and takes a seat, hoping that, with time, the *monyet* will retire back to his original hiding place.

Alfons pulls a chair close, placing a plate of food by her side. He slices himself some meat and takes a seat. 'Annah, tell me about how you came to be in Paris?'

Annah sucks an olive into her mouth, licks the salt from her lips. She rides out the meld of noise, colours, movement as though she's a paper boat dipping giddily over shallow swell. She peers at him across the spuming water. 'A ship. With Marchands. I was servant.' Scraping the last of the olive from the pip with her bottom teeth, she places it onto the knife's flat edge. She pops another one into her mouth.

He smiles, nods, but doesn't press her for more. He doesn't think to ask about the Marchand family who picked her up on their way back to France. Or their two little girls, with hair as yellow as corn husk, who she had to tend. And how could he know to enquire after their older brother, René, who used to stand so close behind her – too close almost – she could barely think of anything besides the heat of him. The olive flesh seems rough as it courses its way down her throat. She places the pip next to the other on the knife.

'And then? How did you find your way to Madame Pack's?'

She stares at Alfons until her vision doubles – triples: the freckles on his face, his ears, his nose. Annah knows what he's asking, but she doesn't want to answer. That time in her life, between René and wandering the streets with the sign about her neck, is stippled with shards of grey. She flinches from its touch.

'Madame Sérusier is still beautiful. Despite her age.' Pol's voice rises like a wave in the ocean before dissipating into the general roar.

'Paul tells me you are fifteen years old,' Alfons says to Annah.

'Yes. Fifteen year old.' This she has also learned to say.

'You are still very young,' he says, pouring more beer into her cup from his bottle.

Annah stares at the portrait above the mantelpiece. Very young. Very young for what? She cannot be sure what being very young means to him, so she doesn't reply. She chews the flesh from another olive. As she lines the grainy pip next to the others on the knife's edge, her tongue tastes where the olive's salt has puckered the skin of her bottom lip.

A short man, largely hidden behind a canvas, bustles into the room.

'Ah, Le Barc, you are here,' cries Pol. 'And you have brought my painting?'

'Yes, Monsieur. It arrived from Copenhagen today. Unfortunately, they were not able to sell it.' He rubs the back of his wrist against his long sideburn.

Pol's smile is sad. 'People don't yet understand my work, my friend. But I am sure once it hangs in Durand-Ruel's gallery, it will find a home.'

The monkey pokes its head out from beneath Annah's skirt and shimmies its way to her lap. It backs up against her stomach and surveys the room with a tilt of its head. Its soft fur is an undulation of grey to white to ginger, and she gently brushes the side of her finger along the long bristles of hair that spring from its ear.

All of the men cross the room to gaze upon the painting Le Barc props above the harmonium. Through a gap between Molard and Pol, Annah can only make out purples and a rich earthen colour.

'Tehura. I was so moved and stimulated by my lovely Tehura in Tahiti,' says Pol, beer sloshing over the side of his glass as he salutes the painting. 'You will perhaps recognise, Messieurs, that this painting is inspired by Manet's *Olympia*. Here, have a look at this copy of the original, and then I will explain how mine differs.'

He takes a photograph from his painting box and hands it to Molard. 'I showed this exact copy to Tehura. Oh, how she sighed over Olympia's fair beauty. And then do you know what she said to me? She said, "This is your wife!" Can you believe it?

How I laughed. And do you know what I did? I lied. I said, "Yes, she is my wife." Ha. Me! Olympia's consort.'

The men laugh; one of them smacks Pol on the back.

Annah pushes the monkey from her lap and stands, curious to see what Pol speaks of. She wavers on her feet, giddy from the beer. Approaching the men crowded around the harmonium, she peers past somebody's elbow. Her eyes take in the sepia tones of the photograph Pol places against the bottom of his painting. A beautiful woman reclines against a cushion, her skin as bare and pale as the pearl in Pol's stick. A flower, its petals drowsy and ripe, is tucked behind her ear. The expression on her face is that of a sultan's wife: proud, yet perhaps a little bored. She wears a ribbon about her neck and a bangle on her wrist. Fine sandals, with a pretty heel, adorn her shapely feet. She lies on dishevelled sheets, and a servant holds a large bouquet for her.

Annah's gaze turns to the servant: a black woman, the outline of her features almost lost against the photograph's pewter tint. Annah eases closer, staring at the curious headdress the woman wears wound about the top of her head. She wonders where the servant is from, and how she found herself working for the pearly lady. Perhaps Madame Pack saw this painting too, just as Pol did, and that's when she decided she needed a Negro girl to attend to her.

'The motif in my painting is savage and quite childlike, you will notice.'

Annah steps back and looks up at Pol's portrait. She likes the violet floor, the lilac background. A girl is stretched out across a bed. She lies on her front and, as Annah's eyes sweep across the supine figure, she realises it was the girl's brown skin that caught her eye earlier, not the toasted earth. Like Olympia, Tehura is naked, served up on a white sheet.

'See, by the lines and the movement of Tehura's body, the gesture of her hands, how she seems frightened by something?'

Alfons nods; another man says yes.

'You must understand that Tahitians have a great fear of spirits.' Pol's words slur slightly. He squints at the painting as though he's trying to bring it into focus. 'I named it *Manaò tupapaú*, which in their pidgin language means *spirit* and *thought*.' He pauses to gulp down more beer. 'But I rather think I might rename it. Something to do with how she knows she is being watched – that is what frightens her, you see – by this.' His finger taps a dark figure in the background of the painting. 'The spirit of the dead.'

The simple figure is hooded in black with a wide eye on Tehura. Annah looks again at the black servant in the photograph of the original painting. Pol has turned the servant into the spirit of the dead. Has taken her darkness – its stain a contrast to Olympia's pearlescent vitality – and transformed it into death.

The men's eyes linger over Tehura's sprawled figure. One of the artists tears a handful of breast meat from the roasted fowl, stuffs it into his mouth. Molard draws on his cigarette, examining the painting through the smoke that hangs in the air.

Annah glances to the corner of the studio where Pol's painting of her rests beneath a blanket. Is that how Pol sees her, too? A spectre to watch over those who live? Her shadow so dark, she feels heavy with it. She drains the last of somebody's beer.

Some of the men return to the wine and food on the round table. Two start up a noisy game of piquet. The monkey races across the floorboards, chasing a cockroach along the skirting board. Grasping the bug in his little hand as though he holds a piece of bread and butter, he shoves it into his mouth and munches.

Pol joins the spotty youth and another young man who are looking up at a painting of two women – naked, with garlands in their hair – resting by a copper slick of water. 'Ah. I was a man retired from civilised life, in a place where all was golden and beautiful – never conscious of good or evil.' The spotty youth turns away abruptly, his lip lifting in an infinitesimal smirk as he catches Molard's eye.

There's a drunken stagger to Pol's step as he returns to his painting of Tehura and the spirit of the dead. He drapes his arm around Annah's neck, his palm resting against her breast.

His eyes caress the painting. 'Look at Tehura, my sweet Tehura, who became more docile and loving with each day. In that tropical paradise, Messieurs, we need only know of the basic human sensations. It taught me that I can follow my fancy wherever I am. I can follow the moon, if I so wish.' He takes his heavy arm from her shoulder and, with a little shove, he strides across the room. Snatching up a thin paintbrush, which he jabs in his palette, he moves to the window and paints the words *te faruru* on the glass.

'What does it say?' asks Annah.

'*Here we make love,*' says Alfons.

Towards dawn, Pol bends Annah over the bed. Her head, her breasts, lurch with each thrust. He squeezes her waist, says, 'Make some noise. Make some noise,' and she grunts, in rhythm, until the foolish *monyet* starts screeching, perhaps in alarm, perhaps because it feels left out.

Four

Pol's head is bowed over the harmonium. He's wearing a shirt and overcoat, but his long limbs are bare, his pale toes stroking the silver fur of the wolf-skin rug. Annah allows herself to think of the other one. René. Of his smallish hands, how they swept the smooth skin of her inner thigh. She feels a ripple of desire; not for Pol, though. She watches as his fingers clank out another tune across the keyboard.

Pol pauses for a moment mid-tune, and Annah returns to sit before the easel. The upholstery of the armchair, the colour of claret, is worn thin where it is most disturbed by the pressure of countless hands and buttocks. She can feel the roughness of its torn fabric against her bare skin, so she raises herself into a squat and perches on the edge of the seat like a starling.

She looks at the portrait Pol has painted of her, finished now, where she is seated naked in this very chair. In the painting, though, the chair is the colour of the ocean's blue shallows. Pol said it reminds him of that place called Tahiti. And Annah knows that the painting's russet heat and basking yellow are further deceits – bold exaggerations created by Pol's brush. The painting's cheery shades are purloined from the flickering flames of an evening's fire and the tubes of paint that are strewn, twisted and abandoned, across the tabletop. Staring at the painting – at the expression on her face that imitates the fair Olympia's, and the silly *monyet* fidgeting on the floor – she decides that she rather likes it. Likes how its lustre cuts though the mute hues of the morning.

She draws the *pareo* around herself more tightly. Pol says it's too early to light the stinky tallow candles, but she's sick of the dreariness – the ash on the hearth, the blanket of dust, the mould on the one apple that sits, pockmarked and lonely, upon the sideboard.

'Can we have fire?' she asks him, raising her voice above the music.

He looks over his shoulder at her, and his eyebrows lift, as though he's surprised at her presence. He rubs his big nose.

'If we light it now, Annah, we will not have a fire tonight.' He nods towards the solitary, charred log in the fireplace. He starts up again, and the wild notes jangle in her ears.

'You get more firewood,' she says.

His back stiffens. She knows he hasn't enough money left to purchase more. Her heart races a little, but not because she's scared of him. She studies him, a buffalo in the field, gauging just how far his temper will reach. Perhaps he will jump to his feet, knocking the piano stool back. He might bellow at her, spittle brimming his moustache, and wave his arms, or hit her across the head like he had the other night when she served roasted sheep's head for supper. He screamed at her that such fare was only good enough for peasants and vagabonds.

She wishes he would storm out of the apartment, leave her alone for once. She would immediately light that log.

Instead – worse – he ignores her. His fingers find the notes again, slowly this time, sulky.

'I am hungry,' she says. 'The monkey, he is hungry.'

Pol slams his hands down on a cacophony of notes. The *monyet* squeaks.

'*Merde*, Annah, will you never stop?' He rummages in his pockets and brings out a few coins. 'Buy some bread. But go somewhere new, for heaven's sake. I am sick of the stale rubbish you bring me.'

Annah ties the money into a handkerchief, places it into the bottom of a basket. She takes Pol's wide-brimmed hat and pulls it as low as it will go over her head. It is not every day that somebody spits at her, or calls out, or refuses to serve her when she goes about without Pol or, earlier, without Madame Pack or René's mother, but it has happened enough times for her to be careful. Sometimes she thinks she should perhaps cover her face with black lace, like the women who have lost their husbands, but some nugget of resistance has crystallised deep within her, revels in the flicker of fear at the back of their yellow eyes when they are confronted with the dark spectre of herself. And, in any case, she has not the money to purchase a length of lace.

She passes the *boulangerie* on the corner and keeps walking until she reaches the Italian bakery further down the road where the woman gladly sells Annah yesterday's bread. Annah hands over a coin – calculating how she can save one, perhaps two, of the remaining centimes for herself – and drops the hard, round loaf into her basket. Stepping from the shop, she hesitates, not wanting to return to Pol's apartment just yet.

She makes her way towards the small market crammed behind the glue factory, familiar with its stench of mud and manure, the snorting pigs and crates of chickens, barrows of vegetables still crusted with dirt, the tables laden with used clothing, patched and stiff. Add one more sweet note and the market would smell like durian. The man from whom she buys the very cheapest cuts of meat cries out from where he squats in the back of his wagon, a greasy mutton carcass nudging his shoulder. A woman tugs at a goat's teat, the milk squirting into a boy's pail.

Annah's eyes snag on a pear that teeters atop a wooden crate, imagines sinking her teeth into the pink blush that freckles its green cheek, the roll of peel and pulp against her tongue. She wants to buy the pear, wolf it down immediately so she doesn't have to share it with Pol. Her fingers press against the coins still in the handkerchief. She takes a deep breath and turns away, deciding against it. If she spends money on the pear, that's one less sou to save for herself. Instead, she stops to buy three gooseberries for the *monyet* from another vendor and some cocoa for Pol from an old woman.

As she leans forward to pay, a fragrance reaches her nostrils, lurches her into brightness, a blanket of heat, a sharp undercurrent of dried fish and salt. Tears press at the back of her eyes, congest her nose. She looks around as though she will see her own people on the wooden dock that creaks and sways above the water, but of course there is nothing more than the red brick of the factory and the alley's dry chill. She folds back the lip of a small hessian sack in the woman's barrow, revealing a mound of ground nutmeg.

The woman clamps the bag shut. 'This is a very precious spice. Too expensive for you.'

'What money remains?' Pol asks, coming in from the bedroom.

Annah places two sous on the table and while Pol rifles through the basket, she takes a bronze coin from where it's tucked inside the cuff of her sleeve and slides it under one of the carvings from Tahiti.

When she first decided to save what coins she could, she considered hiding the money in an old coffee tin. But what if she is taken away suddenly, like last time, and isn't given the opportunity to fetch her savings? And she wouldn't want Pol to notice the tin's rattle, wrest the money back from her to buy more wine or that salted meat he loves so much. Instead,

34

when Pol is distracted, she sews the coins into the hem of her gown so that now there is a satisfying heft to the swing of her skirt. She realises, though, that her gown would have to be very heavy indeed before she would have enough centimes and the occasional franc to escape.

Pol swears. 'Annah, you have brought me nothing more than stale bread again. What must I do to convince you that I do not want to sup on your delicacies of hard bread and beef stomach?'

Annah shrugs. 'More money for good food.'

Pol slams the bread back into the basket. 'And look at this place!' His arms take in the dirty crockery stacked by the basin, the monkey droppings and ash strewn across the bare floors, the clutter of paint tubes and jars. 'You are supposed to keep this place tidy. You are no better than that monkey of yours that just shits and eats.'

'Not my monkey.' She doesn't look at Pol as she leans across the table to take the gooseberries from the basket, but she tenses for a slap across the arm or face. Instead, he thumps the table and swears again. She carries the berries across to the cage and squeezes each one through the bars, breathing in the monkey's familiar odour.

'I can't spend another minute here,' Pol says, striding to the door. 'Put your coat back on, Annah. Alfons said the photographs of my work should be ready today. And he's bound to have beer, and better food than what you provide me with.'

Annah gladly tugs Pol's old coat on and follows him out into the street. She enjoys their visits to Alfons's studio, where Alfons is cheerful, as are the other artists who work with him. Sometimes Alfons gives Annah a box of pink sweets to eat from – rosy squares covered in a puff of sugary powder, so soft they squish between her fingers.

But when they arrive at Alfons's studio they find him locking the front door.

'I am just on my way to the print shop,' he says, shaking Pol's hand. His eyes rest on Annah. 'The photograph I took of you should be ready as well. Why don't you both join me, and we can pick up some wine on the way back?'

As they walk, a light drizzle sets in. Annah curls her fingers into her coat sleeves, hunches against the cold drips of water on the back of her neck. A cherry tree's budding leaves flicker in the breeze. Rain slicks the cobblestones, and Annah's careful to avoid the specks of mud that flick from the wheels of passing buggies. A vendor, huddled beneath a tattered awning, roasts potatoes in a brazier. She knows better than to ask Pol for the money, but perhaps if she says something, Alfons will buy her one. By the time she thinks of this, though, the vendor and his potatoes are far behind.

Finally, they reach a narrow shopfront squashed between a pharmacy and a café. *Imprimerie* is lettered in gold across the plate glass window, beneath the name *Leblanc*.

As Alfons pushes open the door, he says to Pol, 'I work here three days a week. Helps to pay for the studio space.'

Pol nods. 'Ah, yes. I too used to keep usual work hours in an office. That time was not entirely without worth, but be cautious,' he says to the younger man. 'Don't let it leach your creativity.'

Alfons greets two middle-aged men, Hugo and Coupeau, explaining to Pol that together the three of them design posters. 'So our work can be quite creative, you see.'

Pol's mouth turns down, unconvinced. Alfons fans the photographs of Pol's work across the counter, and Pol's pleased with the pictures, commends Alfons on his use of the light. When Alfons rifles through a drawer, withdrawing the photograph of

Annah, Pol turns away and strolls to the back of the shop to inspect some paintings stacked against the wall.

Annah slides the likeness close. This is the third photograph she has seen of herself, but in the others she stands among the men, as drunk and foolish as they – buttoned into ridiculous costumes, with silly hats on their heads – frozen in the few seconds it takes for the camera's shutter to click. When she sees her dark features among their fair ones, she always wonders – feels a pinch of discomfort with it – if the others are reminded of the shadowy figure in the background of Pol's painting of Tahura.

But this photograph is of Annah alone, seated in the armchair in Pol's studio. She remembers the scent of the wildflowers Alfons poked in her hair, how the tiny, fragile petals tickled the side of her face. How the *monyet* scrambled up the curtains, escaping Pol's swatting broom. The sound of a pedlar down on the street below, drumming the side of his soup pot as he wheeled past. But none of that is visible in the photograph she scans so greedily. All is serene as she sits among statuettes and ornaments, the scalloped arches and cabriole legs of the dark furniture. She reclines in the chair, calm in her blue-black gown, like the woman in the red dress. Perhaps this photograph will be even more forever than Pol's painting of her in the bright room.

'Why do you have this portrait here?' Pol's voice is sharp as he calls from the back of the room.

Annah follows Alfons to where Pol stands in front of a framed canvas resting against the wall. She breathes in, breathes in, as she stares at the painting of a pretty Javanese dancer.

'It's a work by Sargent. I'm to send it on to him. He had to leave for Chicago in a hurry,' says Alfons.

'Ah, the American artist, you mean?'

Annah takes a step back so she can take in the full figure of burnished grace: the curve of the dancer's left hand, how her chin tilts towards it. The arched lift of her bare foot, the angle of her hips.

'He painted a whole series of Javanese dancers during the Paris Exposition.'

'But so did I!' says Pol. 'Yes, yes. These people had a village to themselves at the Exposition, did they not? With a small musical band of drums and queer bamboo instruments. I too made several sketches and paintings of the dancers.' His eyes narrow. 'I had to leave them behind when I travelled to Tahiti. I must dig them out.'

Annah feels overwhelmed by the other girl's presence. The portrait is as tall as the men – unlike Pol's paintings, which are small enough to fit on most anybody's drawing room wall.

'The fantastic things I saw at that Exposition, Alfons – the ethnographic displays of the colonies, Africa, the South Seas – it all made me want to be rid of civilisation's influence. I needed to immerse myself in virgin nature. See no-one but savages. I wanted to live their lives!'

Annah thinks of the bold colours and casual beauty of Pol's painting of her. Monsieur Sargent's portrait of the dancer is truer, with its earthy hues, the flecks of almost-gold. The dancer's skin gleams, perhaps dampened by the heat of summer. The anklets, the bracelets, the gilded crown and the rich batik that swathes her body, sheathes her legs – all glisten against the press of gaslight. A golden armlet is clasped around the dancer's upper arm and Annah wonders if it has the same strength as the grip of a man who claims ownership. She imagines the heavy earrings swaying to the *gamelan* music, and rubs her own empty earlobes between finger and thumb, feeling for the tiny lumps where the holes remain.

'Beautiful,' she says.

Pol rubs his chin. 'His brushwork is too loose.'

The longer Annah stares at the shimmer of beauty in front of her, the more conscious she becomes of her own stolid limbs, her wiry hair that can't be tamed into a straw hat, the dull cast of her brown skin that seems incapable of ripening when away from tropical sunlight. Here, aglow in front of her, is the real spouse of a sultan. Annah is nothing better than a villager. A grubby, hot flush dapples Annah's chest.

'When he paint this?' she asks Alfons.

'Three, four years ago, I should say.'

Three, four years ago, pretty Javanese dancers from a place near Annah's own island were here, in Paris. For Annah, a whole lifetime has disappeared in those intervening years. A whole life. She shuts her eyes and resists covering them with her hands. She will not go over it all again.

The pall of those moments in Alfons's print shop remain with Annah throughout the rest of the afternoon. She feels like a poorly exposed figure in a photograph, there but not; a sparrow that flits only where the string tied about its ankle allows. Does Pol wish the dancer in Sargent's portrait was here with him now, in all her golden splendour, to hold court at his soirées? Does Alfons? She smarts when she thinks of the Javanese girl, thinks of the freedoms she might have. Wonders if she's returned home. Annah bites down against the envy that curdles her stomach, claws its way up her throat. She kicks at whatever stone or scrap they pass, refuses to eat a piece of the *palmier* Pol buys from a bakery.

When they arrive back at the apartment on Rue Vercingétorix, she immediately takes a seat in front of her portrait and studies it.

The portrait that is not really of her, of Annah. Even the name *Annah* is merely a fragment of her real name, a sliver that can be schooled around their foreign tongues. She takes to her feet and stands by the side of the easel, her gaze flattening out the perspective. This Annah, this slice of colour with its reveal of flesh, is all anyone will ever really know. She is no more than another one of Pol's *exotiques*. She glances at the paintings that cover the walls: portraits of the Tahitian girls who have come before her. Annah is yet another *étranger*, Pol's *orang asing*.

Her eyes linger on the orange of the *monyet*'s fur in the painting. Pol has left out the patches in its coat, and it's impossible to see how cold and blue the pads of the *monyet*'s fingers and toes are, how it shivers against her leg.

She reaches out and places two fingertips against the canvas, runs them across the russet paint of her lower stomach. Skin taut again. By the time Annah had arrived at Le Havre with the Marchands all that time ago, she knew René had left a tadpole swimming in her belly. His mother knew soon enough, too. Annah never did see their home near Lillebonne that René told her so much about – the manor house with the red door; the wooded hills that surrounded it – for Madame Marchand took her straight to her sister's place in Paris. Annah vomited most of the trip, the tadpole sloshing to the pitch of the carriage. And Madame Marchand wouldn't speak to her, look at her even, just stared out the window through red-brimmed eyes, handkerchief pressed to her lips.

Annah blinks. Brings herself back to the darkening room. Her eyes flick over Pol's statues, his works, the man himself, whistling under his breath as he sketches the mouldy apple. Her gaze comes back to rest upon her painting. She will continue to dress up as Pol asks. She will wrap herself in *pareos*, pose in the nude for pictures and even allow the smelly *monyet* to drape itself about her shoulders when Pol has guests. Because this is not her. The girl in the painting is not her. Annah will hug her real story close to her chest, as tightly as a mother might clasp her baby. A baby with amber eyes.

Five

The thin man takes a seat at the round table. He opens his briefcase, from which he withdraws a sheaf of paper. Peering through his spectacles, he slips one sheet from the rest and places it in front of Pol.

Pol's voice is low, aggrieved, as he peruses the document.

From where she is perched on her armchair, Annah hears the men murmur 'long life', 'uncle', 'you will find quite generous'. The *monyet* settles into her lap, as warm as a newly baked loaf of bread.

Pol escorts the thin man to the door, his shoulders stooped, shaking his head, yet, once the door is closed against the other man, Pol turns, his eyes wide, mischievous almost, cheeks lifted in a grin.

'Annah, we are saved,' he says, shaking the piece of paper still clasped in his hands. 'I have come into some money. We can travel to Brittany after all.'

This is the first time Pol has smiled since the art dealer visited several days ago. Whatever news he delivered made Pol smash a bottle of whisky against the wall, a glass splinter nicking Annah's ankle. Since then there has been no fire, no meat; only some nuts and a sour wine Annah sneaked from Pol's glass as she clutched the *monyet* close to keep warm. Pol continued to work by the daylight that streamed through the windows, sullen, scraping at lengths of timber with a collection of sharp little knives and chisels. He disappeared for hours to work in Alfons's studio, returning with prints that mirrored the slate and ochre shadows of the apartment.

This time, though, he doesn't leave Annah for long before he returns with pâté, roasted mutton, pastries and Alfons. The men circle the room, discussing the storage of Pol's paintings. Pol talks of the exhibition he will stage when he returns from Brittany. 'I'll show that *connard* Durand-Ruel. Vollard will help me.'

Annah's tongue scoops up one of the glazed blackberries from atop a croustade, savouring its tart sweetness. She picks off another, balances it on her finger to offer to the *monyet*.

'When will you leave?' asks Alfons. He refills Annah's cup of wine.

'As soon as possible, Alfons. You really should join us. Have you been? You too will love Brittany. I always find a certain wildness and primitiveness there. When my clogs echo across its granite soil, I hear the matt, powerful tone I seek in my painting.'

The last flake of pastry melts inside Annah's mouth. Her hand is sticky with the croustade's syrup and she presses her finger and thumb together, feels the tiny wrench as they separate. As she licks her fingers, the *monyet* tugs on her elbow, and she has to show him her empty hand.

As the buggy rocks its way across pebbly lanes, Annah steadies her weary body. She had thought the train journey from Paris tedious – what with staring out at meadow after meadow dotted with the occasional church spire, and only an apple and half a baguette to eat for hours on end – but this buggy trip between the station and Pont-Aven is trying indeed. At least she no longer has to watch Pol sleep on the train, though, his lower jaw hanging loose, revealing a lump of liverish tongue.

It took Pol three days to have all of his work delivered to Vollard, to cram his painting gear into two tin boxes and have them sent on to Pont-Aven by coach, to purchase a smaller cage for the *monyet*. It took a matter of minutes before they left the Rue Vercingétorix apartment for Annah to fold her old dress from Madame Pack, two hats, some rags, her comb and the *pareo* into an old, scratchy valise Pol gave her to use, which now rests at her feet next to the cage as the buggy lumbers through the countryside. It is still light, but the evening sun has lost its heat and she bends to retrieve the *pareo* from the valise. The *monyet*'s little hand reaches through the bars to grasp hers, but she gently disengages her fingers and sits upright again.

'We are near, Annah,' says Pol, a hum of pleasure in his voice. 'That is the river.'

The water is dark, as green and opaque as the glass of a wine bottle. The air smells fresh, like a sprig of thyme or spinach freshly pulled from damp soil. They pass a number of granite cottages with thatched roofs, and the river divides away into tumbling estuaries. A man steps to the grass beside the road, peers at them from beneath his straw hat. His cart is laden with seaweed. The buggy veers left, follows the water along a well-trodden track towards the village. A pale-brick building crouches over the rapids, a large wheel creaking through the gushing water.

'A watermill, Annah. It is used to grind the local black wheat.'

Brackish fronds of water crest the slippery rocks; moss-covered stones line the stream. Annah looks out the other side of the buggy at the trees webbed in ivy, the occasional shrub – a rash of purple against the green – the wild copse that reminds her of her island, of the grove behind her aunt's hut. The only tame thing here a square of grass, emerald green, that lies across the road from the inn.

'Come, hurry, Annah,' Pol says, grasping his bag and hers as he climbs from the buggy. 'If we hurry, we will find company in the local tavern after we have dropped our belongings at the lodging house.'

They don't have to walk far before they arrive at a neat building that shares a façade with a stationer's shop. The front door is newly lacquered and shiny, and iron balustrading encloses a tiny balcony on the floor above.

When Pol knocks, the landlady greets him in a friendly manner – says that she would hardly recognise him it's been so many years – but as he pushes past to climb the stairs, Annah close on his heels, the woman's mouth falls open, her gaze alternating between Annah and the monkey cage she holds.

Once locked in their room, Pol strides to the French doors and flings them open. He steps out onto the narrow balcony that overlooks the street, rubs his hands together. 'Right. Don't sit down, Annah. Straight to the tavern before it's too dark. See who's at hand.'

They only need trot down one narrow laneway before they reach the squat sandstone building. A sign, not unlike the one that hung about Annah's neck when she wandered Gare de Lyon, sways above the doorway. Inside, the tavern is stuffy, the still air suffused with the odour of stale ale, damp shoes, sweat and tobacco.

Pol leaves Annah at a corner table, and she feels hemmed in

by the dark panelling, the low wooden beams, the leathery men garbed in an endless mire of brown flannel. The whitewashed walls are yellow with soot and smoke and the shadowy gloom thrown by weak gaslight. A balding man, his bulging stomach sheltered beneath a white apron, stands behind a counter strewn with bottles. He leans closer to hear what Pol has to say over the din, pours two wines, pushes a plate of food forward.

By the time Pol returns, he has gathered a coterie of friends. One man flops his hand over Pol's shoulder, gesticulating wildly. Another brings out his sketchpad, flips through to a drawing he wants Pol to look at. The men are all younger than Pol, smaller than him, enthusiastic with wine and admiration. She catches a few names – Maret, Jourdan, Séguin – and O'Conor, who she recognises as the Irish artist from Pol's soirées in Paris. He asks her something that she cannot understand through the burr in his speech, but when he bandies his legs, scratches his armpits, she realises he is asking after the *monyet*.

Annah sinks her teeth into the slab of bacon on buttered bread that Pol hands her and looks about. Two men at the next table scrutinise her from beneath their caps, the creases about their mouths stained red with wine. Something about their gaze slows Annah's chewing, until the bacon and bread are a moist lump at the back of her tongue, too difficult almost to swallow. A buxom woman, only slightly older than Annah herself, leans against the counter and glares at her. Nudges the farmer next to her, who makes a show of recoiling at the sight of Annah. They laugh together as they turn away.

One of the men at the next table slides off his stool, sidles over to Pol's side, says a few quiet words in his ear. They both look across at Annah. Pol says something sharp to the man, which

Annah can't hear. The Irish man says something too. The man pokes Pol in the chest, says loudly, 'This will be the last night,' and returns to his stool.

Each evening Pol visits the tavern, for their room is far too small for entertaining. Annah stays behind, though, happy not to be burdened with the villagers' disgust of her. Each time someone stops to stare, the skin on Annah's face tightens, her body becomes rigid, aloof, but deep inside a part of her curls in on itself, takes on some of the taint.

She hears the front door slam and, through the glass of the French doors, watches Pol step out onto the pavement. He hooks arms with his new friend, Gustave. With jaunty steps they turn left to walk the lane towards the tavern, to join Pol's 'disciples', as he calls them.

The barber across the way has a very handsome red awning, and two shrubs, like a set of bushy side whiskers, sprout on either side of the windowsill. The building next to it is neatly trimmed in navy blue. Annah's eyes run the length of the dapper street: not a shadow of soot or grime to be seen. Tiny raindrops patter against the glass as Annah stares, fresh air puffs between the doors' gap, whistles against her lips, her nose, her forehead. *Aduh*, she sighs. It is hard to fill the hours. Sometimes she brings out the *monyet*, combs his hair, feeds him grapes one by one. Once, she tried to paint his portrait, but Pol wasn't pleased when he woke the next morning to find she'd used his canvas.

She crosses the room and takes a seat in front of Pol's easel. He is painting from the bowl of fruit on the table: plump citrus, china-blue shadows. A peach nestles among the lemons, and Annah plucks it from the bowl. Her lips rest a moment against its velvet skin before she takes one bite, carefully returning the peach to the same position in the bowl, bite-side down.

Yesterday, Pol said he would paint her again. Here, in Pont-Aven.

'Like this?' Annah pulled on the Breton bonnet she loved so much, with its crisp *coiffe*, as white as a ship's sail. Alfons had given it to her before she left Paris and she felt a slight twist of disappointment that she might not meet him again.

'I don't want to paint a Breton maid, Annah.' Pol laughed. 'I can leave such boring fare to the other fellows here.'

The rain falls more heavily, ringing an insistent tune against the balcony's iron balustrade. Returning to the French doors, she peers out. The village is cloaked in a wash of India ink. Resting her forehead against the gap in the doors, she breathes in the scent of rain, wet stone and a bitter note lifting from the river's brine.

It rains for three more days, keeping them indoors, apart from Pol's visits to the tavern. On the fourth day, when the showers ease, Annah wraps a blanket tight about her shoulders and follows Pol out into the street and around to the path that runs alongside the teeming millstream. The lemony sunlight transforms the morning into a pretty watercolour, washing over the boats with the *jaune* hulls, the fawn spaniel that lopes past chasing a gull, the washerwoman with flaxen hair scrubbing something against the laundry step.

The rain has bleached the buildings of colour, leaving them the buttery hue of sweet *petits pains*. The water seems paler today, as though silt rises to the top. The golden leaves of the chestnut trees rustle above as Pol and Annah leave the road, their clogs grating against pebbly soil. Bits of sand and straw cling to Annah's damp heels, wet grass tickles her shins. Wading through brushwood, she stoops to sniff a flower, disappointed that its yellow flute doesn't hold a pretty scent. Instead, she plucks a flower nearby that has straight, cheerful petals. Its stem is damp against her fingers, its centre as delicate as duckling down.

Strolling back to their lodgings, they pass two women leaving the butcher's shop. They are almost identical, despite the older woman's iron curls and watery eyes. Pol sweeps off his hat and bows, waiting until they are out of earshot before his lip lifts in a slight sneer, and he mutters, 'You can tell by looking at the mother what you can look forward to if you are to marry the daughter.'

Annah studies him as they walk, taking in the furrows of skin about his neck that remind her of the scaly lizards of her island. She thinks of the thick pleats of fat around his middle, his lumpy feet, the yellowing toenails. Does his son's wife know what she has to look forward to?

Pol lifts his hat again, this time greeting a young woman who pushes a white wicker pram, its large wheels lumbering over the uneven pavement. The baby, a linen bonnet framing its plump face like the petals of a sunflower, is propped up against pillows.

Annah's shoe slips into a cleft between the cobblestones. A fisherman tries to sell them a basket of sprats, a black cat lies sprawled on its back, revelling in the sunlight. But the day has dimmed for Annah, dipped her back into the cold embrace of the past. Whenever she thinks of that morning, her memories are shrouded in grey. The bedding, her skin, the tiny thing bundled in her arms. Dawn reaches into the gloom, a leaden wash of light turning everything to clay. Even Madame Marchand's face is ashen with lack of sleep and resolve. And Annah's own despair is dark, sharp, like a jagged piece of granite.

All that gleamed in that dreary room were the baby's amber eyes as Madame tugged her from Annah's clasp.

Six

Pol has done away with the gaudy waistcoat and cloak with mother-of-pearl buttons. Here, he goes about looking like a Breton fisherman in baggy trousers and a blue sweater, a red beret covering his grey curls.

'You certainly resemble one of the locals, Paul,' Séguin shouts above the rumble of the buggy wheels as they bowl towards Concarneau. He laughs, his boyish face flushed, as he takes his wife's slender hand in his.

Annah thinks that perhaps Madame Séguin is a great deal older than her husband. Her hair is still dark, but there is a slight sag to her jowls, wrinkles around her bright eyes. Annah didn't catch her name, but Séguin calls her 'Comtesse' each time he presses a kiss into her palm. They are seated on the bench opposite Annah and Pol, travelling backwards.

The others chatter, passing a bottle of claret between the four of them – even sharing it with the driver when they think of it. The sandy road snakes its way across a series of gentle rises. A fretwork of fields unfolds before them, verdant squares occasionally interrupted by a field of burgundy or yellow. Two tawny birds swoop low, hover and dip with the breeze. The claret has left a pleasant buzz in Annah's ears. They overtake a farmer in his trap, and his dog leans out the side, barks at them. Madame Séguin screams, jumping with fright, but Annah thinks she is pretending, wants Séguin to wrap her in his chubby arms.

'First, I will show you the point,' Séguin says to them, twisting in his chair to instruct the driver where to pull over. 'It is magnificent. You will enjoy it, Annah.'

She is glad when he helps her alight, for she has begun to feel ill with the sway of the buggy. They stride through long grass towards a low stone wall. The sea is almost as dark as Annah's dress and, before Pol can stop her, Annah kicks off her shoes and runs onto the beach.

Joy slips through her blood as her toes sift the fine sand. She lifts her nose, flares her nostrils to sniff the salt in the air. It is almost like being at home, except there is a chill undertone to the wind that buffets her skirt. She gazes down the beach, at a monstrous black boulder, beached on the sand like an exhausted whale. Further again, the long stretch of the point, covered with large rocks the shape of shipwrecks reaching for the sea.

'Come, Annah, eat some pie, and then we must move on,' Pol calls from where they have spread their midday repast across a blanket.

By the time they arrive at Quai Péneroff, the day is overcast. They clamber down from the buggy, returning once for Madame Séguin's parasol and once more for Pol's walking stick. As they approach the inlet, four boys jostle past. One halts, his clogs skidding in the dirt as he gapes at Annah. He lets out a sharp whistle to alert his friends, who turn back to see what he's found. As always, Annah pretends she doesn't notice the stares or the foolish grins as they tail her onto the quay.

'Ignore them, Annah,' says Pol, which annoys Annah, for his comment calls Séguin's attention to the boys, who are now openly leering at her, murmuring *nègre* to each other. Séguin waves his hands at the boys, tells them to leave.

Strolling the uneven pavers that form a wide path alongside the quay, Séguin points out a café with a yellow and black striped awning where they can enjoy a glass of champagne before their journey back to Pont-Aven. Boats of all sizes clutter the marina, masts aloft, sails folded away. The oyster-grey sky mirrors the water, its monotone separated by a narrow strip of stone wall and clumps of bush. Annah pauses to look at the limp body of a dead pilchard that's half squashed into the pavement, wondering why a seabird has not supped on it yet, when she feels a sharp sting at the back of her neck. A pebble drops to the ground, rolls to a stop near the toe of her shoe.

Two fair heads bob up from behind a shrub, and another pebble whips past her face, grazing her cheekbone. She claps a hand to her cheek and glares at the boys.

'You! Stop that.' Pol's voice cracks over the boys' laughter.

A larger pebble strikes Annah's forehead, closely followed by another that bounces off her skirt. A group of fishermen lugging crates from a trawler watch on, chuckling. Two women walking arm in arm shake their heads but smile indulgently at the boys too. Annah's ears burn and she turns away. Wants to shut them all out. Flushed with humiliation, she wishes the heat of it would blaze through her, turn her to fire, transform her into an angry wisp of ash that is whisked away on the breeze.

Pol grabs Annah's elbow, tries to steer her onwards, but Séguin bounds towards the boys, seizing the ringleader. As he tugs on the boy's ear, he shouts, 'Where are your manners, you rascal? How dare you throw stones at this lady.'

The boy yanks himself free with an ugly pout and runs off, closely followed by his companions.

As Séguin dabs at Annah's forehead with his handkerchief,

showing her that there is only a spot of blood, after all, Pol rants about provincial arrogance, that it is exactly this type of peasant attitude that makes him determined to move away. He explains to Madame Séguin how much it sorrows him that so wild and rustic a landscape harbours peoples with such narrow-minded views.

'Which one of you *connards* struck my son?'

The boys have returned with a large man whose face is crumpled with sleep. He breathes heavily, his breath reeking of rum and salted fish. His thick arms flex beneath his sleeves, his hands clench. Black eyes take in Pol and his group, a look of distaste sweeping across his features when he sees Annah.

Séguin lifts his hands, placatingly, says, 'Sir, they were throwing stones at this woman here and they did not stop when asked. I think—'

'You struck my boy over a dirty *nègre*?' the man bellows. He draws his arm back and lunges forward, the bones of his fist cracking against Séguin's nose.

Séguin's head snaps back, his hat toppling to the ground. He staggers a few steps and falls on his rear, his eyes watering. His wife screeches his name over and over, calls him her baby, her sweet child, kneels by his side. Séguin cups his nose, but his fingers can't stem the blood that splashes across his lips, drips onto his shirtfront. The large man bears down on him again, fist held high, but Pol grasps him by the shoulder and, growling with the exertion of it, throws the man to the ground.

Three sailors run across from a café, shouting. One of them heaves the boy's father up from beneath the armpits. He kicks out at Séguin again, but his boot connects with Madame Séguin instead. She yelps, clutching her side, limps a small distance away.

As the men fall upon Pol, Annah crouches down onto her haunches, shelters her head with her elbows, but she's still able to see the flurry of punches and slaps; she can still hear the grunts, the smack of skin, the squelch of gristle. Séguin scrabbles backwards, like a crab in retreat, flings himself over the side of the quay into the water.

Fear and shock roil Annah's stomach. She pants with the nausea of it. She watches as Pol resists their attack the best he can: whacks one with his cane when gripped by the hair, headbutts another when held in a tight tussle. They drive him backwards towards the road, and then something happens and Pol howls, drops to the ground clutching his ankle. But the others aren't deterred. The boy's father leans down, bangs Pol's head against the ground. The others kick him, in the side, in the thighs, in his stomach, with their wooden shoes.

A waiter from the café runs across the road, yells at them to stop, holds his arms wide, barring them from Pol. The three sailors and the boy's father stand back, bent double, winded with the exertion of beating Pol. The waiter beckons for them to follow him, twitches a sailor's sleeve, remonstrates with the other. Hesitating, looking over their shoulders like they might like to return, the men make their way into the café's dim interior.

Annah crawls to Pol's side where he lies by the edge of the road. His face is black with blood. One eye is closed over, the other blinks up at her. He makes a strange clucking noise at the back of his throat as he inhales.

'My ankle,' he whispers. He rotates his left foot, but the other one lies fallow.

She lifts the hem of his trousers, revealing a long gash of vermilion. A gleam of white breaks the fold of pale skin, not unlike the brittle bone that pokes out from a leg of mutton. She vomits into the gutter.

'Well, it seems your right leg is broken at the point of the internal malleolus, and you've dislocated the foot,' the doctor says, stepping back from the bed. 'Quite shattered, it is. I've splinted it for now, but in a few days I will return to put it in a cast. No moving about. Take one drop of this when required.' He places a brown bottle on the cabinet before taking his leave.

Pol's face is as white as a daub of lead pigment. He fainted twice from the pain when he lay in the farmer's cart as it rumbled back to Pont-Aven. As soon as they arrived at the lodging house, Séguin and the farmer carried him upstairs and the landlady ran to fetch the village doctor.

Pol wriggles his fingers towards the medicine. Annah draws out the dispenser and drops one bubble of the clear tincture into his mouth, watches as it dissolves on his tongue.

Pol's good eye squeezes shut. 'More.'

Annah releases one more drop of fluid onto his tongue. The creases of agony that pucker his forehead and mouth, that tighten the skin about his jaw, gradually release, soften away. His shoulders relax to the mattress, his head nestles the pillow. He snores softly.

For three days they follow the same routine. Pol's friend, Gustave, brings fruit and wine and tonics. He sits by Pol's bed for hours, sometimes reading to him, sometimes drawing. Annah slumps low in a chair at the foot of the bed, her feet hooked over the footboard, her attention monopolised by Gustave's conversation and a dizzy fug of memories. Her sleep is broken by Pol's demands for more medicine or drink, and Gustave's visits.

On the fourth morning the doctor returns with an assistant.

Pol gasps through gritted teeth as the doctor prods his leg, declaring the swelling to have gone down sufficiently to dress the wound properly, and the two men get to work on wrapping the ankle in a cast. The doctor soaks lengths of cloth in a basin of water the landlady fetches for him, then gently binds the bandaging about Pol's leg, sponging it smooth. Pol's fingers claw at the bedsheets, and Annah drops more of the tincture onto his tongue, until he sags into the mattress again. When the men are done and gone, Annah runs her hand over the cast, surprised at how hard it's become. By the end of the week, with Gustave's assistance, Pol can pull himself into a seated position, pillows banked behind his back.

'I will bring action against those sailors, Gustave, I swear it. The doctor alone will cost me five hundred francs, God help me. I will be ruined. It is very unusual for me to need such an amount of money. I am like Jesus – the flesh is the flesh, the spirit is the spirit. Usually, the smallest amount of money satisfies my flesh in order for my spirit to be left in peace.' He accepts a glass of the wine Gustave has brought him, places it next to the pouch of tobacco, also a gift from Gustave.

It's raining again, but the room is stifling, even when Annah flings the French doors open. She feels like she's drenched in the stench of liniment, Pol's unwashed bed linen, the *monyet*'s fruity farts. Leaning over the balcony railing as far as she can, she inhales deeply, but can't be rid of the room's smell, feels it cling to the fine hairs in her nostrils.

'I knocked the boy's father down with two punches,' Pol tells Gustave. 'But then he fetched the crew from his boat, damn him. It must have been fifteen men who set upon me, but I took them all on, Gustave, and kept the upper hand, until my damned foot caught in a hole. That's how I broke my leg.' Pol's voice quivers with anger. A rush of blood colours his throat and he clutches his damaged leg.

Annah watches three girls skip past, their clogs drumming hollow notes across the cobblestones. An older man enters the barber's, while another hobbles towards the stationer's shop below. She reaches her fingers as far as they will go, so she can feel the sun's heat upon her skin. She hasn't been out since that day. Envies the girls below who can feel the sun's touch upon their scalps.

'I have brought these magazines for you to read, Paul,' says Gustave, his voice high-pitched, fluting, at odds with his stout figure. He places three old copies of *Le Figaro Illustré* on the bedside cabinet. 'I've also cut this news clipping from *Le Finistère* for you to read. Another account of that dreadful incident in Concarneau. These newspaper features will help your case, no doubt.'

Pol scans the words, murmuring as he reads. He tuts. 'They've spelt Gauguin wrong again. Look!' He waves the clipping under Gustave's nose. 'And they say Annah is of the black race, *imbéciles*.'

He remains cranky for the rest of the afternoon. Throws a book at the cage when the monkey chatters too much, calls Annah a *salope* when she accidentally bumps his foot. He is only calm when working. At first Gustave positions the easel so Pol can continue with his painting of the fruit, but one morning Pol catches sight of Annah as she peels stamps from his correspondence, bored.

'Bring me those,' he demands. She scatters the stamps across the sheet, a confetti of black, blue, red, yellow. His long fingers pick out a blue one. He flicks its edge with his nail before tossing it aside for another. Flipping open the closest magazine, he stares at a picture of a handsome woman wearing a moss-green gown. She too has a dark servant, and she stands upon a lion-skin rug. Pol sweeps the stamps nearer to the page, matches the black of a stamp to the jewels in her hair, the green to her gown.

'Annah, take some coins from my purse and buy some glue from the shop downstairs,' he says to her, still arranging the stamps by the magazine illustration.

Annah stills. Shakes her head.

He frowns at her. 'Don't be stupid, girl. It's just down the steps.'

She takes a seat at the table. Eyes Pol where he is trapped on the stinky bed.

What if someone is to throw stones at her again? Hurl abuse? She will not go out alone. She recalls the sailors' faces, teeth clenched as they kick Pol; she hears the dreadful thwack of fist splitting flesh. Fear rises in her chest, peaks somewhere behind her eyes, blinds her. Her head is almost too heavy to keep upright.

When her vision clears, she feels giddy; everything seems to wobble, drowned in aspic. The walls close in on her, press against her skin, but she knows that if she is to leave, if she is to try walking out the door, the yawning space of outside will be too much for her. She will shatter in the glare.

There's a knock on the door, and Gustave pokes his head inside.

'Gustave. Thank God you are here. Annah's as useful to me as that fucking monkey. She needs a good beating – and the sulking! It's unbearable!'

'What is it you need, Paul? Tell me,' Gustave says.

'I have an idea for a new project. You can fetch the equipment for me, if you please. I'll need some glue and something to ...'

Annah turns in her seat, stares outside, her eyes scanning the strip of blue sky above the building across the way.

Annah peels another stamp from an envelope and drops it into the small bowl by Pol's side. She watches as he selects a faded orange one, carefully rips away its edge until it's the shape of a crescent, dabs it against the surface of a ceramic tile. With deft fingers, he tears up another stamp, then another, arranging them on the tile, until Annah recognises the handsome woman's waves of auburn hair.

As he works, he tells Gustave of that Vincent man, and she thinks she too will slice the ear from her head if she has to listen to that stupid story yet again. She drags a chair to the French doors and, taking a seat, she leans her elbows on her thighs, hands over ears. Although muffled, she can still hear the drone of his voice. Madame Pack's yellow canary comes to mind: how it used to flap itself senseless against the bars of its cage, a torrent of twittering and damaged feathers floating to the floor.

Annah squeezes her head tighter. Thinks of smashing her body against the walls, so hard the cloudy mirror crashes to the floor, the glasses on the table spill. She wants to shed her gown, scrape deep trenches in her skin with her fingernails. She hugs her arms about herself.

'Perhaps if you use your walking stick in one hand and lean on me with your other?' says Gustave.

Annah looks over to see Pol standing next to the bed, leaning on his good foot. Gustave wedges himself under his left arm, while Pol grips his stick, manoeuvring it so it is comfortable in his hand, taps it twice against the wooden floor. He grimaces as his left foot shuffles forward. Lets out a grunt of pain as he limps forward. He tries two more steps before he halts, breathing heavily, perspiration beading his forehead.

'That's enough for today, my good friend,' he says. 'I will try again tomorrow.'

Gustave helps him hop back to his bed. He notices Annah staring, and smiles. 'You see? It will not be long before Paul walks by himself. I just need to find him another crutch.'

Annah turns in her chair to gaze outside. A starling lands on the barber's tiled roof, spies something below. For the first time in days Annah's mind feels sharp, as clear as the turquoise water of home, a sparkle of fish darting to and fro. When Pol is sufficiently healed to walk, they can leave this smelly room, and she should feel relieved, jubilant. But she doesn't. Dread lies cold and heavy in her stomach. She pictures herself trailing him, as she did before, like the black servant in that painting of Olympia, or the dark man who waits upon the handsome woman in the magazine. Nothing more than Pol's shadow. A reminder of death. Waiting for death. And even though they will no longer be cooped up in this room, like the poor *monyet* is kept to his cage, she will still have to continue to do as Pol bids, listen to his never-ending lectures, hear the same stories. Annah sits straighter in her chair and lifts her skirt, feels the weight of the hem.

The slant of the afternoon sun inches across her skin as she thinks on what needs to be done so she can leave this place, leave Pol. A young lad leads a cow along the road towards the dairy, switching its rump with a length of straw. The barber locks his front doors; a maid hurries past carrying a basket of linen.

The landlady brings their supper – roasted *rouget* and a bowl of boiled courgette – and Annah tears away half of her bread and slips it into the scratchy valise with one of the peaches Gustave has brought them. The men talk late into the evening, and anxiety squirms in her stomach, rising higher and higher in her chest until it rings in her ears. She almost closes the door on Gustave's heel when he eventually leaves them, but has to wait almost another hour for Pol to find sleep.

Her fingers tremor just a little as she slides the *pareo* and comb into the valise next to her Breton bonnet and her other dress. She rifles through Pol's painting gear for his sharpest palette knife to nick the stitches from her hem, releasing copper coin after copper coin, four brass coins and two precious silver ones. Weighing the small mound in the palm of her hand, she wonders if she has enough.

Glancing across the room, her eyes take in Pol's leather purse on the bedside cabinet. As she creeps across the floorboards, Pol mumbles something in his sleep. Annah snatches up his purse and retreats to her chair. She takes half of his money and adds it to her savings, tying the handkerchief in a tight knot.

Annah dims the lamp and positions the chair so that it faces the balcony. She pushes her buttocks against the chair's hard back, folding her legs up beneath her. She's worried if she lies down, she might fall asleep and not wake in time to escape. She must leave before the village stirs. Before there are too many people about who will stare at her, accost her, perhaps return her to Pol. With anxious eyes, she watches the night sky, dozing only once in a while, waking each time to a sore neck and numb legs.

Finally, a feeble cock's crow reaches her ears. She leans forward in her chair, straining to hear its call again. Rising to her feet, she collects her bag and pauses at the end of the bed, watching the rise and fall of Pol's chest as he sleeps. By his legs, a glimmer of white catches her eye – a corner of the ceramic tile, the collage of the handsome lady almost completed. A tiny spark of spite lights her sleep-deprived mind. Picking the tile up, she slips it into her valise. She decides she will take his walking stick too. The pearl alone will be worth something to someone.

Annah finds the netting that the landlady throws over the food to keep the flies away and drapes it over her head. Clamps her hat down over it. She pulls gloves over her brown fingers. Dragging the valise's handles up over her left shoulder, she tiptoes to the door and turns the handle. She startles as something shuffles in the darkness, but it's only the *monyet*. His tiny face presses against the bars. She can't possibly take him. His eyes glisten up at her, and her shoulders drop. She can't leave him behind either. He is like her, a frayed thread torn far from the tapestry of home, searching out some form of selvage. Annah picks up the cage and clamps it under her other arm and leaves, not bothering to close the door behind her.

She steals down the stairs, her heart thrumming as she lets herself out through the front door onto the street. Dawn's light mutes the village canvas, reminding her of the gentle purples in that painting of Tehura. She wonders if she will always see Pol's colours in the world, a constant reminder of this time, drawing her back – immediately, unbidden – just as a flavour or fragrance might do.

She walks to the end of the lane, stopping for a moment to listen to the rush of water in the millstream. Draws strength from its familiar rhythm, imagining for a moment she is home, standing on the creaking dock. Brave enough to be alone.

Hearing the clatter of shutters opening somewhere behind her, Annah clasps the cage more firmly to her body and hurries towards the inn on the other side of the village. She will catch a stagecoach, a train, walk if need be, to Paris or Le Havre, or anywhere else her money will take her.

She gazes up at silver clouds, a frottage against the lavender sky, and feels a ripple in the waters of her stomach. The tiny flick of a tadpole's tail.

She breathes in, breathes in.

Invitation

THE INVITATIONS ARE IN YELLOW envelopes this time. They're pigeonholed into the pockets of the wall-hanging decorated with orange lions with sunshine manes. Arum peers over the shoulder of another mum but can't tell if the invitations are for a girl's party or a boy's. Brianna has an invitation but so do Josh and Sam.

Her eyes find their way to Rafi's pocket – last row, three from the right. Empty.

Last week the envelopes were pink, for Letitia's birthday. He wasn't invited to that one either.

The kindy doors open and the waiting mums shuffle along the corridor. The two women in front of Arum chat to each other, talking too swiftly for her to keep up. Her English is getting better, but she understands only snatches – *the Woolworths in Annerley … sweet and white*. One of them reaches over, tears open the envelope, reads it to the other. *Mott Park … Sunday*.

The closer Arum gets to the kindy room, the more the dusty smells of the corridor recede, replaced with the familiar odour of stale wee, orange peel, antiseptic cleaner. The mum behind her, the impossibly thin one, reads something on her phone. Her toddler son leans against her legs, claws at her T-shirt so that it gapes low, reveals the top of a pink bra. His fingers leave their trace on everything they touch, reminding Arum of a frog's sticky pads. She places a hand on her stomach as it lurches. It was like this when she was pregnant with Rafi, too, like everything is overexposed, bleached in light, but fogged and distorted. Her lips part, the fat part of her tongue rising as she silently gags.

The children are sprawled across the squares of scratchy carpet while the teacher reads the final page of a book about a wombat. Two boys at the back of the group squirm across the floor, but most are seated cross-legged as they listen to her, mouths open, eyes glazed, like cold snapper on beds of ice at the supermarket. Rafi is in his special chair, the one with the blow-up wedge cushion that's supposed to keep him attentive. He's watching the two boys roll around on their bums, but he stays put, his fingers pressing and stroking the rubbery goosebumps down the side of the cushion.

When they finally notice their parents, the kids sit straighter, twist around to see better. One of the squirming boys looks like he's ready to burst forward, like he's a sprinter, poised against a starting block. Other children smile shyly, while one boy even gasps, as if this daily ritual is new to him.

Arum moves to Rafi's side, places her hand on his shoulder. 'Get your bag, Rafi,' she says, careful of the English words.

He stands up, kicks his chair – showing off for her – and stomps over to the bag rack, head down, like a steam engine.

'The dentist came to kindy today.' Little Harriet's voice, high-pitched with excitement, carries above the others as her mum wriggles her green jelly sandal onto her foot. Harriet balances on one leg by planting her hand on the top of her mother's head. 'We all got to see him, Mummy, even the naughty boy, Rafi.'

'The teacher says Rafi might be "on the spectrum".' Arum says the English words for 'on the spectrum' because she doesn't know how to use the term in her own language.

'What's that?' Her husband, Dani, is seated at the pine table in their kitchen, and she has to squeeze around him to reach the fridge.

'I'm not sure.' She takes out a tray of diced beef. A taut layer of cellophane covers the meat, neat and fresh, no sign of blood. Once, Arum spent three hours in the supermarket, inspecting all that was on offer. She marvelled at just how many types of cereal people here in Australia need, how many types of rice.

'The teacher says Rafi sometimes hits the other children, or even kicks them.' Her eyes search her husband's, seek out a reaction.

'But he never hits,' says Dani, surprised.

'I told her this. But she says that maybe he does it because he doesn't know how to get their attention in a better way. He doesn't speak well. Can't communicate.' She wipes the bench down with Spray n' Wipe, its antibacterial tang reminding her of her work at the nursing home. Dani had brought them here on a special skills visa, when his work at the Nike factory outside Bandung had dried up, but she can't return to nursing until she does a bridging course. So in the meantime, every Tuesday, Thursday and Friday she cleans tiles and floors, maybe helps hand out meals, at Hopetown Aged Care.

'Will he need to see a doctor?'

Arum shrugs. She wonders if he's worried it will cost too

much. She pours treacly soy sauce over the sizzling onion and meat and thinks she should've bought chicken instead of beef for the *semur*. Chicken's cheaper.

While the beef simmers, Arum moves to the lounge room. Rafi is at his red plastic table, staring at the television. Behind him is the small bookcase that houses her nursing textbooks, the only things she'd brought from Indonesia besides clothing and a few bits of jewellery.

'*Makan*,' she says to him, pointing at his plate of strawberries. He's watching Mr Bean cartoons again, his favourite. She promised the teacher she'd wean him from them because Mr Bean doesn't talk properly. But she also promised they would speak English more often with him at home, too.

Her eyes take in his long lashes, the curve of his nose, the way his stubby fingers play with his right ear, pleating it in and out. Does he even notice he isn't invited to parties, that he doesn't have any friends? Sadness weighs heavy on her, like a sack of rice has been lowered onto her chest.

Rafi looks up at her and dimples. He places his hand under his armpit and flaps his elbow. He learned this trick from the man who came to fix the taps in the kitchen. The man noticed Rafi trying to hide by the side of the fridge and he grinned, showed Rafi his trick of making farting noises by cupping his underarm. Now Rafi does it whenever he wants attention or even when he is embarrassed and doesn't want attention. But his little hand can't catch the air in his armpit; he makes the noise with his mouth. Brrrrp. Brrrrp.

Dani comes up from behind and wraps his arms around her, resting his hands across her rounded stomach. 'You worry too much. He's fine. Look at him.' Rafi sees them watching him, rolls off his chair, laughing at Mr Bean falling down a broken elevator shaft in a wheelchair. 'He's fine.'

The TAFE campus where Arum learns English is small – much smaller than the university she attended in Jakarta. But she likes that the TAFE is surrounded by forest – dry trees that rustle in the breeze, so tall that when she looks up between them it reminds her of when she was little, gazing up at adults, their hands and heads filtering the beams of sunlight. Nerves no longer clench her stomach tight, and she's no longer confused about how to find her way around. She has a white folder in which her notes are organised neatly, nouns written in solid blue biro, verbs in eye-catching red. She uses yellow highlighter for past tense, pink for present and green for future, but sometimes she gets it wrong, has to re-highlight, so that she creates new colours of blue or streaked orange. But she feels proud every time she speaks in English, uses a new word. 'Can I please buy two pies? Yes. The beef pies, please,' or 'Does this bus go to Garden City?' Although some words – words like 'tongue', 'shower', 'school' – still trip her up.

And she has made new friends at TAFE, two women who make her feel like herself again. Sabeen, from Iraq, with heavy, black kohl around her eyes, her friendly, pudgy face framed by a hijab. Arum doesn't wear a head covering anymore. She'd stopped bothering within a month of arriving in Brisbane, but she keeps a scarf in her handbag, just in case they run into other Indonesians in Sunnybank, at one of the restaurants – women who are wearing their *kerudung*. Then Arum feels naked almost, brings the silk square from her bag, slinks it across her hair. Laleh, Arum's Iranian friend, doesn't use a scarf either, although she, too, is Muslim. She's younger than Sabeen and Arum, and her hair has been lightened to the rusty colour of autumn leaves, and Arum wonders how she can be bothered to curl the ends each morning.

At lunchtime they sit at the park bench next to a cluster of bamboo palms, and Arum tries to tell them about how Rafi is being left out of parties, but she needs to reach for her *kamus*, look up the English word for 'invitation'.

'But that is not kind,' says Sabeen.

'It's rude,' says Laleh, popping a piece of pineapple in her mouth. 'You need to just go.'

Arum stares across at her. 'What do you mean?'

'Just go to the party.' Laleh starts to say more but can't think of the word, even though her English is much better than theirs. She flips through her own dictionary. She taps at a word on the page and pronounces, slowly, curling the 'r': 'Pretend. You need to pretend you get one of these invitations. Or pretend you do not understand.'

Arum draws back and laughs. 'No. I could not.'

'Yes. Yes, you must.' Laleh waves her fork. 'And then you have a big birthday party too. Invitation all the children.'

Arum shakes her head. 'But Rafi's birthday is already finished.'

'We were supposed to go to Basra for my sixteenth birthday,' says Sabeen.

Arum turns to look at her. A tiny mole teeters on the bottom eyelid of her left eye that always reminds Arum of a tear. She knows Sabeen escaped to England before finding her way to Christmas Island. Out of the three of them, she's the one who always says she will return home, as soon as all the trouble is over.

'My mother come from there. She used to say it was like Venice. Beautiful. You ever been to Venice?'

Arum shakes her head, but Laleh says, 'Yes. It is beautiful.'

'I will go back,' Sabeen says. She turns to Arum. 'Do you miss home?'

Arum stares at the palms, how the higher fronds cast their tiger-stripe shadow across the lower leaves. She thinks of how excited they were when they were contacted to say the visa was approved. A new life in Australia! But then she thinks of her mother, of her firm hug at Soekarno-Hatta airport, how her eyes were smiling but her bottom lip jerked. She feels a dip of sadness, but then a flutter, like the tremble of powdery moth wings against the inner wall of her belly. Her baby.

She lifts her shoulder. 'No. This is my home now.'

On Sunday she catches the 175 bus to Mott Park with Rafi. At kindy drop-off on Friday morning she heard Josh talking about Luke's birthday party, so she has a gift-wrapped box of Lego in her bag. She thought about Laleh's words for three days, uncertainty slippery in her guts. By Saturday she'd formed a plan. She'll sidle up to the party. If the parents seem aghast to see her, she will say they are passing through the park, looking for the swings. If they are friendly, she will pretend, like Laleh suggested, that they were invited, offer them the gift of Lego.

Balanced on her lap is a lunch box, warm against her legs. She's cooked *risoles* for the party, Indonesian style, not the lumps of mince they call rissoles here. Arum knows a woman in Runcorn who cooks *risoles* and other Indonesian pastries, but she charges three dollars a piece, minimum twenty pieces. So Arum looked up the recipe on Google, made them herself. She thought that once the other mums taste how delicious they are, they'll ask her about them, talk to her.

But the *risoles* have not turned out well. She couldn't get the crepe layer right – it's too thick, too dry – and there's not enough carrot in the filling. They're supposed to look like soft spring rolls but, instead, they're deflated and greasy. She considered not bringing them, but she'd spent four hours on them and although they're wonky, they still taste good.

She takes Rafi's hand as they step from the bus. From the path, she can see the park bench with balloons bobbing in the breeze, the small groups of parents standing near the children. Uneasiness gurgles in her stomach, like she's swallowed too much soft drink. She wants to turn around, climb back onto the bus, but it's pulling away.

'Oh, look, Harriet, it's Rafi.' Harriet's mum smiles at Arum as she takes a bag from the boot of her car. She tells Harriet to run ahead with Rafi and falls into step with Arum. She tells Arum her name is Jodie, and when she asks for Arum's name, she repeats it twice, like she's tasting it.

Arum sniffs the air, looks up at the blue sky. It is always curious to her that this country has no real smell, besides maybe times like this, among the trees, when it smells of something like crumpled bay leaves and the sharpness of dirt.

As they near the party, Jodie peels off to talk to two other mothers. Arum treads forward, her smile fixed, her muscles tensed, ready to keep moving if she senses the slightest animosity. But she's not even sure which ones are Luke's parents, and nobody seems to notice her.

She approaches the picnic table, and silty dirt slips into her sandals, grass prickles the sides of her feet. She places the container of *risoles* between a packet of pink biscuits and a bowl of stout sausages that are the colour of red balloons.

Jodie beckons and introduces her to the two mothers she's with. They're talking about making something for the kindy, something to do with dinosaurs and green. She wants to join in, but knows her tongue will turn into a snail. Her eyes scout the crowd of children, until they rest on Rafi's black hair. He's waiting by the swing with the scooped seat for small bottoms, watching Harriet swoop up into the air and back. At the table, a kid, younger than the others, inspects the food, his fingers hooked over the side of the table, his nose resting against the edge. He reaches out and places three fingers on the top *risole*, presses, takes his hand back and licks it. Rummaging in a bowl of chips, he takes a handful and runs off.

Arum slaps at a fly that tickles her right shoulder as she follows the others to the table. Her fingers slip across the sweat that trickles into the cleft of her collarbone. Jodie hands her a cup of orange cordial and reaches for a piece of watermelon for herself. Nobody is eating the *risoles*. Arum wants to cover them, take them away even, but doesn't want to look like it matters. Maybe, in half an hour, she will put the lid back on, keep them for dinner.

Rafi still stands by the swing, watching Harriet. He turns to Arum, points at the girl as she swings high into the air, kicking her legs forward. He wants a turn.

But her attention is drawn to Josh's mum who leans in close, inspects the *risoles* before picking one up. She's chatting with the skinny mum, brings the *risole* to her lips, pauses as she nods and says something. She waves the *risole* twice before finally taking a bite.

An ant tickles its way across Arum's heel. She can't tell if Josh's mum likes the *risole* or not – she just keeps chewing and talking, reaches for a napkin, presses it to her mouth. Arum's chest swells, wonders if Josh's mum is about to spit into it, but she pulls the napkin away, glances at the lipstick mark she's left on the tissue.

Rafi is still pointing at the swing, glancing over his shoulder at her. She makes her way to him, asks, 'What is it, Rafi?'

He keeps pointing at the swing, pleats his ear with his other hand.

'Why don't you get on the other swing, Rafi?' She points at the empty, flat swing-seat that jangles in tune with Harriet's movements. 'I will help you.'

He shakes his head.

A mother – maybe the birthday boy's mum – buzzes by with a friendly smile. Arum smiles back and catches a glimpse of Josh's mum, as she wraps the rest of the *risole* in a napkin, places it on the table.

Arum's eyes drop to the girl. She watches her brown curls feather across her cheeks each time she tucks her legs in and swings back.

'Maybe Rafi can go on swing, Harriet?'

But the girl just frowns, shakes her head no, surges upward.

Arum looks over at her *risoles*, which are wilting in the sun. A fly lands on one, hops across its glistening surface. She turns back just in time to see Rafi whip the seat out from under Harriet, how the girl lands on her hands and knees, screeching.

'Rafi,' she gasps.

Rafi squints up at her and tucks his hand under his armpit, flaps his elbow.

Hardflip

THE ROOFING SAGS A LITTLE under his weight, but Oskar's not afraid of heights when he's on his skateboard. He can see his friends below. Gav has his camera ready, and Amadi gives him the thumbs up.

'Mate, it's no higher than a ten-set,' Amadi calls.

He's bullshitting. The deserted Mexican restaurant is squat, but its roof is much higher than ten stairs. It's more like a fifteen-set, easy, but Oskar's jumped that before anyway.

The sun is behind him, stings the back of his neck. Another perfect Sunday. The best time to street-skate – when all the schools are empty, the city buildings deserted. He drops the bow of his skateboard forward, holds the back of it steady under his left foot. The roof tiles are flat, patched together, but his board rumbles as he rolls the wheels back and forth.

It's weird. When he sees heights on TV, like that time his mum was watching the movie with the two men grappling over an icy crevasse, or when they show a fish-eye view of a bungy jumper on one of those survival shows, Oskar's hands become clammy. He feels a prickling in his fingertips like a Christmas beetle is crawling across them. But when he's on his board, he's fine. He's in control.

He pushes off. He feels his own heft, his feet steadying the board's wheels as he scoots across the roof. Crouching, his calf muscles tense, ready to spring. It's just him and his board, movement, the wind cool against sweat. He knows he will fly.

Oskar rolls his shirt sleeve up so it doesn't brush the graze on his elbow. It took him four goes before he got the roof jump right. The first two times he'd fallen off his board, rolled against the hard ground of the car park, the bitumen pebbly and glittering up close. The third time he landed, the board slumped in the middle, and he thought the fucking thing was going to snap. Gav had to lend him his flick-knife to tighten the deck bolts. But Oskar got it on the fourth go. Lucky. He could tell Gav was getting a bit bored filming him by then.

It was Gav who'd taught Oskar to roll with it when he stacked it; just let the momentum take you, don't resist. Later, whenever they look through the video footage of Oskar somersaulting off his board, they always laugh. When Oskar shows these parts to his mum, though, she glances away, like she's watching a horror movie.

Hitching his backpack onto his shoulder, he fist-bumps his mates goodbye. Gav pulls his car keys out from his pocket, walks towards his Milo-green ute. As usual, Amadi tries to clack his knuckles against Oskar's, a sharp crack of pain. 'Not cool.' Oskar grins as he turns towards the bus stop.

The sun's lost its bite by the time he takes a seat on the bench. It's only him and an old woman. His board rests beneath his right foot and he rolls it gently back and forth across the cement. A slight breeze has picked up, swooshing dirt and a chip packet along the gutter. The music beats loud in his ear, his earphones vibrating with Joey Bada$$, telling him he can't change the world unless he changes himself, and Oskar doesn't realise the old woman is talking to him until she glares at him and shakes her head.

He pulls the left earbud out, says, 'Sorry?'

'I asked you to stop moving that thing,' she says, pointing at his skateboard. 'I can't think with that racket.'

Oskar's brows lift, but his foot pauses.

'Where you from, anyway?' she asks.

'I live up the road. In Holland Park.'

She shakes her head, impatient. 'No. I mean where are you from?' Her voice stressing the last word. She's wearing a cloth hat, and the store's plastic hook is still attached to its brim.

'I was born here.'

Her eyes, as bleary as a dead mullet's, flick over his face. 'If you say so.'

'I was.' He smiles politely at her, looks up the road for the bus.

'Too many foreigners here. Too many.'

He nods but doesn't say anything. He thinks of Gav, of how Gav says to just smile along, be polite. Prove to people that skaters aren't the dicks they think they are.

'But where are your parents from?'

'Vietnam.'

'Well, they should go back, is my opinion.' She clasps her handbag closer onto her lap. 'I've got nothing against them personally, but youse just don't fit in.' Her bony finger points at the pathway. 'Like you, riding up and down.'

Heat creeps into his cheeks, but he just keeps smiling like a fucking idiot. His chest feels like it's burning, like an army of ants swarm up from his abdomen. Two girls, older than him, handbags bumping against high-cut shorts, approach the bus stop. He wishes the old woman would shut up. He doesn't want the girls to hear her, maybe agree or, worse, cast sympathetic eyes over him. He picks up his board, steps to the side of the road, peers along its length, like he's searching for the bus. Suddenly, he's aware of the frayed hole on the side of his shoe, of the damp gaminess of his stained shirt. The grime on his brown skin that now feels like a heavy jacket he wants to shrug off.

When he arrives home his grandad is on the back patio, hosing water into a wide bucket. Oskar pauses close by, and gazes down at the bulbous goldfish that bobs in the water.

'Why don't you put that thing in an aquarium, Gong?' he asks.

His grandad grunts. 'Easier to change water like this. Every day I change water and he grow this big. When your mum got him, he only this big.' He holds his thumb and forefinger up, about an inch apart. He squats, his knees spread either side of the bucket. Beads of sweat bubble between the sparse strands of hair on his pate and his shins shine like polished chopsticks.

'You want some noodles? I'm going to cook some,' Oskar asks, but his grandad just waves his hand, says, 'You make them wrong anyway. I'll wait for your mother to get home.'

Oskar shrugs off his backpack in the kitchen, kicks it under the kitchen bench. He props his skateboard against the wall. After filling up the kettle, he plugs it in, then tears open a packet of Indomie. He drops the noodle cake into a cereal bowl, taps out the spices from the sachet. When the water's boiled, he pours it over the noodles. He prods the still-firm noodles with a fork, breaking them apart in the steaming broth. In his room, he places the bowl on his desk and turns on his PS4.

He's just fighting off a pack of feral ghouls when he hears his mum arrive home.

'Oskar,' she calls, one of her shopping bags banging against the sliding door as she struggles through into the kitchen. 'Oh, there you are. Help me unpack these.' She leans in to peck a kiss on Oskar's cheek. She smells of her Beyoncé perfume, cigarette smoke, oven fries.

His grandad watches from the TV room, his eyes blinking slowly. He doesn't greet her or offer to help.

She plonks three grey plastic bags on the table and drops her handbag to the floor where it slumps against a chair leg.

Oskar peels a soggy plastic bag away from a bottle of cold orange juice, unscrewing the lid to pour himself a cup.

'I said unpack, Oskar, not help yourself.' She's smiling, shaking her head at him. 'You can also take out the recycling.'

He suppresses a groan. It pisses her off when he does that, and he wants to stay on her good side. 'Don't forget I've got that party tonight,' he says as he lobs the bread onto the bench. 'Can you still give me a lift?'

His mum heaves a loud sigh, her hands resting on her hips. 'Oskar, it's Sunday. You know your Uncle Danny is coming over for dinner. And who has a bloody party on a Sunday, anyway?'

'But Mum ...' He can feel the ants start up again, one or two stinging under his skin. 'You said I could go.'

Her shoulders drop. 'Who's going?'

'Amadi.'

She nods. 'Your Sudanese friend?'

'Ethiopian, Mum. You're thinking of Abdi. You're so racist,' he says, joking.

'Okay. Who else?'

'Beck, Laurel, Sebastian.' Actually, he's not sure if Seb is going, but his mum likes him. It might sway her. 'And Gav will be there.'

She frowns, causing two neat slivers between her brows that leave their mark even when her face is relaxed. 'Is it a grown-ups' party?'

'No, Mum.' He works hard to keep the exasperated tone from his voice. 'It's a girl from school – her birthday. A grade eleven girl. Kat. You don't know her.'

'Why's Gav going then?'

'I dunno. He's just one of the guys from the skate park. She's invited all of us.'

His mum presses her lips together, shakes her head. 'You have school tomorrow, mate.'

'Come on, Mum. We've had all our assessment. The last week's always a total waste of time.'

She looks tired. Her coffee-bean eyes are magnified by her glasses, and some of her mascara has smudged the skin beneath her eyes.

They hear a snort from the TV room. 'What does it matter, Daughter,' Oskar's grandad says in Vietnamese. 'Your son doesn't get good marks, anyway.' To Oskar, he says, in his broken English, like the boy can't understand his mother tongue, 'You be better stay home and watch news. Learn something. Put something in that head of yours. Not waste time with bum friends.'

Oskar stacks four Homebrand cans of tuna in the cupboard. He rolls his eyes at his mum.

As he leaves the kitchen, she tries to rub his back, but he's moving too swiftly.

'Okay, Oskar. You can go to the party. But I can't drive you, sorry. I've got to get the chicken on.'

Oskar pushes his hair back before replacing his Yankees cap as he walks to the bus stop from the train station. He has to meet Seb and Amadi so they can catch the 579 to the party. On the train he'd thought about his grandad. Living with him was like how Ms Haddon, his geography teacher, described reducing your carbon footprint – avoid heavy traffic, skip bottled water, lower the thermostat. Except in his case, Oskar avoids irritating his grandad by keeping to his room, by being invisible. He skips TV time with his mum, lowers the volume of his music. Once, a few years ago, when Oskar still slept in his mum's bed, she told him that Grandad was just cross that Oskar's dad had run out on them, that he was left to support them. She told him how Gong's shop had closed down when her mum died, not long after Oskar was born. She insisted that he loved Oskar, that he loved her, but Oskar didn't see it. How was constant yelling and criticising love?

'Hey, Oskar.'

Seb grins at him from the bus-stop bench. He has a diamond stud in each ear, and the sides of his head have been shaved so that his black curly hair springs tall at the top. He's wearing his camo pants, too, just like Oskar, but Oskar's got his Only jacket on, much cooler than Seb's Nike.

'Have we missed the bus?' asks Amadi, coming up behind Oskar. He's got on the Bape hoodie that's a hand-me-down from Gav, and a black Supreme cap that doesn't quite contain his frizzy halo of hair. 'My mum made me eat before I could come out. Today, when she went to the shops, I asked her to get me something so I can fatten up.' He holds his hands out, displaying his long, skinny frame. 'And you know what she gave me? Did she get me ice cream? Or Tim Tams? No. A punnet of cherry tomatoes. Tomatoes! Like that's gonna get me fat.'

Oskar loves how funny Amadi is. He feels lighter, looser. Like how he wants to feel all the time.

They wait another eight minutes for their bus and line up to board with their *go* cards ready. The driver's eyes flick over them. 'No more room.'

Oskar looks down the aisle. The seats are all taken, but the triangle hand-straps dangle, empty. 'There's still standing room,' he says.

'No more room,' the driver repeats. 'Off you get. Wait for the next one if you want.'

'We're school students.' Oskar waves his bus card. 'You have to take us.'

Amadi murmurs, 'Yeah' and 'Daniel Morcombe' behind him.

The driver just shrugs, shakes his head.

'Why can't we get on?' asks Seb, over Oskar's shoulder. He points to the aisle. 'There's plenty of room.'

The driver gazes straight ahead, through the windscreen. 'I don't have to give you a reason. Now, get off my bus.'

Oskar glances at a couple of people seated at the front of the bus. The young man just stares back at him, the woman by his side looks out her window. He glimpses a few people behind them craning a little, to see what's happening.

He turns, tilts his head at Amadi, indicating to get off.

'What the fuck, bro,' says Seb, standing his ground. 'I'm not getting off until you give us a legitimate reason for not taking us.'

'Off the bus,' says the driver.

Oskar grabs Seb's elbow. Seb resists, whips his arms back.

After a few seconds of no response from the driver, he too steps from the bus. 'You're a fucking joke,' he says. 'I'm gonna report you.' But the doors squeal shut on his words, and the bus peels away, leaving the boys standing in the dusk.

'We're going to be so late,' says Amadi.

The party is in a two-storey brick house. They're in a suburb that Oskar has never been to before.

'My brother says this is such a sketchy area,' says Seb as they approach the front door.

A faultline of cracks spread across the cement driveway, straggly weeds peeping out from the edges. On either side of the doorway is a pot plant – one holds a sprawling vine of some sort, the other only soil and a gold and purple Turkish Delight wrapper. The door is open, and down a dim corridor they can see the living room, but everyone seems to be out on the back patio. They make their way out, high-fiving, shaking hands, fist-bumping.

Oskar sees Kat standing by a trestle table covered with plastic bowls of chips, fruit skewers, mini hotdogs. Perched on the side of the table is a big blue and white drink canteen next to two stacks of white plastic cups.

'Happy birthday, Kat,' he says loudly, over the tinny music blaring from the small speakers on the ground. His mum wanted him to bring Kat some chocolates, but he doesn't want her to get the wrong idea. His eyes scan the crowd for Hayley. He thinks it might be her sitting with her mates in the dark corner of the patio on a day bed. 'You got a good crowd here. Where's your parents?'

Kat shrugs. 'Mum went out with her friends, and Dad's upstairs watching the footy with my uncle. He doesn't care what we do.'

Oskar nods, out of things to say. He watches as a kid he doesn't know lifts the lid of the canteen and pours in half a bottle of vodka. He winks at Oskar and hands him a cup of the spiked orange cordial. Oskar raises the cup to say thanks, then joins Amadi and Seb.

Handing the drink to Seb, he says, 'Here, you have this. It's got vodka in it.'

'Cool. Thanks.' Seb takes a large gulp of the drink. 'You not drinking?'

Oskar shakes his head. 'Nah. Got a trick I want to practise before school tomorrow. Don't want a cloudy head.' He thinks of the bigflip he wants so badly. Down a fifteen-stair set. He's watched the footage of Max Summers hardflip down that thirteen-set a thousand times. Mostly, he watches the end of the footage when the guys, Gav and the others, lift Max onto their shoulders, carry him away like a king or a footy legend or something. Oskar knows if he pulls off the bigflip, the others will raise him up too, embrace him. He will really belong. His heart swells at the thought, banishing all the ants, leaving him feeling hollow and good.

'Boys.' A hand claps him on the shoulder. Gav. 'Been partying?'

He's brought a few guys from the skate park, who come in behind him, carrying two cartons of beer. The kid who spiked the cordial cheers, and Gav beats his chest like a gorilla. Kat squeals, claps her hands, points them towards the eskies.

In the commotion, Oskar edges to the side of the patio, peers over at the day bed crammed under the kitchen window. By the glow from the fluorescent kitchen light, he can see two girls he doesn't know sit on one end of it, bare feet swinging, and at the other end is Hayley, lighting a cigarette.

'Hey, Hayley,' he says, taking a seat next to her. She's wearing a black singlet and a denim skirt. She smells nice, and glitter shimmers high on her cheekbones.

'Hey,' she says back, closing her eyes as she draws on her cigarette. A slick of eyeliner arcs across the rim of her eyelashes. 'Can you get me another beer?'

'Sure.' Oskar stands again, goes to the esky. Gav makes him take two, won't listen to him when he says he doesn't want one. But maybe it's better that he holds a stubbie, Oskar decides. Less conspicuous. More a part of things.

Hayley pours a neat amount of beer into her mouth, managing to keep her matte lipstick intact. Wiping the corner of her mouth with the back of her hand, she offers Oskar a cigarette.

He laughs. 'No, thanks. Don't smoke.'

She stares at him, narrows her eyes. 'Whatever. Think you're a bit of an athlete, do ya?' She smiles at him, though, and her teeth are small and straight. Taking another draw on her cigarette, she blows the smoke away from him in one fast, long breath.

'Okay, give me a drag,' he says, hand out. If the night goes the way he wants it to, he might as well make sure his breath tastes the same as hers. Sucking in the smoke, he holds it in his chest too long. He tries to blow out smoothly, but the last bit catches in his throat, behind his nose, and he splutters.

She laughs at him, taking the cigarette back. He feels dizzy, like he's been drinking beer after all. He's just asking her how she thinks biology went when tyres screech out on the road, and raised voices can be heard from the front lawn, billowing over the roof. Oskar and Hayley get to their feet, look through the kitchen window.

The crowd of kids surges from the patio towards the front of the house like an outgoing wave, the ones at the back clogging the corridor. Oskar goes too but hesitates in the patio doorway. Some of the guys are yelling now, a girl screams, glass shatters against cement. Amadi jostles his way back into the house from the front, jogs towards them.

'There's a fight,' he says, eyes wide. The plastic cup in his fist is crushed. 'Some guys from down the road tried to gatecrash, and …'

Oskar walks towards the front door to see for himself, ignoring his friend's restraining hand. Gav heads in from the opposite direction, brushes past him into the living room. 'Where're my keys?' he says, but he's not talking to Oskar.

The crowd in the doorway breaks apart as the tide of kids roll back inside, mouthing the words 'stabbed', 'neck', 'never seen so much fucking blood'.

'Call the police,' someone shouts. 'Has anyone called the fucking police?' Kat runs up the stairs, and her face is crumpled like she's about to cry.

Hayley grasps his wrist, and her fingers are cold, clammy, and for the first time he notices that her fingernails are short and painted dark blue. 'What's going to happen? We've been drinking. My dad will fucking kill me.' Her voice rises, in tune with the police car's siren.

'It'll be fine. It'll be fine,' Oskar says through clenched teeth. His shoulders and neck are so tense it's painful. 'Just calm down. Be quiet. It'll be all right.' He sounds snappier than he means to, but can't help himself.

Amadi's dad drops Oskar home. Oskar stares up at his house, at the double garage, the verandah above. The house is still a shadow against a sky lightening to dawn, and his mum's window is shrouded in darkness. She won't be awake for at least another hour. He walks around to the back and, taking the spare key from beneath the mat, he slides the door open silently, reaches inside for his skateboard, closes the door.

Out on the streets, he just skates. His wheels clatter across the grooves in the pavement, rumble along the uneven road, and he imagines a chasm rips open behind him as he rolls, swallowing up his thoughts, his memories. He has to keep moving or it will swallow him up too.

The police had divided up those at the party, breathalysed the ones under age. That was the last Oskar saw of Hayley. She was bundled into the first of three police vans, along with most of the kids from the party. In the end, there were only six of them left in Kat's living room.

Oskar presses his hands to his ears, the wind whistling past his elbows, remembering how loud Kat's dad bellowed, how Kat screamed and cried.

He passes the Mitsubishi car yard, and thinks about the policeman who questioned him and Amadi. He seemed nice. He reminded Oskar of his mate Alex's dad. But Oskar's not a snitch. He knows that dobbing gets you into more trouble than it's worth. So he'd told the policeman he'd seen nothing. Wasn't even out the front. Ask Hayley. Ask Amadi. The policeman stared at him, until the ants rose to Oskar's throat and nearly choked him. But he didn't say anything. The policeman grunted, sounding just like his grandad did.

Dobbing can get you stabbed. His thoughts snag on the word. Stabbed. Stabbed.

He rolls past Red Rooster and scrapes to a stop at the foot of Mount Gravatt. He can't see the top of the mountain for all the trees, but he's heard there's a lookout with some good benches to tre flip and grind. He pushes off again, kicks against the ground, glides, kicks against the ground, glides, until the road becomes too steep. Stopping, he lifts his board and walks the rest of the way. Beneath the eucalypts it's cool and dark, the dawn light just flickering through the leaves, but he's moving so swiftly up the twisting road he's soon winded.

The car park at the top is deserted, the café empty. He skates over to the cement benches. They're a bit awkward to tre flip. Too much grass on one side. Looking around, he sees the toilet block, painted in candy stripes. Its roof is low. Maybe a fifteen-set? He tucks his board under his right arm and clambers onto the block's handrail. With a teetering step, he treads onto the top of a metal box that's attached to the outer wall of the toilets. Holding on to the edge of the roof with his left hand, he tries to fling his board over the top but, for several seconds, his arms are jelly and he thinks he might fall backwards. With a surge of strength, he manages to lift himself and the board onto the rooftop. He holds the board clamped to the roof so it doesn't slide down the slope, and lies flat on his back, panting. He presses his eyes shut. Just roll with it. Roll with it. He can hear Gav's words.

Oskar gazes up at the sky, blue now, but with a shimmer of pink on the horizon that looks like someone has taken a graphite pencil in art class and smeared lines across it. The sky is so wide it's like he's trapped under a snow globe, and he finds he can't thrust the memory to the back of his mind anymore. He thinks of Gav coming in from the front yard, shoving something into his back pocket. Of Gav's glazed eyes, as he checks the kitchen counter and scouts around the eskies, looking for his keys, his movements jerky.

In his mind, Oskar tries to rewind the clip, erase it but, no, he sees the blood smeared on Gav's right hand, flecked up his forearm, a dark flash as he disappears out the back door, flees to the right.

But Oskar's no snitch. Could be millions of reasons Gav had blood on him. Millions.

He pulls himself to his feet and walks to the edge of the roof. At the front it slants upwards, so he knows he can't tre flip it. Glancing behind, he sees that if he skates down the slope he'll land among shrubbery. He stares at the road again, clasping the skateboard to his chest. The toes of his Adidas inch closer to the lip of the roofing. His eyes are scratchy, and he feels a bit sick in the stomach from lack of sleep. He thinks he might be swaying, forward, forward, and he's scared of how drawn he feels to the edge.

His mum'd kill him if she saw him now. Turning, he moves to the back of the toilet block and drops his board onto the grass and then scrambles down.

Oskar skates twice around the car park, trying to shed his thoughts. Stopping at the top of the mountain road, he steps off his board.

The narrow, winding road disappears about fifty metres ahead. He should skate down. Surely longboarders have given it a go before. He thinks of the many bends in the road, the tight corners. Maybe his wheels will get the wobbles, throw him headfirst against a tree. Maybe he'll pick up so much speed he'll slam into an incoming car.

Maybe, though, if he films it and makes it to the bottom, he'll be a star on YouTube. Taking his phone from his pocket, he opens up the video camera, glances down at the moving screen. A green text comes through. Hayley. *You said it'd be alright.*

The ants start up again. He can hear them in his head. He feels like he might fall to his knees, cough them up onto the road.

Oskar places his left foot onto his board, slides it forward a centimetre. He thinks of his grandad. Of the old woman at the bus stop. And he thinks of Gav. Gav, who tells him to roll with it.

'Fuck it,' he says.

Hazel

HAZEL LOWERS HERSELF INTO THE ARMCHAIR by the window. A slight ache burns down the front of her thighs, as though she's been on a long bicycle ride.

She looks about the room she's been shifted to, only slightly different from the one before. Single bed, three framed photos atop a sideboard and a small television she no longer enjoys watching thanks to her failing eyesight. Sometimes she puts the volume up, though. The noise, at least, is company.

Her outlook is a well-kept square of grass and a tall, yellow-brick wall. Hazel doesn't bother with her glasses anymore, and beyond the dark patches in her vision, everything else has the pleasant blur of a Monet. Below her window, to the right, is a lone pot plant, a fern of some sort. Its plumage is sparse, its outer leaves brown. A radiator above the bed buzzes, keeping the chill of the day at bay.

She rests her head back and closes her eyes, and imagines that her son is visiting. Chris will drag a chair in from the common room, and Tracey, his wife, will take a seat on Hazel's bed. Even when Hazel is lying in the bed, Tracey still perches on its edge, which Hazel finds a little irritating. Hazel decides, seeing as it's only a little game in her own mind, that Chris will visit her alone this time. More peaceful that way, yet there are now silences to fill. Hazel reminds her son of how much he loved chicken cacciatore when he was young, tells him to add two slippery fillets of anchovy to the recipe. And he tells her about how Abby is going with the new baby. How he's not keen on being called poppy or grandpa. Five months old now? No, Mum, almost seven, and got some heft on him. He'll be a footballer one day. Hazel smiles, thinking of how chubby Chris was, too, as an infant. Yet he was never interested in playing anything but backgammon or chess.

A nurse enters Hazel's room, wearing a surgical mask. Hazel is quite certain she's never seen her before. This nurse is tall, has bright pink hair. Hazel doesn't catch what she says.

The nurse repeats herself more loudly. 'Hello, love, how are you doing today?'

'Where's Olivia?' Hazel asks after her favourite.

'She's just a bit off-colour, love,' the nurse says. She has to repeat herself twice before Hazel can hear her through the dreadful muffle in her inner ear.

Hazel feels quite cross with her daughter. She doesn't understand why Andrea perseveres in bringing her gadgets to help her read when the whole rigmarole turns out to be so tedious it takes any joy out of the business. But Hazel probably shouldn't have told her to stop interfering, that she wasn't one of her godforsaken pupils. Hazel's eyes blink open, and she wonders if that's why Andrea hasn't visited for such a long time. But then Hazel remembers.

'Of course, I was just dreaming.' Her voice is wavery and almost childlike in the silence of her room. She experiments with speaking out loud again. 'She hasn't visited because of the virus.' Her voice fades towards the end of the sentence. She allows her eyes to close, and pictures her daughter bringing her a bunch of flowers because she knows they are her mother's guilty pleasure. Andrea will burst through the doorway, an armful of carnations, or perhaps lilies, held aloft, or most probably Hazel will hear Andrea's voice first, as it draws near along the corridor, chattering with whichever one of the staff she comes across on the way. And Andrea might gossip about the parents she has to deal with at school, and Hazel will tell her something from when she and Chris were kids. That always delights her. 'Did you know, Andrea,' Hazel will say, 'I never allowed you children to have the wishbone because I couldn't bear one of you not getting your wish.'

The new nurse – Hazel has learned her name is Josie – comes through the door, interrupting her reverie. A young man in a powder-blue uniform is close upon her heels, and Josie says something but Hazel finds it so difficult to understand her when both her voice and lips are hidden away behind that face mask.

Josie places a plastic tray on the bed. 'This man just has to give you a little test, darling. Sit up.'

Hazel gags as the paddle is pressed against her tongue, but it's nothing compared to the frightful jab up each nostril. She feels an urge to grasp the man's arm to yank it away.

'It's a bit stingy, isn't it, love?' Josie squeezes Hazel's thin forearm with her gloved hand and, as usual, Hazel finds it a little shocking, this personal touch from another human being after so many weeks. Almost as thrilling as when Jim first took Hazel's hand at the town hall dance back when she was twenty-two.

~

She has a dull headache that makes her eyesight worse than usual. She's propped up in bed, huddled under the floral quilt bequeathed to the nursing home by the local craft ladies. Josie sails in, looking as though she might be about to deliver a baby – she's wearing a surgical gown, and besides the mask she also has what looks like a shower cap over her pink hair and bags over her shoes.

'Your daughter called, Hazel. YOUR DAUGHTER.' Josie stands a few feet away but bends to be more on Hazel's level. 'She says HELLO and she LOVES you. And she wanted me to tell you that Monty – YOUR CAT – is okay.'

'Maybe she's overseas,' says Hazel, wanting Josie to know she's loved and there'd be a reason for Andrea not visiting her in so long. 'She's a big traveller, you know.'

'No, darling, I don't think she'll be going anywhere for a while. REMEMBER?'

'Oh, of course,' says Hazel.

When Josie comes to collect the lunch tray, she guides Hazel to her chair by the window.

'What's this then, Hazel?' she says, pointing outside.

A small group of people stand with their backs against the yellow wall. Hazel leans forward, peering the best she can. Her fingertips find her mouth. Could it be Chris? And Tracey? Hazel gives a little whoop of joy and claps her hands together.

Her daughter-in-law approaches the window. The glass is cool as Hazel presses the palm of her hand there but when Tracey places hers against the outside of the window, Hazel is sure she feels her warmth. Tracey is saying something, perhaps asking her how she is, and Hazel nods, enunciating the words, rounding her lips, 'I'm well. I'm well.' Chris steps closer to the glass, too, holding up a computer screen of some sort, and she sees a wash of russet hair. Andrea. Her darling heart. She's probably sitting on her deck, glints of the blue Queensland sky dapple the edges of the screen. Hazel catches a flurry, guessing that Andrea is waving at her. Hazel waves back and then throws a series of kisses her way. Chris grins at her and slowly closes the case back over the screen and returns to the others by the wall. Hazel thinks that perhaps it is Abby, her granddaughter, there. Yes, it's definitely her, although her fair hair looks softer than usual, doesn't have the brash gold from the pool's chlorine, and her boyfriend, Dev, stands a little behind. Abby's baby, little Elliot, is clamped to her chest. Hazel's great-grandson. He's swaddled against the cold so all Hazel can see is a shock of black hair rising from his cocoon. Abby brings the baby up close to the window, and although Hazel can't really see the sweet thing's face, she smiles extra hard for Abby.

But how cold they must be. She wants to yell her thanks, tell them that it's time to go home, they have a long drive ahead of them. She'll be fine, she wants to say, but her throat is tight. Her voice is too puny for such things, not like it used to be, booming through the house to *finish drying the dishes, you tearaways* or *do your homework, Andrea, I won't write another note.* Instead, she tries to wave them goodbye, but they only wave back, so she makes little shooing gestures, sorry that they might think she wants them to leave, that they won't realise it's just that she's worried about them freezing to death or becoming too bored. The little table has been wheeled to her side, and she looks down at the plastic cup of tea with a lid and straw, at the sealed cup of fruit and plastic spoon, and she makes a small noise of frustration that they can't come in for a biscuit and tea. 'Sorry,' she mouths through the glass.

Chris puts his hand to his brow, and Tracey looks up at him, stroking the back of his head.

Hazel doesn't like to cry in front of others. Nobody wants to see their mother, their grandmother, cry. Instead she closes her eyes and takes a deep breath in. She feels her diaphragm creak. Opening her eyes, she sees her family are still there. Tracey waves once again. Hazel throws them three more kisses and then closes her eyes, waiting a little longer before opening them on the exhale. Abby shifts the weight of the baby to her other arm.

Closing her eyes, Hazel settles back into her chair as though to rest. She breathes through five cycles this time, slowly, like she learned at yoga at the senior centre. In for four – thinking of the time Andrea was so sad when her doll lost all its eyelashes in the bath – out for four – when Chris ran up the beach, terrified of the scuttling ghost crabs. She breathes in again, deciding she'll give Abby some money for a clothes dryer or a rice cooker or something useful.

When Hazel's eyes finally open, she sees that they have left. The yard is quite empty except for the poor fern, its withered leaves trembling in the breeze.

Dignity

I HEAR THE MUEZZIN'S CALL TO PRAYER. His chant pulses through my body, dredges me up from my sleep. I grasp Asep's chubby wrist but not too tightly. I don't want to wake him. I don't want to lose him. I nuzzle into the nape of his neck, sweet with sweat. But the dream flickers, the grey light of dawn seeps through. He is not here with me. His tiny form is not cradled into mine. My nose is pressed into the pillowcase, into where I have dribbled in my sleep, not into his wispy baby hair. I even dreamt the muezzin's call, for all that can be heard in this place is the roar of the machinery, the groans of the cranes, as another building claws its way high into the blue skies. My nightdress is damp with perspiration because the air-conditioning in the kitchen doesn't quite reach my tiny room.

The delivery boy places the bag of groceries on the tiled floor. He's new, maybe from Myanmar. Or Bangladesh. Not Indonesia, though. Few of us are coming over here anymore. Our president has called us home. Wants to preserve our dignity.

I lock the door behind the boy and return to the kitchen to finish preparing the porridge for breakfast. The flakes of oat puff into the saucepan from the red box that has travelled all the way from Australia. I add milk and stir it over the gas flame. I'd like to cook the family some *bubur ketan hitam*. I think they'd like the black rice sweetened with palm sugar, but I know if I ask Mrs Bowman, she will shudder, say no.

When the porridge is ready I ladle it into three bowls. I retrieve a banana – organic – from the basket. Its skin is yellow and soft, easy to peel. Not like the green ones that grow on the trees in my village, that are as small as my thumb and tough to peel. But sweet. Sweeter than these bananas. I slice its firm flesh across the top of the porridge.

I lay the table how Mrs Bowman likes it. Cutlery at attention next to her white plates, a jug of milk, dewy cold from the fridge, a carton of juice. Three place settings. Three glasses. The coffee machine is switched on, gurgles once in a while. I've heard Mrs Bowman tell her friends that she doesn't know what she'd do without me. That makes me happy.

The family is not up yet. It's Sunday. No rushing to the office for him, no protein shake before the gym for her. And I won't have to walk Noah to the mini-van that takes him to the international school. I, too, have the day off as long as I make breakfast and return home in time to prepare dinner. There's not much to do during the eight hours I have free, but I sense the family like to have the apartment to themselves for their day of rest, so I usually go to the shopping mall.

The lift in the Bowmans' apartment building is stuffy, bodes of the heat that lurks past these air-conditioned walls. I travel down to the basement, to the second level of the car park, because servants are discouraged from using the main entrance on the ground floor.

As I walk towards the exit, I see that the woman is still there, still seated in her big, shiny blue car parked over in the furthest corner. The shadow of her head moves behind the tinted windows. About a week ago I caught a glimpse of her when she was taking a blanket from the back of her car. Her hair was faded orange, her skin the shade of bleached coral.

'You have noticed Mrs Alice,' says Laksmin, the parking attendant. His English is better than mine. He's told me he learned some English at school. I like him the best of the men who work in the car park. He's a little older than the rest, and friendly. But friendly in a way that doesn't creep up my back as I walk away from him, that doesn't make my smile tense until my jaw aches.

'I will be in a lot of trouble if the bosses find out she is parked here,' he says. The bristles of his black moustache remind me of the shoe-brush I use when I shine Noah's school shoes. 'But I don't have the heart to make her leave.'

'Why she live in her car?' I have seen many people who live on the streets among the dogs and the chickens. I have seen whole families living under a bridge, near rubbish heaps, even crammed into a car like that Mrs Alice. But never a white person.

'Her husband ran out of money and had to go to jail. So, until he pays back the government or does all his jail time, she is stuck here, too,' says Laksmin. 'That fancy Range Rover is all she has left.' He laughs, but he's shaking his head as well.

I walk up the ramp and Laksmin presses the button so that the garage door trundles open. The glare of sunlight bleeds into the darkness, but the heat slams in, searing my face, baking my clothes. I walk to the bus stop, and tiny granules of sand crunch and skittle under my shoes. I'm used to hot weather, to hanging out wet clothes in the blinding sunlight, to the line of sweat that trickles down my spine. But the heat in my country is lazy, drapes over your skin like a blanket, not like this ravenous heat that shimmers off the desert, pursues me into the enclosed bus stop. I wipe the layer of silt from the bench before taking a seat. I know that if I sit here long enough, I will become a pillar of sand. I will disappear.

Gazing out the bus window, I think of Asep. Hendra sent me a photo of him yesterday, to my phone. Asep is losing his baby fat, but his eyes are still bright, still pretty with those long, inky lashes. Every time I think of his soft skin, the creases under his chin, his throat, it feels like my chest is being squeezed tight, like all my tears are on the inside. A boy grows a lot in seventeen months. And there are still another seven to go before my contract is up, before I can see him again.

Hendra said my mother is taking good care of our boy. He called me last night, like he does every Saturday night. I never ask him about his work. I wait for him to tell me.

'Pak Sudirman says he still doesn't need a driver,' he said. His voice dragged, was resigned. 'Even the Chinaman doesn't want a driver. He has some fancy boy from Bali.'

'How are your vegetables going?'

He grunted. 'The cassava is nearly ready to take to market, but the *kangkung* needs more time, more rain.' I heard him suck on his cigarette – bap bap bap. I could almost smell the thick clove smoke. I pictured him, hunkered down on the doorstep of our house in Gunung Batu, the ragged banana trees by the roadside, litter strewn in the rubble.

'My money? Is it still reaching you?' I asked. My pay provides the rent for the three-room cement house we share with my parents, the weekly rice stipend, maybe some fish to fry, some chickens to raise. My stomach curled away from the question, from rubbing against Hendra's pride, but I wanted to make sure all of this is worth something, to someone.

'Yeah. I picked it up from the agency yesterday,' he said. Two years ago they had offered him work here too, in construction. But we've both heard of the concrete beehives full of foreign workers, mostly men, who battle against the desert to erect more high-rises and wondrous gardens. Men who sometimes never make it home. It is better this way. I can see that.

The bus pauses at a vast shopping mall, a shopper's palace of steel and glass. Some of the other passengers get off, but not me. I'm not even sure the security guards would allow me to pass into its marble halls, not with my scuffed shoes and my black handbag that's peeling away at the edges. I wait five more stops until we arrive at a more modest shopping centre. This one has Mrs Bowman's favourite supermarket, where I can pick up some vegetables for dinner. Mrs Bowman likes that the produce is organic, from farms far away. But I will never get used to the prices. One little punnet of tomatoes costs the same as feeding Hendra and my parents for two nights, I am sure. They could go to the local *warung*, sit cross-legged on the blue plastic tarpaulin and eat a bowl of *nasi goreng* each. They could even get a fried egg, or a chicken-leg, on their fried rice for that sort of money.

I wander past the shops slowly, for there is no hurry. I have the whole day to fill. Once I went to see a movie, but the subtitles were in Arabic, and I could not keep up with the American actors' shouts between gunfire. I felt conspicuous seated alone in the dark cinema. There were four men a few rows back from me.

Three times I felt popcorn hit the back of my head, land near my foot. But I didn't look around.

So I pass the purple carpets of the cinema and make my way into the department store. I ignore the clothing and the cosmetics. They are beyond any price range I will ever know. I take the escalator to the basement level, to where there is row upon row of boxed colours, plush toys, baby dolls with golden hair. Every Sunday I stroll these aisles, wonder what my boy Asep would like. I think he might enjoy the tiny piano, the one with five fat keys, each a different colour. I imagine him pressing the blue key, laughing at the tune it plays. But the packaging says it is recommended for a child up to thirty-six months. He might be too old for it by the time I get home. Maybe it is better to buy him the toy with the yellow plastic steering wheel. He can learn to be a driver like his father. But maybe not. We should work hard to keep Asep in school, is what I think. I don't know what Hendra thinks.

I pick up the toy and pull the steering wheel to the left, press the red button. It drones out the numbers from one to eight in an accent I think is American. It sounds like Mrs Bowman's friend, Miss Linda, who sometimes picks her up for the gym. It costs a little more than the piano, but if I keep saving some of the money Mrs Bowman gives me for my Sunday lunch I should be able to buy it in only five more weeks.

I snatch my hand away as a sales assistant approaches me. She's young and very pretty. Her long black hair is slicked back into a plump bun, and her large lemur eyes are dark, velvety. I think she might be here to usher me on my way, but her lipsticked mouth widens into a lovely smile.

'May I help you?' she asks.

I wave my hand towards the toys. 'I was choosing toy for my son.'

'How old is he?'

'Two year old.'

I am used to the look of boredom that sweeps across the faces of sales assistants or waiters who serve me. The lack of eye contact, the short speech. But this girl is interested. She searches through the toy boxes, reads what is on offer.

'I like the piano, but maybe he be too old for it,' I say.

'This one is very popular, madam,' she says, showing me a colourful train that has letters and numbers printed across its body.

I look at its price. It would take me six months of Sunday lunches to pay for it.

'Yes, it is a very good toy,' I agree.

I wonder if she is from Indonesia. She has the high cheekbones, the smooth mocha skin of the local Bandung girls. But I do not ask her. She might be from the Philippines, or Malaysia, and people can get offended by this sort of thing.

She shows me a spinach-green dinosaur, with a jaw that snaps up and down. A mother, pushing a pram, walks into our aisle, asks the assistant for help. When they turn aside I slip away.

The food court is near the supermarket. I used to treat myself to a glazed doughnut and a small bowl of curry, but now I am saving that money for Asep. My lunch box of leftover rice and canned tuna is tucked away in my bag, but I will eat it later at the bus stop, not now surrounded by others eating their burgers and noodles from clean, white styrofoam. I take a seat on a bench, sip my Coke, watch other shoppers pass me by.

That's when I notice Mrs Lee. Seeing her makes the skin on

my thigh itch. I'm surprised to see Pramiti shuffling behind her. Pramiti looks too skinny, much skinnier than when I saw her last. She needs to eat goat soup for a full week, suck the marrow from the bones. I look away quickly, into the shop to my left, at the khaki shorts, the row of blue shirts with a pineapple print. I'm sure Mrs Lee and Pramiti don't see me, though. Mrs Lee is not interested, and Pramiti has her gaze to the ground. From the corner of my eye I see Mrs Lee turn into the supermarket.

The scar on my leg rasps against my black pants. It's like a tree-root traversing my flesh, leeching across the tender skin of my inner thigh. Whenever I brush the sensitive skin with my fingertips, I feel a thrill of revulsion, even though it is no longer sore. It is soft, ridged, like the crocodile leather of Mrs Bowman's handbag.

Someone sits down on the bench beside me and, turning slightly, I see it is Pramiti. She had noticed me after all.

I glance around, but I can't see Mrs Lee. 'Pramiti. How are you?'

She shrugs. 'Nothing has changed.'

Her black, wavy hair is clasped in a red barrette, and she wears faded jeans and a baggy T-shirt. My eyes are drawn to her throat, to the scar that is the twin of mine. It creeps from below the frayed neckline of her shirt, reaches for her right earlobe. When Mrs Lee had thrown that bowl of laksa at us, screaming, *Can you once and for all stop putting so much fucking salt in the soup*, it had landed mostly on Pramiti, over her chest. I was seated beside her, in the kitchen, slicing snake beans. What hadn't splashed across Pramiti dropped into my lap. I think it was the coconut milk, and the palm oil, that burnt so bad. I don't think a plain chicken noodle soup would've done so much damage.

'You are still with Mrs Lee?'

'I still owe them money. For my board, my agency fees. I cannot leave until that is paid,' she answers, staring ahead. Her cheeks droop.

'Can your agency not help?'

'No. No help. Mr Lee, he has my passport. My papers.'

Three days after Mrs Lee had hurled the soup on us, I'd packed my things, crept away while she was at the hairdresser's. I'd been there for nearly four long months by then. But I was luckier than Pramiti. My agency had kept my passport, and although they couldn't get my pay out of the Lees, they found me my new position with Mrs Bowman.

Glancing around to make sure Mrs Lee is nowhere nearby, I slide over a little closer to Pramiti. Her hands and wrists are darker than mine, but long, almost impossibly slender. She still has the same nose-ring, a golden stud with a red stone. Plastic maybe. I breathe in her scent, a pungent combination of layered sweat and sandalwood. Oh, how I've missed her company, her cheerful chatter, her truly terrible stories that left me feeling skittish as if I'd drunk too many cups of coffee. When we lay down to sleep on our mats on the kitchen floor, she told me terrifying tales of servants who were beaten, even starved. She told me of the time she saw a woman tug on her servant's hair so hard that big clumps fell out, leaving a bald, bloodied patch. And of the servant girl who hated her masters so much she murdered their baby. I could never keep up with whether she'd actually seen the dreadful things she told me of, or if she caught snatches from the television news like I now do. Watching Pramiti's dark face, I suddenly remember the time the master ushered her into his office, locked the door. I shied away from knowing, busied myself with the pots, the scrubbing. I shy away even now.

'Did the Lees replace me?' I ask.

She shakes her head. 'No. I am alone.'

When I walk back into the garage at the Bowmans' apartment building, I see that the faded lady, Mrs Alice, is still seated in her car. The window is down. She has a phone to her ear. Her other hand pounds the dashboard. Then her head falls forward and rests against the top of the steering wheel. She is trapped, like many of us. For one reason or another.

For dinner I am cooking Mr Bowman's favourite – Swedish meatballs and mashed potato. Mrs Bowman taught me how to cook it soon after I started working for them. While I marinate the lamb mince, I take out the ironing board, pull the clothes from the dryer.

'How was your day off?' Mrs Bowman pours herself a glass of icy water from the fridge. She is tall, much taller than me, but still she wears shoes with a high, thin heel, even when she is just at home. Her toenails are hibiscus red this week. 'Hit the shops again?'

I dip my head. 'Yes, thank you.'

She glances into my room, at the small pile of clothes Noah has grown out of. She lets me keep them so I can take them home for Asep. Pausing in the doorway, she gazes at the baby photo of my son that I keep next to where I sleep.

A small frown puckers her brow. She looks a little sad. 'You must miss him.'

I press the collar of Mr Bowman's shirt with the iron and nod. 'Yes, I miss him. But I like working for Mrs Bowman too.' I smile for her.

'And he lives with your parents?'

'Yes. And my husband.'

'You should tell them to get the internet put on,' she says. 'Then you can skype whenever you want. You can use my computer.'

I keep smiling, and think of the erratic electricity we must buy on credit in my village, the grainy television picture, the phone kiosks.

Pouring stock over the garlic and cabbage, I imagine the *ayam serai* I will cook for my son when I get home. I will rub turmeric powder into the chicken drumsticks, until my fingers are stained yellow. I will layer lemongrass, ginger, onion and garlic over the chicken, add a dash of water, wait until it simmers. I will let its fragrant steam mist across my face. Last, just before I serve it to him with boiled rice, I will add short stalks of shallots. I know my son will enjoy this.

I really hope Hendra is managing to save some of my pay. I must remind him to plant more vegetables in time for my homecoming. I can help him harvest them, take them to market. Maybe I will get some cleaning work too, near our home. Maybe the rich people, in their compound of new houses, will employ me now that I have this experience.

I clean the kitchen and eat a small bowl of the meatballs with some rice. I will leave the mopping until the morning. The Bowmans are still watching television, but I am weary, ready for sleep. I lie down on the single bed, stare at the photo of Asep. I know he's bigger now, but when I close my eyes I picture him as I saw him last, flopped across my chest asleep, heavy.

~

I'm handwashing Mrs Bowman's silk blouse when she asks me to join her in the dining room. I wipe my hands down my pants, the detergent slick across my palms.

Mr Bowman has already left for work, and I have seen young Noah off. Mrs Bowman gestures for me to take a seat. I lower myself onto the cushioned chair. It feels strange to be seated at the glass-top table.

Mrs Bowman sits across from me, slipping on her running shoes. As she ties the shoelaces, I wonder if she is angry at me. I undercooked the bacon again this morning. I will never get used to the smell, the way it curls as it fries.

'Don't look so worried,' she teases. 'I just want to ask you a question.'

I try to smile, nod. 'Yes, Mrs Bowman.'

'Now, I think you only have another six months or so with us, huh?'

'That is right.'

She peels a hairband from her wrist, ties her blonde hair back into a ponytail. 'Did you know that Indonesian people can no longer work overseas as domestic workers?'

'Yes. I heard this.'

'But because you are here, we can ask your agency for an extension. Did you know that?'

I shake my head. No, I did not know that.

Her lips lift into a smile, her pale eyes crinkle, entreat me. I have seen this look – when she is cajoling Noah into eating his carrots or when she wants the concierge to pick up her dry-cleaning. 'I've spoken with Anthony. We would love you to stay on with us. Maybe another year. Maybe two. Whatever you choose.'

Anxiety tightens my breathing, is white noise in my ears.

Her hand taps the back of mine. 'We love having you here. We'd be so sad to lose you. And it will be good for you too. You can save more money. You can send more back for your lovely baby.' She looks at her watch, stands up. 'I'd better get to the gym.'

As she hooks her gym bag over her arm, she glances back at me. 'Think about it. It's totally up to you.'

I rub and rub the suds into the blouse. I won't tell Hendra, I think, as I rinse it with fresh water. If I tell him, he will want me to stay. Make more money. Tears press against the back of my eyes.

Swirling the blouse around in the bucket, I make sure the water is clear of detergent.

I know I should stay. That is more money we can put aside for Asep. For school, for clothing. Maybe we could even buy him a small bicycle like Noah has. I think of the train, the red and yellow one the sales assistant showed me yesterday. I can save up for that, too.

But then I won't see Asep. I wring the water from the blouse, tap it against the side of the sink. I won't be able to hold him again until he's four, maybe five years old. He won't know me. We won't know the smell of each other.

I walk out onto the small balcony off the kitchen where I hang Mrs Bowman's handwashed clothing out to dry, the clothing that cannot go through the dryer.

I won't tell Hendra.

A new building is going up across the road. So far it is only a steel cage, but soon enough it will be clad with cement, marble and glass. I peg Mrs Bowman's blouse to the airer.

Maybe I won't tell Hendra.

I hear shouts. I peer over the side of the balcony. Below me, seven floors down, a shiny blue car swerves out from the garage onto the road, screeches to a halt. One of the parking attendants, I can't see which one, jumps out from the driver's seat, runs back into the building. A few seconds later he pushes someone forward. I see flashes of faded orange hair as he slaps her around the head. She ducks to her car, hands flapping, like there's a myna bird swooping around her ears. Her cries float up to me on the still desert air before they are drowned out by the stutter of a jackhammer across the way.

Growth

IT LIES ON THE CRISP hospital sheet, absolutely grotesque. Dr Arnold tells us it's called a 'fetus in fetu'. Our son's unformed twin. Most likely joined via the umbilical cord in gestation, now just a jumble of elephantine bone and skin, about the size of an apricot. Three canines – there's no denying they're teeth – protrude in a jagged line across its circumference. When we first saw it after the operation, there was a shock of hair pressed to its side, still moist from having Thomas's stomach juices washed away. It looked like the slick of hair and scum drawn from a shower's plughole. I gagged, felt nausea water my mouth. But the hair, the colour of wheat and nearly ten centimetres long, is dry now, almost glossy. It looks like her hair. Like Hannah's.

'It's been living in Tom's abdomen,' says the doctor, glancing over to where Thomas lies asleep, in recovery. 'He should be good to go in a couple of days. No more tummy upsets. No more vomiting.'

'What do you mean "living"?' asks John.

Dr Arnold purses her pale lips, considers what to say. 'It's been growing inside Tom's stomach, growing with him.'

'Like a parasite?' The distaste on his face the same as when he changes nappies.

Dr Arnold bobs her head side to side, a little like the bobblehead dog we used to have on the dash of the Holden. 'Yes. I guess so. A parasite.'

'What will you do with it?' I ask her.

The doctor bends down, scrutinises the small mass. 'They're extremely rare, you know.' She's far more interested in it now than in our son. Her blonde hair is drawn back with a navy-blue ribbon tied in a bow. I wonder if she has a neat row of ribbons arranged on her dresser, a rainbow to choose from according to her outfit. She says, 'I don't think it'll be destroyed. I'm sure the research team would like to have a gander at it.'

'But I'd like to keep it.' I haven't given the words any thought. I watch surprise lift the doctor's brow, the recoil of my husband. 'It was part of Thomas. You said it yourself.'

'Yeah, as a parasite, Shelly. Get it together.' John smirks towards the doctor.

At least it survived, I think.

I'm wrapping salad sandwiches in the tuckshop when I get the call to say I can finally pick up the twin. That's what I've started to call it in my head. But not to John. He's already joked that he wouldn't be surprised if I give the parasite a name. He was only half joking, though. There was contempt in his voice, too, like when he points out the flab that mushrooms over the waist of my jeans, or when he catches me watching *Home and Away*.

I want to peel off my disposable gloves, shove the squares of sandwich paper over to the next mum, but it's nearly eleven o'clock, time to deliver the baskets of food. The other mums already think I'm a bit of a cow, a bit stand-offish, but it's just that I don't have the time or money to hang out with them. I listen to their talk of trips to Fiji or Melbourne, and the packages they receive from stores in the USA, but what do I have to add? The only reason I'm here is to see Thomas's smile when he hands me a sticky coin for a fluorescent iceblock.

I have to pick the twin up from the hospital's pathology centre. The woman on reception pulls the jar from a zip-lock bag, and the twin is awash in formalin.

'What a gruesome little creature, huh?' She laughs. 'I bet your son was glad to be rid of it.'

I'm sorry that it's not dry anymore, that the length of wheat hair is no longer glossy. The hair is darker in the jar, like seaweed, floating around its host.

When I arrive home I'm not quite sure what to do with it. I place the jar on the deck table, and the formalin takes on the bottle-green of the table's plastic surface. Thomas is delighted with it when John collects him from school. He shakes the jar, so that the teeth clank against the glass. I want to stop him, but John's with him, and they are both studying it like it's a science experiment. I watch them through the kitchen window as I prepare a salad for dinner. I follow the recipe I found in a magazine. I have the rocket and haloumi, but not the pomegranate. My salad looks a little bereft without the gleaming ruby seeds, but who on earth can afford a pomegranate at four dollars a pop?

'Can I take it to school?' asks Thomas.

'Of course, mate,' says John. 'How cool will it be to tell everyone this is the twin you gobbled up in Mummy's tummy?'

John grabs Thomas's stomach, wobbles it, until Thomas squeals. But then John sees my face.

He comes to my side, rests his hand on my shoulder. It's reassuring, but has weight too. 'It's not real, you know. It was never a real ... you know.'

I shrug off his hand, slice the haloumi. 'I think we should bury it.'

'Bury it?'

'Yeah.' I think of the flat grounds of the crematorium. The straggly rosebushes, the square plaques. 'Yeah. In the backyard maybe.'

'Like the guinea pig?' He's grinning at me now.

'Yeah. Maybe.'

John calls Thomas in for a bath, and while the chops are on the griller, I return to the deck, pick up the jar.

I stare at it for a long while and, not for the first time, wonder if it was a boy or a girl. Its hair is not as dark as Thomas's, so for that reason alone I think maybe it was a girl. Another daughter I've been robbed of.

For a few months after Hannah was born I didn't want her. Before that, when I was pregnant, I thought I was ready for children. Thought life with a baby was going to be like in those nappy advertisements, full of a carefree love as soft and sweet as talcum powder. But then the pulsing wound that surged against stitches, the sore bosoms as taut as balloons. Splinters of resentment lodged in my heart for that poor baby, whose cheeks held the blush of a seashell, whose earlobes were as velvety as a peach. I wasn't prepared for how truly potty I became from lack of sleep. It took a while for my skittling thoughts to gather, to grasp the fact that I wasn't Shelly anymore. I'd shifted. I had become Hannah's mum.

I can't sleep well again. I listen to the clock tick, to John's snoring. I lie still, let sweat prickle my scalp. But at least I'm not in pain anymore, not physical pain like after the car accident. I should ask my doctor for more sleeping pills, but I've always felt like that's cheating, like I'm trying to shut out memories of her.

I also spend hours wondering what the twin would have looked like had she survived. Would she have had Hannah's thin face, or Thomas's more sturdy features? Hannah's hazel eyes or Thomas's blue ones? And I fret about what to do if we ever move house. Will we dig up the twin from where we buried her in the yard?

After Thomas had his day of show and tell, John took me to Bunnings to choose a plant to bury the twin under. He wouldn't let me get a citrus, said it was gross, said he wouldn't eat the fruit from the parasite's tree. And, anyway, it was too expensive. So I chose something called a *plectranthus*, which had little bell-shaped flowers in Angel Pink. I thought that was appropriate. It was on special for eight dollars.

The soil in our yard is dry and stubborn. I chose a spot behind the mulberry tree, and my little garden spade chiselled against rocks and roots, but I couldn't ask John for help. Eventually, I had a hole deep enough. I inspected the twin one last time, a swirl of flesh and hair, and then nestled the jar deep into the ground. I pushed the dirt back into the hole, leaving enough room to plant the *plectranthus*. And then I leaned over it, my palms resting against the ground. I didn't cry.

~

123

We take Thomas back to Dr Arnold for a check-up. She's wearing a purple ribbon this time, to match the pinstripe in her blouse. She's pleased with Thomas's progress, pleased he's put on a little weight.

'Did you ever pick up that specimen we found in his stomach?' she asks us.

I nod.

'Did they tell you it was just a teratoma, after all? Not a fetus in fetu.'

I can only stare. It's John who asks her what she means.

'It can be difficult to tell them apart, you see,' she says. 'A teratoma is a tumour. It's made up of various tissues, which is why it can resemble a fetus in fetu. But when pathology had a look at the mass we found in Thomas's stomach, they couldn't detect a spine or other organ matter. So they think it was only a teratoma.'

My mouth is open, but no words come. The doctor pushes her hand across the surface of her desk towards me. 'Don't worry, Shelly. It was benign. Nothing to worry about.'

'But the teeth? The hair?'

Her head bobs from side to side. 'Yes. Common.'

I smile. I don't know how to respond. There's an uncertain frown on John's face. Thomas flicks through a Bluey book.

On the drive home I look out the window, squish as close to the passenger door as possible. The tips of my ears feel hot, as I wait for John to tease me. I buried a tumour in the backyard.

As soon as we pull into the driveway, I walk through to the back and unfurl the hose from its rack. I turn it on full blast and yank it over to the *plectranthus*. Its plump leaves wilt under the midday sun and the flowers have taken on a pulpy brown tinge.

I need to soften the soil, dig it up. The water pools on top of the tough dirt, refuses to sink in.

'Shelly, what're you doing?'

I stare at John. I can see he's on the edge. He teeters between sarcasm and concern. But I feel as hard as the soil, as barren. 'I'm digging up the teratoma.'

'You don't have to do that, honey. Just leave it.'

I shake my head. 'No. I don't need the reminder.'

'The reminder of what?'

The sun's rays sting the skin at the back of my neck. 'Of what I've lost.'

'But, baby, you never had it in the first place.'

I fall onto my knees and tear at the soil, rip my fingernails into it. The soil is damp at first, but dry beneath. I rest back on my haunches. My shoulders are shaking.

I'm laughing.

Cinta Ku

THE OIL POPS IN THE PAN, bites the skin at the base of her thumb and she thinks of Jakub, of the first time she met him in her stepfather's sitting room, surrounded by porcelain vases, eggshell-white and blue. He stood across from her on the Persian carpet. His eyes took her in, this rich girl who was being tossed to the poorest fishing family of the village, all because her mother had been foolish enough to follow the waves that beckoned to her from the sea. He'd murmured her name, *Maya*, and, even then, right then, she wanted to rest her face against his chest, inhale the scent of his skin that was as glossy and dark as tamarind.

But that was a long time ago now. In another land. Later, when she moved to Australia, she taught her language at university – a mere assistant to the lecturer, Professor Malcolm. Her students would never have imagined their neat little Bahasa tutor, Bu Langkun, in her button-up blouse and pleated skirt, had once been a lowly fisherman's wife who lived in a hut, who dried and salted sardines until the pungent flesh crumbled in her fingers.

After scooping garlic into the oil, Maya makes her way into the lounge room and opens the mahogany display cabinet, the one with the leadlight glass. From it she takes out a pink dessert bowl in which are nestled five gleaming shells. Betrothal gifts from Jakub, left by the ebony tree in the garden each morning leading up to their wedding. As she lifts them out, the shells clack against each other. Pressing the cowrie shell to her ear, she closes her eyes and for a moment she can hear their beach, their waves, the whistles and coo-coo-coo of the birds. She can smell the brine, the seawater fug. She runs her fingertips over the metallic peacock swirl on the underside of an oyster shell, while her gaze takes in the milky gleam of the clam. Her favourite is the mother-of-pearl on the mussel shell. She brings it to her mouth, and the tip of her tongue searches out anything – a granule of sand, a hint of salt – in the shell's scalloping. But there's nothing left.

She smells burning. The garlic. She hurries back to the kitchen and whisks the pot from the stovetop. The slices of garlic, charred so that they look like woodchips, still bubble in the oil. That's okay, though, isn't it? Staring at the garlic for a moment longer, she shakes her head. No. She will start again. It has to be just right.

While the fresh garlic cooks, Maya glances out the kitchen window, the foggy glass a barrier between the warmth inside and the damp chill. The eucalypts in the backyard are paler than the teak trees of her childhood. Their leaves are dry, crackle between her fingertips, but she likes the little plants, the ones called 'pigface' – what a funny name to call a flower with such friendly petals, but that's definitely what Pat had called them when she'd popped in from next door to welcome Maya to the street.

Placing shallots into the mortar with the chillies, ginger and candlenuts, Maya grinds and pushes until the spices are pulpy and her hand cramps. *You two will be like a mortar and pestle*, Jakub's grandmother had croaked at their wedding, and then, leaning in close to Maya, *You'll be the mortar.* Maya could smell the cardamom on the old woman's breath from the betel nut she chewed, the red cud wrapped in sirih leaf.

Each morning, at dawn, Maya waited on the beach for Jakub's fishing boat to return. At low tide, sea foam frothed across the sand like honeycomb and had the orange tinge of paprika. She had to step around bluebottles that washed up on the shoreline so that their whip-thin tails didn't sting her toes. One day she was inspecting a tangle of the tiny jellyfish, strung together like a bunch of fairy lights. Jakub came up behind her, stomped the bulbous bluebottles under the soles of his sandals so they burst.

'Jakub,' she screeched, jumping out of the way.

He grinned at her and shrugged. 'I can't help myself.'

Smiling, Maya mixes turmeric into the paste, scrapes it all into the pan. From the fridge she brings out a bowl of cubed lamb, and the meat sizzles as soon as it hits the spices. Seasoning the meat, she watches as crystals of salt sink into the pink flesh, and thinks of how she used to lick the salt from Jakub's skin, from the flat planes of his shoulder blades. Of how, on the very hottest days, when the heat thrummed through her blood and left even the furniture warm to the touch, he'd purchase a handful of ice to place on the back of her neck, and then slowly suck it away. She shivers, stares at a speck of sauce on the white kitchen tiles, can almost feel the trickle of water down the middle of her back.

But her skin is no longer smooth like it was then. It's as dry as a desert – elbows, throat, her hands – an arid mosaic of drifts and creases. Arthritis tightens her joints and aches in the bones of her right foot.

After thumping four stalks of lemongrass with the base of her knife, she adds them to the pan. The lemongrass lies atop the lamb, bruised and knotted like Jakub's body that bright morning they'd brought him to her on a makeshift stretcher made out of a shattered door, a sarong stretched across its beams. The waves had smashed his body against the rocks for so long his eyes were as milky as tapioca balls, and bloodberries were scattered across his chest, except they weren't berries. She couldn't keep her thoughts straight as Jakub's father told her of the storm that had claimed five fishermen, as Jakub's mother pressed her cheek to Maya's swollen belly and wept.

Maya's chest tightens, and her breaths are shallow. She adds lime leaves to the curry, and the fragrant steam rises from the *gulai kambing*, a shroud of silk against her face. It will be all right.

The wheels of Riley's skateboard clatter down the driveway, scrape to a stop. As he walks through the door, he pulls his sweater off over his head so that tufts of his hair stand up. 'You have the heater up too high again, Gran.' He grins and drops his backpack to the floor, drapes his sweater over it and goes to the bathroom, locks the door. The pipes squeak as he turns on the shower.

Maya wonders where he's been all afternoon, but her daughter, Ina, told her not to worry about him, that they like him to be a 'free-range' kid. Ten days ago, when Ina and her husband left on their cruise, Riley showed Maya a video of him skateboarding in the city, flying over a set of stairs, his board skimming the handrail. She'd clutched at her chest and murmured, '*Adu, adu.*'

Maya has long enough to fold the towels and sweep the kitchen floor before she spoons the lamb curry onto steamed rice. Some of it splashes over the side of the bowl and her hand wobbles as she carries the heavy bowl into the dining room and calls Riley to dinner.

He drags a chair out from the table. He's much taller than Jakub was, but his wiry hair has the same blackbird sheen, and his nostrils flair when he's annoyed, just like Jakub's did. He takes a seat and she stands beside him. The bruising on his cheekbone has sallowed, is no longer the colour of an eggplant. The tiny cut is also healing neatly, and doesn't tell of the fracture beneath.

Her fingers follow the line of his jaw, find the soft skin beneath his chin. '*Makan*,' she urges. 'This was your grandfather's favourite meal.'

She watches him dip his spoon into the curry.

'It's not too spicy, is it?' he asks as he presses his earphones back into his ears, scrolls through the music on his phone.

'Maybe I'll make those *pandan* crepes I told you about?' she says. Jakub used to love them. Sweet. She always added extra palm sugar to the coconut filling when she made them for him.

He takes a bud out of his ear and raises an eyebrow. 'Sorry?'

'The crepes? Those green ones?' She holds her breath. Somehow it's important that he wants to try them but, of course, it doesn't matter too.

He shrugs. 'Sure. Thanks.'

She smiles, pats him on the shoulder. Returning to the kitchen, she hopes weevils haven't gotten into the desiccated coconut. Her hand rests on the plastic container as she glances over at the boy again. The facial swelling is fading, but what of his anger at the boys who waylaid him and his friend, Kedus, last week? Worse than the phone call to collect him from the hospital had been the squall of Riley's rage. The swearing, the calls for revenge, as he circled his bedroom, muttered on his phone. Her stomach clutches into a sick knot. She wonders again where he's been all day.

'Riley, how much longer do you have of your holidays?' She has to repeat herself twice, louder each time, before he turns his head and removes his earbuds.

'Two more weeks.'

Nodding, Maya mentally calculates her savings against airfares, wonders where his passport might be found. She can already smell the curl of smoke from a *kretek* cigarette and the charred lamb *sate* smouldering on a barbecue plate.

Only four days into their journey, and Maya's already feeling sickly. Riley, though, is fine. Safe. When Maya had called Ina to tell her of their trip to Java, her daughter was pleased – disappointed, almost, that she was missing out on a holiday with them.

From the lookout, the ocean appears overexposed, blurred, in the afternoon light. Pelabuhan Ratu's shoreline scallops to the north, and white houses with shingled roofs rise like small anthills from the hectic foliage that covers the land from the sea to the mountain. Closer in, banana fronds wave; closer still, a scattering of sun-bleached rubbish litters the dirt directly behind the *warung* where they sit on a rattan mat, waiting for their black tea.

Riley crunches on *krupuk* chips and Maya's gut squelches, shifts. She turns from the food, gagging. She wonders which meal in their two-day visit to Jakarta has turned on her. How foolish, arrogant even, to have eaten that bowl of delicious goat soup by the side of the road, blasted from all sides by the heat of the gas burner, the cars beetling by, the midday sun. Or was the *bubur manis* she enjoyed at the hotel's breakfast buffet the culprit? She can't believe it was her niece's rice porridge, but she's wondered about the slices of fruit; were they washed in local water? Local. The word reminds Maya that she is no longer from here, that her body betrays her time away from this place, and she feels a dip of sadness.

Maya gazes on Riley as he reads something on his phone. Luckily he's a little fussy and only eats from styrofoam cups of Indomie, bananas, crisps.

Shops, timber shacks and makeshift petrol stalls flash by on the drive to their hotel by the beach. She wants Riley to see the chickens that scoot out of the way of the traffic, the heavily laden banana trees, the colour of the soil she is from, but he's opened up his laptop, taps hard at the buttons as he plays a game.

When they reach the hotel, Maya holds her breath a few moments. The hotel, white and brick, looms large on this part of the coast. She's never stayed here before. Has avoided it, in fact. But it's the finest hotel along this stretch, and she wants Riley to experience only the best. The reception area is vast and bare of people, except for a young woman standing behind the reception desk.

After receiving their room key, Maya asks the girl in Bahasa, 'You have a room here for Nyai Loro Kidul, don't you?'

'Room 308, Bu.'

'Can we see it?' Her pulse quickens as she asks. She's heard this hotel has a bedroom set aside to honour the Queen of the Southern Sea.

'Of course.' The girl picks up the phone and speaks to someone and, not many moments later, a man, also in uniform, joins them. His skin's the colour of mocha, much darker than Maya's and, although his face is sunken and lined, he has the physique of a wiry adolescent. He leads them to the lifts, and they proceed to the third floor. They follow a long balcony that overlooks the gardens and beach. And there is so much light. Maya shields her eyes. She's feeling nauseous again, giddy. Riley stands by the railing and peers out to sea.

The man turns the handle of number 308.

'No, wait,' she says. 'I've changed my mind.' Her heart pounds. How foolish. She didn't realise she still believed.

'Yes, Bu.' The man bows and moves away.

Suddenly Maya's tired. The joints in her fingers ache. She joins her grandson.

'What's in there anyway?' he asks.

'A room dedicated to Nyai Loro Kidul.'

'Who's she?'

'A goddess, Riley,' Maya replies, rubbing her dry hands up and down her face. 'A beautiful goddess.' Who stole your grandfather away. From me. From you. 'She doesn't like anyone to wear green. Green is hers.'

She points at the aqua flowers on his board shorts, and he grins.

After settling into their room, Maya opens the sliding doors, and a warm draught billows the curtains as she steps out onto the balcony. Sitting down on the plastic chair, Maya takes it all in. It's been many years since her last visit. That time, her steps had been heavy, had dragged through the sand as her eyes sought out tiny bluebottles or familiar sand-polished stones. Now, she sees ancient fishing boats, naked and lonely, resting high up on the beach; the long shed-like buildings of the fish market. The bougainvillea, dashes of pink against the blue of the sea.

Maya's gazing at the swelling, lava sunset when Riley pulls a chair closer to hers and hooks his bare toes up against the balcony wall.

'Can you smell it, Riley?' she asks him. Can he smell the fragrance of what once was her home? She wants to clasp his hand in hers, but he's almost a man now, not the little boy she used to squeeze and sniff. From where she's seated it's awkward to pat his shoulder, so she taps his knee.

He closes his eyes and lifts his nose to the breeze. His nostrils flare and in the half-light he looks like Jakub. 'That curry smell? It smells like your curry, huh? That one you make me, yellow, with chicken drumsticks.' He opens his eyes. 'Except yours smells better.'

He's being kind. Or maybe he means it.

When Maya wakes the next morning, she is curled into the fetal position. Her body has tried to cradle itself from the pains that cramp her stomach. Sitting up, she groans softly as she gets to her feet, her knees creaking in the quiet of the room. Riley's not in his bed.

By the bathroom sink he has left her a note. *Gone to the beach. There are surf lessons.*

Alarm spirals through her body like a rising siren as she staggers out onto the balcony, leans over the railing. There he is, paddling through the shallows on a board, one among four. He mentioned going for a swim the night before, but she just said that his mother wouldn't like it, that the surf was too rough. She thought that was enough. How can Maya tell him she doesn't want him to go into the ocean because that's where her husband died? How could she convince him that her fears were not unfounded?

She doesn't bother with shoes, a comb, her bag. As she wheezes down the two flights of stairs, as she scrambles across the stark white tiles of the foyer, as she shields her eyes from the glare of the sun, she knows she will not catch him in time. Even as she makes slow purchase across the hot sand, she can see the surfers are out of calling range.

Maya wades into the sea a few steps and crouches down. Her nightie trails in the water, and the gentle waves lap at her underpants. She will wait here all day, if need be. Riley and the other surfers have paddled out far, beyond the lacy ripple of the coral lagoon. They are just dark dots bobbing in and out of sight. Her eyes take in the blue water, so dark, so bright, if she squints it's almost as if the sea merges with the sky – a cerulean world, an underwater dome. She can't believe that there are large waves, even past the reef break.

Maya's gaze drops to her feet, hazy under water, half submerged by sand. She swishes her hands in the warm sea water. The skin of her arms is papery and sunspotted above the water level but appears as smooth as a hazelnut beneath. Like it used to be. She mutters a short prayer, not to Nyai Loro Kidul, but to Jakub.

Bring him home safely, *cinta ku*. My love.

She Is Ruby Wong

RUBY CAN HEAR THE LOW murmur of the London crowd being ushered to their seats. She drops her cloche hat and cloak over an armchair and slips out of her dress. Holding it up, she admires the flower that adorns the low waist, the lustre of the blue silk. Later, she will go dancing with Bert; she wants to try that new quickstep he learned in America after the war.

She pencils a thick line of charcoal across her left eyelid, then pencils the other. Just as the Chinese women do in her grandfather's photographs, Ruby pins a fragile cascade of silk flowers behind her ear, before sliding the tortoiseshell comb into her hair, the one with the silvery butterfly that dances with each nod of her head. Drawing three filigree bangles from a velvet pouch, she pushes them onto her left wrist where they jangle as she moves. Sitting back, she contemplates herself in the mirror, satisfied with the transformation. Glad she'd packed the props into her trunk at the last moment. Hopes Larry doesn't miss them from the costume wardrobe at the Enmore.

Of course, her narrow, tapering eyes, and her olive skin, dark with both Chinese blood and the Australian sun, are of no artifice. What she had tried to disguise in the schoolyard of St Bernadette's, Ruby now accentuates with paint and ornaments. What had once made a secret corner of her soul curl in on itself has been smothered beneath this brazen deceit. Although – her hand pauses as she daubs red on her lips – it is not entirely a deceit. With each day, she becomes less certain of where the line lies between what is embellished and what is real, or even whether a line actually exists.

A sharp rap on the door. 'Miss Wong, the Circle is ready. Quite a crowd, as usual,' says Hutchison, the stage manager. 'What will you be talking of tonight?'

'I am thinking of simply reading some poetry,' she says, in her carefully cultivated voice. She's almost completely lost the Cairns twang. She tries to modulate her speech somewhere between what she learned from her elocution teacher and what she knows of a Chinese accent. In particular, she thinks of her Great-Aunt Moy Wong's speech pattern: the back-to-front sentences and how she dropped prepositions willy-nilly. 'Perhaps Li Bai. Poet, very old.'

She waits for him to leave and stands from the dressing table. Allowing her petticoat to fall to the floor, she folds it over the back of the chair and steps into emerald-green trousers. Over her blouse, she slips on a black Chinese jacket, running her hand across the nap. Admires, yet again, the pale yellow dragons embroidered into the silk. She tugs the jacket straight and returns to the mirror. Content with the Chinese woman she sees reflected. Ruby may not be fair enough to play Juliet or Rosalind in the Shakespeare plays she adores so much, but this part she performs to perfection. London's premier Chinese Reciter. Oriental Actress. Exotic Expert.

She pulls a face as she thinks of the tutor who teaches her Mandarin here in London – a sallow ghost of a bloke who spent years in Shanxi with his missionary parents. It's as though an eel worms its way through her guts when she wonders how the men and women who flock to her Circle each week would react were they to find out that her knowledge of Chinese culture is merely an inheritance of blood and stories and half-forgotten customs stubbornly carried out in a blue weatherboard house that rises out of the eucalypts like a plume of smoke. But her British audience's trust in her is as great as their arrogance. Ruby knows it's unlikely they will ever twig that she's never even set foot in China.

'Don't forget there's a private reception after your performance,' Hutchison says, as he leads Ruby towards the stage.

'In my rooms?'

'No. At the Ormonde this time. An American couple and chums. They want to talk to you of your travels in the Orient. The wife seemed particularly interested to know what you eat over there.'

Ruby pictures her favourite braised chicken, and her appetite stirs as she recalls her grandmother's eggplant stew. But that's not what the Americans want to hear about. They want to be shocked, titillated, by stories of fried insects, perhaps an eyeball soup of some sort. Ruby peeps around the curtain to see how many people are in the audience. The Keane is only a small theatre, but she's gratified to see that most of the seats are taken. Mainly women, as usual. She scans the crowd, admiring the glitter of the jewelled evening gowns, the sheen of brilliantined hair. Her gaze snags on a fine string of pearls looped across the ample bosom of a young woman in the first row, and her eyes lift to take in the owner's features.

Ruby steps back. Holds her breath.

Fran.

But it couldn't be. Here, in London. The last Ruby heard of Fran she was selling hats in Melbourne. She was a shopgirl, not a fine lady in a West End theatre.

Ruby edges forward and has another quick look at the woman. She's laughing at something her companion whispers in her ear, and Ruby clenches her hands until her nails bite her palm. Despite the crimson lipstick, Ruby would know that mischievous curl of the lips anywhere, the slightly crooked nose in an otherwise pretty face. Fran. Here. At her show.

Ruby was only twelve when she first met Fran. She was new to Cairns, sent up to town from Innisfail. Still smarting from being wrested away from her younger brother, and sad that she could no longer run barefoot across the red soil to her mahmah's blue house.

Another girl – Gwen – was showing her around the classroom, pointing out the watercolours they'd painted to decorate the hall, when Fran wandered in. She'd edged her way around the girls, watching Ruby from the corner of her eye.

Finally, she took Ruby by the wrist, her fingertips blunt and cold. 'You don't want to play with her.'

As Fran led her away, Ruby remembers looking back at Gwen, feeling a little bad, but not resisting either. Fran took her out into the schoolyard. It was a mild day, the sun buttery, and they settled on either side of a seesaw.

'My name's Fran. What's yours?'

'Ruby.'

'Ruby what?'

'Ruby Wong.'

The seesaw jerked Ruby into the air.

'You a Ching-Chong?'

Ruby shrugged, whooshing to the ground with a bump. 'My dad is. But my mum is half-white.'

'Like a mongrel?'

Ruby knew better than to show offence. Knew that was the fissure that allowed a germ of malice or mischief to sneak through. And she could tell Fran wasn't trying to be mean. She seemed curious, a little pleased with herself for making the connection. Ruby nodded, pushing from the balls of her feet so she swooped up into the air.

'What does your dad do?' Fran asked.

'He's a farmer. In Innisfail.'

'What does he farm?'

'Bananas.'

'My dad's a policeman.'

They lazily jockeyed up and down several times before Fran said, 'Well, where do you live here?'

'I'm staying with my aunt and uncle. Behind their shop on Grafton Street.'

Fran nodded. 'I know the one. Do you think you could get me some peppermints?'

Ruby watches Fran from behind the stage curtain. As Fran takes a cigarette from her purse, Ruby has an aching urge to run to her, pull the other woman into a close embrace, despite all that has happened. She had once found such comfort in their friendship, such glee. That first year, taking turns to hide Miss North's reading glasses when she was out of the classroom, and filching boiled lollies from her uncle's shop when he was serving a customer. For two years they tried to catch the other one unawares as they walked past old Mr Morrison's fishpond. Fran had succeeded in pushing Ruby in three and a half times. Ruby only managed once to get Fran into the green water, but Fran made such a fuss about her drenched shoes, Ruby only pretended to push her after that. But now, mostly what Ruby yearns for is the lovely detritus of their girlish friendship. The little things, so banal, so personal, they could never be explained to another. Ruby's fingers stretch, remembering the exact width, the texture, of the fold of freckled skin she would clasp on Fran's forearm to get her attention. Her fascination with watching Fran speak as she tore through a cold sausage sandwich, collecting damp clumps of dough in the gaps between her teeth. How Fran blew her nose on the inside of her skirt when she didn't have a handkerchief to hand. Only in front of Ruby, of course. She would never have exposed herself so in front of others.

Glancing up at Hutchison, Ruby says, 'I've forgotten something in the dressing room,' and before he can remonstrate, she turns, hurries back down the corridor.

She closes the door behind her and crosses to the dressing table, her fingers sifting through combs, jars of greasepaint, hairpins, anything to justify turning back. She needs a little time to *think*.

Why is Fran here? Does she realise that the Ruby Wong on the poster is her? Ruby feels heat flush her face, prickle the skin of her chest, as she thinks of the preamble with which she begins her evenings on stage. A tale of an idyllic childhood in a Chinese village, filled with kite flying, moon festivals, firecrackers. The horror, when a scholarly father is murdered by bandits. A beloved mother, wasted away with sadness. Siblings sold off to work in far-off lands. But Ruby tells the audience she was lucky. She had found work with an English lady in Canton, who had brought her to London, leaving Ruby a modest amount of money when she died. When she arrives at that part, Ruby drops her eyes and says softly, 'All I have left of my life in China is my father's robe,' and she presses her fingertips to the yellow dragons on her silk coat.

It's an intricately woven tapestry of lies that Fran can unpick.

Ruby stares at herself in the mirror. At the heavily kohled eyes and the ornaments in her hair, on her wrists. The wild hope that Fran may not recognise her flares in Ruby's heart. How long has it been since they've seen each other? Eight years? Nine? She stares up at the ceiling, dismayed it has been so long, but despairing too. Of course Fran will know her.

Hutchison knocks on the door. 'Find it?'

She picks up a silver opium pipe to take back with her. She's not even sure how to use it but finds that its presence adds to her Oriental mystique. She takes a deep breath in, feels the swell of it in her belly. Closing her eyes, she imagines her mahmah pressing her abdomen with a wrinkled hand. 'Remember, Granddaughter, this is where the real Ruby resides. This is where your strength lies. Your power. This is you. It doesn't matter what others see.'

Ruby sucked warm sarsaparilla up through the paper straw and then handed the bottle back to Fran. They huddled together on the wooden steps of the hall attached to the parish church, waiting for their turn to audition for a part in *The Merchant of Venice*. School had finished for each of them as soon as they turned fourteen: Ruby in July, Fran in November. Since then, Ruby helped her aunt unpack and organise stock in their store, while Fran had found work at the lemonade factory. But one of their former teachers had a love of theatre and had started up a small repertory group. When Sister Celsus pronounced the word 'thespians', something within Ruby had shuddered in response, in delight. There was something about inhabiting another life, uttering unfamiliar words, that thrilled her.

A midge settled on her ankle. She caught it beneath her thumb, leaving a short smear of black and blood. The skin on her face stung with sweat, yet a slight afternoon breeze tickled the hair at her nape. She pointed at a fading bruise on Fran's thigh, and said, 'Licked by a ghost.'

'Is that what you people think? You're so strange.' But she laughed, nonetheless.

Ruby had a hard time gauging what Fran found charming or funny and what she found peculiar. Usually, she hid her Chineseness more carefully, but she wasn't thinking straight. She was so nervous – so excited – about their audition that she could feel the tickle of vomit burn her throat. She inhaled, tightened her abdomen, and thought of her grandmother's words, of strength, of knowing herself. But today she wasn't Ruby, not entirely. She was Portia too, beautiful and strong. She thought of the engraving of Portia in the book she had borrowed. The waves of golden hair, the tapering, fine nose. Ruby felt as though she understood Portia – her desire to stay true to her father's wishes, but likewise, the appeal of finding a way around such rules. And didn't Ruby also know something about disguising herself?

Several people filed past them into the hall: Mrs Cooper, the butcher's wife, and her daughter, Doreen; Mary and Geraldina from school; the Harvey twins. Ruby eyed all of them, trying to guess their level of talent by how they walked or what they wore.

Fran nudged Ruby when three youths pushed through the squeaky gate. 'You're not auditioning, too, are you, Ted?' she asked.

'My mum made us. Old Sister Celsus was onto her. Said there wouldn't be enough men for the male parts.'

They loped past the girls and entered the hall. Fran threw the bottle into the grevillea next to the steps and, grabbing Ruby by the upper arm, dragged her to her feet. 'Now I know why I'm here.' She winked at Ruby.

The hall was cooler than outside. As Ruby's eyes adjusted to the dim light, she took in the scattered chairs, the smudges of chalk on the floor left over from the ballet class, the stacks of cups and saucers on the corner table for morning tea after service. The air was still, smelt of dust and the violet scent with which one of the women had drenched her handkerchief.

Sister Celsus clapped her hands, calling them to attention. She was a pale woman, not long arrived from Ireland, and her skin glistened in the heat like a fillet of perch.

'Who wants to audition first?' she asked.

Everybody fell quiet. Mr Kenwood, the school's gardener, cleared his throat and Geraldina tapped her foot. The agony of waiting was too much for Ruby and she put up her hand.

'Shall I?'

Sister Celsus smiled at her and took a seat. The others shuffled around finding chairs.

Ruby's heels clicked across the timber flooring, matching the beat of her heart. With each step she surrendered to Portia. The velvet of Portia's blue gown enveloped her arms. The heavy skirts draped her knees. As Ruby recited her lines, she stared at a painting of the baby Jesus on the wall, but really, in her mind's eye, she was talking to Nerissa, with her merry black ringlets and freckled cheeks.

'Thank you, Ruby.' Sister Celsus beamed at her when she came to an end. 'That was very well done, indeed. Very well done.'

And Ruby knew it was true. Both Geraldina and Doreen read from Portia as well, but the former kept losing her lines, while the other was too dull. Ruby clapped loudly when Fran read Jessica's part and, as Fran gave the floor to one of the twins, Ruby tried to congratulate her, but Fran didn't glance her way. She turned to the side, her attention focused on Ted and his mates.

The sun was quite low in the sky, and the mosquitos had found them out by the time the auditions were over. Sister Celsus took her place at the front of the hall.

'That was so beautifully done,' she said, in her low, pleasant brogue. 'I congratulate you all. I have already made my decision on who will play each part. It's the best way, you see, so we can get started on rehearsals. Without further ado, I think Mr Kenwood —' she squinted over her spectacles at the gardener '— will make a fine Shylock. I do not mean to give offence, kind sir.'

Ruby tittered along with everyone else, but anticipation jumped beneath her skin like plucked fiddle strings.

'And for Bassanio, I think Master Edward might be best.'

One of Ted's friends struck him so hard on the shoulder he bounded forward a step. Fran clapped and shouted, 'Well done, Ted.'

'And Geraldina will make a lovely Portia.'

Geraldina. The name echoed in Ruby's ears, but she managed to keep her smile in place as Sister Celsus listed off the remaining roles. She didn't allow the slightest quiver of surprise or disappointment to cross her face, although a painful stitch crept into the cavity of her chest as Sister Celsus assigned Nerissa's part to Doreen, and Jessica's to Fran. One of Ted's mates, Peter, a stocky fellow with red hair, was assigned the part of Antonio, while the other, Harry, would play Gratiano.

'As you can see, we do not have enough men to play the male parts,' said Sister Celsus. She turned to one of the twins and said, 'Catherine, you will play the Prince of Arragon, won't you? And Ruby, I would like to see you bring your considerable talent to the part of the Prince of Morocco.'

'Of course,' Ruby answered, clasping her hands behind her back lest their shaking give her away.

As they all streamed back out into the darkening night, the young men pushed ahead, clamping their hats onto their heads.

'At least you won't need any blacking,' said Harry as he brushed past her. He looked back and grinned, and she stared at him, the same silly smile straining her cheeks.

Fran came up beside her and pulled Ruby's right hand loose from where it still gripped the other. She gave it a squeeze. 'Sorry, pet.'

Ruby unfurls her hand, almost dropping the opium pipe. She remembers crying that night, lying safe in her bed, the leaves of the longan bush scraping the window. But they weren't jealous tears. Not wholly. She felt sorry for herself. Not so much because she couldn't be Portia, but because she couldn't be Geraldina.

Ruby opens the door of her dressing room and pauses. Peers towards the shaft of light from the stage. She will have to brazen it out. If Fran does say anything, Ruby will simply deny that she is the Ruby Wong that Fran knew so long ago in some country town in north Queensland. Ruby will say, with a laugh, 'Don't they say we all look the same?' or 'I know we're all supposed to look alike, but this is ridiculous!' Ruby moves towards the stage, thinking about how everyone carries secrets. She's just not sure who has the most to lose anymore.

'What did you bring, Ruby? Usually, she has these strange doughy things,' Fran told the boys as she spread out a blanket to sit on. Ted smirked lazily as he leaned back against an ironbark. Harry pretended to gag.

Ruby stared at Fran for a moment. Fran loved eating *bao*. Usually, she insisted on swapping her marmalade sandwich for Ruby's pork bun. But Fran caught Ruby's eye for one second, an unspoken pact that had evolved over the years that Ruby wouldn't spoil the tall stories Fran told for a laugh.

'I brought some beer like you said to,' said Ruby, and from her basket she pulled out an assortment of beers she'd pinched from her uncle's shop. She had taken only one of each brand – a Dai Nippon, a San Miguel and a Kirin beer – hoping her uncle wouldn't notice. 'I also brought this.' She handed Peter a brown bottle of Dutch schnapps. Her fingers left their mark in the cloak of dust that covered it.

'Good girl,' he said, and Ruby felt a glow at his words, at the approving look from Fran.

Ted's chestnut scuffed the ground where it was tethered to a mango tree next to Harry's grey mare. Rehearsals had finished early and the boys had brought them to a grove not far from the train line near Freshwater Creek. Fran took a sip of the Kirin beer and offered some to Ruby who shook her head, already a little sick with stealing the grog and lying to her aunt. She'd told her she was eating supper at Fran's, and she knew Fran had told her parents that she was visiting her cousin.

'Tell us what other things she eats,' Harry said, tilting his head towards Ruby. He took a swig from his beer.

'Oh,' said Fran, straightening her puce skirt over her knees. 'Whenever I go over to Ruby's house, her aunt is cooking something dreadful like sheep innards or these soggy weeds of some sort and once I lifted the lid from the pot and about ten fish heads were bobbing in the broth!' Fran's laughter, her teasing gaze, embraced Ruby as though Ruby was in on her amusing game.

And, of course, Ruby couldn't refuse her. She laughed too, her eyes fixed on her friend so she didn't have to see the distaste on Peter's face or the repulsion on Harry's.

'Yes, my uncle scoops out the eyes,' she said, pretending to grimace. 'It's so disgusting.'

They settled around the rug, and Fran opened the copy of *The Merchant of Venice* she'd borrowed from Sister Celsus. She practised her lines with Ted, and Ruby listened. In her head, she repeated the lines in the way she would have pronounced them. She imagined what gestures she would have used.

After some time, Peter, still clutching the bottle of schnapps, tried to rise to his feet but only got as far as his knees and, with a snort, fell onto his side where he stayed, eyes closed. His mouth gaped open, and Harry leaned over to tug his hat down to cover his face.

Ted swatted at his jawline. 'Mozzies!' He stood and held out his hand to Fran. 'Let's go find some firewood.'

Fran let him pull her up and, as they disappeared into the cover of trees, she giggled at something he said. Slapped his arm.

Harry took a box of matches from his vest pocket, lit a match, and held it to a blade of grass.

'Do you live near here?' Ruby asked him.

'Nah.' The blade of grass caught alight, and they watched it blaze orange, then black, before he patted it out. He placed a dry leaf in front of himself and held a match to it.

Seeing that he meant to ignore her, Ruby drew the book towards herself and flipped through to her small part. *Mislike me not for my complexion, The shadow'd livery of the burnish'd sun.* When she had first read this line, she had envied the Prince of Morocco his pride. She wondered if Sister Celsus realised how excruciating Ruby would find it to utter these words on stage, in front of everyone. But with time, with each telling, Ruby felt some of the prince's confidence seep into that hard space beneath her diaphragm. Her voice became infused with a coaxing manner, with good humour.

Harry climbed to his feet.

'What's taking them so long? Better go hurry them along,' he said, lip curling. He stepped through the long grass until he was swallowed up by the copse of trees.

Peter snored softly. A grasshopper landed on his collar, rubbing its hind legs together. Ruby watched the gap in the trees, her eyes straining to see any sign of the others through the straggle of gums. She shut the book in her lap.

'I might help them find wood,' she said to Peter, but he didn't stir.

As she walked, the dark foliage cut out much of dusk's light. A narrow dirt path was worn into the ground, and it wasn't long before she caught sight of Harry ahead. He stood behind a stout shrub, holding a branch aloft to watch something down low before him. As she trod closer, a twig broke under her foot and she froze. She heard a laboured gasp, then another, like the sounds her aunt made when she lugged sacks of rice across the floor of the store. Through the gaps in the branches, close to the ground, she caught glimpses of puce.

She jumped when Fran screeched, 'Get away, Harry.' A bird fluttered from the branches above. Harry let out a whoop but didn't move from where he was stationed behind the shrub.

One more gasp and Ruby turned tail, hurrying back to where the horses were. She stood at the edge of the blanket, breathing heavily as though she'd run a mile. Wondering what she'd seen. Hoping Fran would be back soon to tell her. She knelt and reached for Fran's beer and took three quick sips. Concentrated on the burn of the alcohol.

It wasn't many more minutes before Harry came back. 'I'm hungry,' he grumbled, wrenching the bottle of schnapps from Peter's slack grip.

Ruby bent her head to the book. She knew her own paltry lines off by heart, so she turned to Fran's, each page tagged with a strip of newspaper, and tried to memorise hers.

When Ted and Fran finally returned to the clearing, Fran gathered up the blanket. She kept her eyes lowered, and her cheeks were flushed. 'Hurry, Ruby, throw the bottles over there and let's go. Ma will be wondering where I am.'

Ruby leaned over to pick a leaf from Fran's hair, but Fran tossed her head, said, 'Leave me alone.'

With much effort the boys levered Peter onto the back of the mare. Ted moved across to his horse and gestured for Fran to climb up.

'I think we might walk,' said Fran.

Ted shrugged. 'Suit yourself.'

He swung up onto the horse and the boys clopped away to the north.

Fran stared after them for several seconds and then turned back to follow the train line into town. As they trudged home, she wouldn't look at Ruby, wouldn't speak. Ruby tried to grab her clenched hand, wanted to squeeze it, tell her, 'Sorry, pet,' but Fran snatched it away.

A flash of blue light brings Ruby back. A whiff of acrid smoke. Hutchison lights his cigarette, and all those days are gone again, ashen pin bones, picked clean over many sleepless nights.

'Better get out there.' He pulls the curtain back a couple of inches.

Ruby's gaze is drawn to Fran. She's saying something over her shoulder to the lady seated behind. After that evening in the grove, Ruby had tried to visit her six times before she became tired of hearing that Fran felt unwell, Fran was working extra hours at the factory, that Fran had popped to the butcher's for a few lamb chops. Several weeks later Fran was sent south by her parents, and Ruby learned that what had happened to Fran was not to be spoken of, but also, that it was. There had been one letter from somewhere called Toowoomba, but Ruby's aunt had ripped it up before she could read it. And when Ruby had gone around to ask Fran's mum for her address, the woman had said, tiredly, 'Leave it be, Ruby. It's for the best.'

The crowd murmurs. A gentleman shifts in his seat. Hutchison frowns, opens his hands wide. 'What are you waiting for?'

Drawing a deep breath in, Ruby feels it flutter through to her stomach. Time to perform. The one thing she has perfected over her short lifetime. She digs her fingers into her diaphragm and squeezes her eyes shut. Exhales slowly. Perhaps it won't be so bad if Fran recognises her, if Fran does know who she is. This time, it will be Ruby who draws Fran into her game. She will convince Fran that her role as Chinese reciter is no more than yet another mischief, much like the pranks they pulled when they were younger.

And there's comfort in that. Fran, the one person in London to know who she really is. Ruby Wong. She's Ruby Wong. From China. From a little blue house in Innisfail that rises out of the eucalypts like a plume of smoke. Ruby. She opens her eyes and stares down at her embroidered slippers, willing them to stride onto the stage.

Mind Full

'Now.'

'Now?' Jennifer's mind has wandered.

'Keep your active attention in the present. In the now. The Buddhists talk about the monkey mind, swinging from thought to thought.' The therapist smiles. 'Try to still the monkey.'

Jennifer thinks of the dress she has, with its pattern of cheeky monkeys. Of the charcoal drawing of a gorilla that earned Ben an A in art at school.

'And what of Ben's dad? How's he coping?'

'Oh. I'm not sure, really.' Jennifer notices the surprised expression on the therapist's face. 'He works out at Centenary Mine. We haven't been together for over six years.' Closer to eight years, when Jennifer thinks about it.

The therapist pulls a pad and pen to herself. 'Before the next time we meet, I'd love for you to practise mindfulness, Jennifer. Here, try to get your hands on one of these to read.' She jots down the titles of three books.

Jennifer takes the slip of paper and nods. She promises the therapist she will practise this mindfulness, she will concentrate on the present. Except Jennifer knows that on the periphery of every moment her son's shadow will nudge through. That, since losing him, every moment will be implacable.

Now, just as Jennifer settles into an armchair to read the first book on the list, Dawn, a mother from Ben's old school, stops by with a small pot of pumpkin soup. The same soup – too heavy on the cumin, chopped dill scattered across the top – as the one she brought over after the funeral.

'I'm so sorry I haven't visited in a while, Jen,' she says, plonking the pot on the stove. 'Work's been crazy, and I've been chasing after the bloody kids.' She swings around to tend to the soup, but not before Jennifer notices the tiny pause of chagrin. Jennifer's become used to parents being wary of mentioning their children to her.

She takes a seat and watches as Dawn brushes crumbs from the kitchen bench and washes a saucepan and bowl from the night before, telling Jennifer of the new girl working at her hair salon; how she waxed off half a client's eyebrow. Dawn uses what Jennifer's grandfather called 'elbow grease' to scour the bottom of the pan, and Jennifer wants to tell the other woman that it's not grief that makes her slovenly. That, even before, Jennifer would have left the washing-up to some future time.

Dawn insists on eating with her. They sit at the kitchen table and, as Jennifer lifts the spoon to her lips, it occurs to her that she was sitting down to a bowl of chicken soup when Ben's teacher, Mr Connor, phoned her that night from Bali where they were attending the international school debating championships. Jennifer can't remember much of that first phone call – just that Ben had possible gastro and, if he worsened, they would take him to hospital. And she wonders if, in the moments she sipped on chicken soup, Ben was already going blind.

'Jen, have you thought about what you will do on the twenty-seventh? I want you to know we are all here for you.'

Dawn's voice is gentle. She hasn't eaten much of her soup either. Jennifer realises her friend's probably been screwing up the courage to broach the subject with her – of the anniversary of Ben's passing – but all Jennifer can do is give a tight shake of her head.

She gazes down into the soup and pictures the clock face that the therapist had shown her. How the word *now* replaced all the numbers. Wherever the long hand ticked, it was still *now*. Now. Now.

'Thank you, Dawn, the soup is delicious.'

Now, while watching the sports on TV, Jennifer frowns at the football players, their orange and white team colours reminding her of Ben's soccer jersey. She sits forward. His Tigers jersey. What happened to it? Was he wearing it when he was taken to the hospital in Denpasar? He was so proud of that jersey he wore it at every opportunity. Jennifer looks about, as though she might find it draped across the coffee table, the walnut cabinet, the lamp.

She lies back on the couch to watch the rest of the news, recalling how Ben's death was reported on this very program, and in the Indonesian media, too. She's thankful, in a way, that what happened to him had been taken so seriously. Seemed so singular that it was noteworthy. A lesson to them all.

Jennifer knew almost nothing of methanol poisoning before what happened and she dwells on the privilege of Australian teens, who can sneak a sickly sweet UDL or pinch rum from their parents' stash or shotgun bottles of beer and not risk dying from liquor inexpertly brewed. Homemade rice wine, in Ben's case, obtained from a street stall. Alone, too, they think, for none of the other students fell ill.

Pressing her face into a cushion, Jennifer wonders yet again why her beautiful boy bought the *arak*. Was he in a mischievous mood, perhaps? Feeling rebellious? Worse, was he lonely, left out of things like he was the previous school year? Maybe he just wanted to be mellow for a little, like when, around the same age, Jennifer drank half a glass of her mum's Baileys to see through a chemistry exam. If only Ben had waited until he returned home.

Her fingers search the back of the couch for the second book the therapist recommended, recalling that there's something inside about not brooding on the *what ifs*. She throws the cushion to the floor and, sitting up, flicks through the pages for something, anything, to calm her thoughts. She reads that she must look more deeply in order to see herself and others and her present situation clearly. Drawing a deep breath in, she concentrates on the wineglass in front of her, noticing that each time she's shifted it, the base of the glass has left a damp imprint on the coffee table. She breathes out slowly, taking in the cloudy wine stain on the inner surface of the glass. The crusty claret puddle at the bottom where her tongue couldn't reach. She breathes in again, already a little bored. Thinking of what she will do on the twenty-seventh.

Her eyes linger on *mindfully, awaken, enlightenment*. She takes in the words *our surroundings*, and glances about her living room, at the same old TV cabinet, the beanbag Ben used to fall asleep in, the rug the silverfish have feasted upon. Deciding that, if she has to live in the moment, perhaps those moments can be occupied where Ben spent his last few days, seeing, experiencing the last things he did. She can breathe the salt air he once did, watch the same glint of sunlight play across the ocean's surface. Then it will be in her present; not in the past, not soon, but now.

Jennifer hurries into the study and takes a seat at the computer. It blinks open at the article about mindfulness she was reading the evening before. *Living consciously with alert interest powerfully affects your interpersonal life with loved ones.* The words smite her and she closes the webpage with a click, and types in *flights Bali booking.* While she waits for the results to load, she glances up at one of the framed photos on the wall, taken perhaps two years before, of the last time her family were all together at Burleigh. Jennifer stands beneath a towering Norfolk pine, one arm around her sister's waist, the other about her mother's. Her father – Ben's grandad – grins from beneath the broad brim of his straw hat and he has a stubbie clasped in his hand. Ben's not in the photograph, though. He's the invisible one behind the camera. Not there, but there.

Now, her elbow tucked in close so she doesn't nudge the passenger sleeping next to her, Jennifer thinks of all she must do as soon as the plane lands. First, she hopes the driver that Dawn suggested has received her message and meets her at the airport. And then she has a whole list of places to visit, taken from the itinerary Mr Connor forwarded to her the week before. The last time Jennifer was in Bali, she had seen no more than the airport, the hospital and what she thinks was a government office. But the smells have stayed with her, of something like cinnamon; a medley of cigarette smoke, incense and smog; the floral antiseptic used in the morgue. Jennifer turns her head to stare out the window, wondering if the opalesque expanse below is cloud cover or sea.

The last book on the therapist's list lies in her lap, and she flips through to where she has dog-eared a page, re-reading *to have a fulfilling future with your significant other* – and Ben is, was, her significant other, wasn't he? – *you must inhabit the present.* Jennifer puzzles over these words, trying to work them into some sort of shape she can use. Reaching into the seat pocket in front of her, she withdraws her phone. She plugs her earphones in and scrolls through her stored videos, until she finds the one where Ben is only six years old, singing the national anthem. She smiles at the footage, listening to the words lisp through the gap where his front tooth is missing. When he ends on a scowl, having forgotten the beginning of the second verse, she presses the refresh button and watches again.

Now she can cross Tanah Lot off the list. She climbs out of the car, and the Balinese driver, Wayan, grins at her, urging her to move towards the market stalls ahead. It's stiflingly hot as she scans the T-shirts, fans, sarongs, keychains, coconut handbags and all the other souvenirs. She buys herself a lemonade iceblock, wondering if the boys – if Ben – enjoyed one too, when they were here.

Following the small crowd and the roar of the surf, she makes her way through massive carved gates that rise to a tip, pointing to the heavens. Pauses, as the vast ocean stretches before her. The water sapphire blue; the froth of the waves a lace fringe scalloping the dark sand. She walks closer, the iceblock dripping between her fingers, down her wrist. Her eyes take in the outcrop of black rocks that graduate their jagged way from beach to clifftop, meeting impossibly green gardens that edge the fenced pathway. Quick breath in when she catches sight of the Hindu temple perched atop a massive offshore rock, crouched over the sea.

The temple quite cut off by high tide. Waves crash against its walls, slap its winding stone staircase.

Jennifer keeps walking the neat path, passing pretty shrines with pagoda-style roofs, pink frangipani trees, hawkers selling bird whistles. She has to look twice before she realises that coiled complacently in a huge basket under a pandanus is the largest python she's ever seen. She murmurs with wonder at its muscled girth, as do the Chinese tourists behind her, and, pressing her clasped hands to her chest, she prays that Ben saw this snake too. How much he would have loved it.

She arrives at a set of narrow, steep steps carved into the side of a cliff, which she climbs slowly, so oppressive is the sun's glare. She passes a couple of gift shops and a café selling *luwak* coffee, where a civet, perhaps nervy on a surfeit of caffeine, prowls an elevated log. On the front bench lies another civet, curled in sleep, and the café owner runs his fingers through its luxuriant fur.

When Jennifer reaches the very top, she finds a row of open-air restaurants overlooking the sea, and she stops at the third one along, thankful for the breeze that rushes through. Too early for dinner, the restaurants are mostly empty of custom, and Jennifer chooses a table near the edge and orders a Bintang and a packet of crisps.

She stares out across the ocean as she sips the beer. The surf is rough and, despite the tremendous heat, nobody swims the narrow coastline between the headlands. She pulls the boys' itinerary from her handbag and peruses it. She's already spent a day in Ubud and wandered the beach in Legian. After this she will visit Kuta and the famous silversmith village, but she needn't see the sunset at Jimbaran Bay because Ben hadn't made it there. She takes a gulp of beer.

Turning her gaze to the sea temple again, she notices three men bustle about, perhaps priests arranging evening prayers. She supposes they will be stuck there until low tide returns. Black and white checked cloths flicker in the warm breeze.

Packing the uneaten crisps into her handbag, she pays the waiter and heads back down the stairs, once more staring in on the pacing civet. She can see that it's not tethered and wonders what it's so restless about. Perhaps it is bored, straining for a future filled with adventure, or dreams of an earlier time, a happier time, roaming a distant woodland. Jennifer continues on her way but feels something of the civet's agitation simmer through her own body, jumping beneath her skin with each step.

Once at the bottom, she returns along the pathway that leads to the headland. As she approaches the shoreline, she squints out across the darkling water, thinking of all the half-naked bodies baking on towels and sun chairs at the beaches further south. She comes to the sand and drops her bag to the ground, slowly peels off one sandal, then the other. Her eyes trace the huge black rocks to her left, take in the temple perched high above. The sun shimmers as it sinks towards the horizon, a shot of gold across the violet sky. If only Ben were here to see it. With her. Right now.

And the extraordinary beauty of the moment leaves her greedy for the past. Squeezing her eyelids shut, Jennifer thinks of how all those tremendous, mad, heartbreaking moments led to this very point. The Tintin tuft of Ben's hair when he was born, the mole above his lip. The time he ate the small chilli straight from the tree, shushing the heat of it through clenched teeth. How he cried for three whole days after Florence, their little white mouse, died. The tiny scar at his temple from when he was clowning around in the bath and knocked his head against the soap dish.

The familiar heat of loss tightens her chest and her mind grasps for some line from one of her books. *Clear the clouds of your thoughts.* Jennifer opens her eyes, dragging her mind back to the present. To the sand, scorching the soles of her feet as she hops, then runs, towards the water. To the waves that gobble at her ankles, slap her shins, sting the soft skin of her thighs. Her skirt billowing about her, nudging her raised elbows. Her bra soaked through, somehow heavier than her drenched dress.

Now, as a man points at her from the temple and two women lean against the clifftop railing the better to see. Now, as a white bird dips with the breeze, and the water – deliciously cool against the back of her neck – draws her close. Now, when nothing really matters.

Now.

What Would Kim Do?

THE KARDASHIANS ARE ON TV, and Kim looks tired, says she has to have sex five hundred times a day.

'Youch.' Liv grins, clutching the crotch of her jeans.

Georgia tells her to keep still as she draws the hair-straightener down the length of Liv's tulip-red hair. We're in her room, getting ready to go out.

I peer into the mirror and apply glittery, black eyeliner, carefully avoiding my spidery lash extensions. Each mink lash balances on one of my own pathetic lashes, which are as straight and short as the bristles of a kid's paintbrush. *does kim actually look that bored when she's having sex for the 478th time? does she droop, exhausted? or can she keep the act up for that long? grunting, gasping with each bump, uh uh uh uh, her legs wobbly, her neck strained while she wonders if north will eat banana if it's mashed …*

'Pass me the hair-straightener,' I say to Georgia, who rolls her eyes, says, 'Milly, your hair couldn't get any straighter.'

We catch a bus into town because none of us wants to drive tonight, and Georgia's mum is already too pissed to give us a lift. It feels weird sitting on the bus all done up. There's an old guy across the aisle from us. He's eating a pie or something, and there are crumbs on his chin and his blue shirt that stretches across his whale belly.

Liv turns her head towards Georgia, smirks, and mouths, 'Your dad's here.' I look out the window. I don't want to egg her on.

I have to press my knees together with each swerve of the bus to stop from flashing my undies. Georgia and Liv are seated across from me, and I can see a small triangle of Georgia's white undies between her thighs and the hem of her taut, short skirt. *i know that under there the skin on her vajayjay is as smooth as a peach. i only got a brazilian once. knee to the side, peeled open, searing hot wax. raw, a blush of pimply chicken skin. mum would crack it if she knew. reckons you can't tell whether you've got a real man or a pedo down there if your vagina looks like a kid's.* Our feet meet in the middle, a huddle of stilettos and straps that scrape the bus's black-speckled floor.

We stalk off the bus in those high heels, and we haven't gone three steps before Liv topples forward, straight onto her knees. We gasp and laugh, haul her to her feet.

'Great,' I say. 'We're not even drunk yet.' We've only had a couple of vodkas at Liv's place.

More vodkas, house whites and one tequila shot.

The club is loud, like really loud, and dark, all deep blues and blinking orange like a deep sea cavern in a dodgy theme park.

Liv grabs me around the waist from behind and we sway, cheeks pressed together. We love each other. We are best friends.

She drags me over to some guy she recognises at the bar, and her wine splashes down my leg.

'Milly, this is Joel. We go to the gym together.' She pats him on the chest. 'Joel, this is my friend, Milly. She's Asian.' This always happens when Liv gets pissed. She starts introducing me to people as her 'Asian friend'. It doesn't piss me off, exactly, because I am fucking Asian. I'm fine with it. But what's with the little giggle that follows the words? Like it's a good joke that I'm in on?

Joel, or whatever his name is, smiles at me. 'Yeah, I can see that.' He looks nice. His hair is curly, and he has a nice shirt on, but he looks so young. Like a boy. *there was this thing on facebook, that asian women are the most sought-after ethnic group in online dating. they're seen as submissive but sex-starved or something. they haven't met mum obviously. but that was in america, anyway, it'd be different here. most of the guys here, their eyes flick over me and come to roost like a couple of lovebirds on girls like georgia, i think it's the blonde hair i really do. god and i'd like bigger boobs too. liv got a boob job for her nineteenth birthday. five weeks later we squished into a toilet cubicle at chop chop changs and she lifted her shirt and we prodded her boobs like they were a couple of pork buns. firm but bouncy. 'no, the left nipple does not look crooked.' it did.*

Georgia pulls me away, tells me about how her boyfriend, Scott, did something something his mate Matty something. I have to concentrate on her nose to keep steady, but her face looms in and out. I'm not really sure if she's happy or not about whatever Scott did, so I just nod, say I have to go to the toilet.

I peer at myself in the mirror. God, the lights are so bright. Surely I don't look this bad out in the shadows of the club. My eyeliner has smudged a little, looks kind of sexy. My lips are still stained 'Are You Red-dy', but I wind up my lipstick, press it to my mouth, and the fucking thing breaks off, falls into the damp sink. I try to squish it back into the tube before I think of all the germs.

I lurch from the restroom, disorientated for a moment. Left or right down the short corridor? And a hand grabs me around the waist. The downlights are dim, but I can see it's that man-boy, Paul or Joel or whatever. He pushes me against the wall, holds my hips against his, smiles down at me. I can do this. I smile too as he lowers his mouth to mine.

It feels kind of hot kissing there in the darkness of the corridor, as girls totter past to get to the toilet. He's a good height for me, not too tall, and my hand coils around his back, clutches the hair at the nape of his neck, like in a movie. I lift my knee a little, lean into him.

But he is a way bad kisser. He thrusts his whole fat tongue in my mouth, and I have to kind of push it back with mine. It's difficult not to gag.

I wipe the spit from around my mouth, and he squeezes my bum, says, 'Where's your butt? You should do twenty lunges a day. I can show you how if you like.' Then he comes in with that suckerfish mouth of his again. *i hate my butt. i want a bubble butt, like in those hip-hop music videos, all grinding hips over swinging flesh. a girl at work says she has a butt like kim's, she can balance a wineglass on it, but i don't think it's true, you can't always believe what charlotte says. i told mum that i was thinking of maybe butt implants, maybe a boob job and she got mad, waved her spatula at me between scraping at the stir-fry, but what would she know with her flabby wide hips and those boobs — bigger than mine! — sagging beneath her jumper, pouring* kecap manis *over the frying potatoes. and anyway, iggy azalea says it's normal to have plastic surgery, that it's fine to want to change for the better.* I pull away, spin back into the restroom to smudge some more lip colour onto my damp mouth.

~

Another vodka or wine? I'm leaning on the bar, wondering if the barman will ever look my way when I see Xavier seated in one of the booths, and suddenly there's a slippery eel in my guts. *he used to call me his black sparrow, he used to stroke my hair like I was a pretty spaniel, curled up in his lap.* I glance around, make sure that the man-boy is nowhere around. I just couldn't bear it if Xavier saw me with him.

The barman nods my way, and I shout that I want a vodka soda, and I try real hard not to look at Xavier again. But of course I do. It'd be stupid to ignore him. If I go right up to him, smile wide, look delighted, he won't know how sick I feel at seeing him. I walk towards his booth, and my stiletto heel skittles out from under me on the cement floor, but I right myself in time. There's another woman ahead of me. She's tall, her dress is strapless, the tips of her fair hair dyed turquoise. And she stops at Xavier's booth. He stands, and I see the look on his face. I know that look.

I turn back, just as he kisses her on the lips, his hand resting on the curve of her hip. I race for the other end of the club.

The door thuds behind me. I'm in the fishbowl room, the music so loud all I can do is close my eyes, allow its pulse to take over my heartbeat. The dance floor is pretty full – a few couples, a group of girls dancing around their handbags like they're some precious offering. *once, his head between my legs, Xavier said this is how i'd trapped him, with my honey, and that he was the bee. i laughed and said it felt more like i was the poor little bantam hen and he was the python. he grinned, baring his canines, as he snaked up my belly.*

Light strobes through the darkness, faces flaring at me in flashes. Some guy takes my hand, leads me onto the dance floor. I sip the vodka through the straw as I slowly gyrate my hips, shift back and forth, but my feet ache now and, looking around, I can't see Liv or Georgia. They're at the other side of the club, near Xavier. *who used to say i had such beautiful, sad eyes as he traced their edges with his fingertips, and so i'd pretend to be that sombre person, that girl with something sorrowful hidden deep, deep down in the tissues of my soul. but it wasn't enough. he was once married to this thai woman, that's what he called her – woman – but he said i was still a girl, still needed to have my own adventures, meet other men, or women, even. he wasn't mean, he squeezed my fingertips across the café table, the relief softening the edges of his face as he let me go.*

'You want to get another drink?' the guy shouts, his breath warm in my ear.

I nod, let him lead me to the bar.

His name's Daniel. He's pretty hot actually, says he works in the mines in Moura, as a fitter of something. I like that when I lean on his arm to hop off my stool I can feel the muscle in his forearm flex. We kiss in the back of the cab to his place. He's a good kisser, firm, teasing tongue, and his hand presses against the top of my inner thigh, nudging, so I feel pretty ready by the time we get to his unit. He says he has a female flatmate, but she's out too, might not even come home if she stays at her boyfriend's.

He's one of those guys who likes to peel his clothes off immediately, helps me do the same. His sheets are soft, well-worn and smell of sweat and his aftershave. I lie back, wait for him to join me, but he just stares down at my body by the light of the bedlamp, gazes at me like I'm food, like how my dad examines a platter of gleaming chilli mud crab. I want to cover myself with my hand, wonder what he's thinking. *sometimes i look at porn to see what i'm supposed to look like down there. at girls with vaginas as dewy as orchids, shades of dragonfruit pink and fairy floss. i worry mine is less … pretty.* He straddles me, and his hands and tongue map out his territory for the

178

night. I arch my back, *like i see the girls do in the sex videos,* wish again I had round, hard boobs that point to the ceiling.

He lies on his back, guides me over him.

'Protection?' I'm perched on top of him, ask the question quietly, lightly, like it doesn't really matter. I'm on the pill, but still.

'Babe, I forgot to get some. I can pull out if you want,' he offers. *i've seen this in porn too. kneeling girl, rosy tongue seeking communion, waiting to be baptised in his holy water.*

He slips into me, and my head falls back, the tips of my hair tickling the small of my back. I want to ride this wave with him, crash on the sand together, but I know I won't make it. I won't be in time. I can feel he's close. The closer he is, the louder I get. It sounds like I'm sobbing almost, *like those women,* I press my boobs together between my arms, *uh uh uh uh,* arch my back, and when he climaxes, I cry out, too. *i think i sound convincing. i'm pretty good at this part.*

When it's all over I slide off him, slick with sweat.

'What a workout,' he says. His eyes are shut, but he's smiling.

He rolls onto his side towards me, and his heavy arm pins me down across the stomach. His breathing slows, and I wonder if he's already asleep.

But I'm still awake. His skin is warm and moist against mine. I angle myself so that my breast brushes his, and I wriggle under his arm, will him to wake, to continue what has not finished for me, but his mouth has fallen open a little. He is definitely asleep.

I raise his arm from my belly, tuck it against his chest and step from the bed. Pulling on my undies and his shirt, I pad out to the kitchen on shaky legs. I find a glass on the draining board, fill it with water, but a drink is not what I've come for. Not really.

Leaning on the bench, I stare out the kitchen window, at the sky lightening over the neighbour's roof, like the aura that shimmers above a bonfire. And I can see my reflection in the black glass. A dark girl. Still.

My fingertips are cold as I slide them down the front of my undies.

This I know how to do. Silently.

So Many Ways

THE FIRST THING ELLA DRAWS from the box that her Uncle Joe has sent from Innisfail is a brittle branch of longans. The fruit's skin is as raspy as she imagines the hide of a scaly lizard might be. Sliding her fingernail beneath its skin, she strips it away, taking her back to her grandmother's lounge room, when she and her younger brother, Shaun, used to peel the wallpaper from the walls on those sticky, boring afternoons. Ella tries to recall if Ma ever scolded them for such vandalism but only remembers the feel of her grandmother's cool fingertips when she cupped Ella's cheek, and the rings of talcum powder caught in the wrinkles of her throat, the jade earrings swinging from her stretched lobes.

The longan flesh is plump, moist. She knows it will taste sweet, a bit like a lychee, but instead of taking a bite, she lifts it to her nose. There's only the faintest scent, thank god. For the past month, most smells make her gag, even the fragrance of her mother's Clarins face cream. The other day, at the restaurant, she nearly vomited when the cook was slicing cucumber. Cucumber! Who knew it even had a smell? And yesterday she had to cross the road to avoid the salty musk coming from the fish and chip shop, even though a handful of hot chips is the only thing she can possibly keep down.

Dr Chin said that if she goes ahead with the procedure, she'll need to go to the northside to have it done. Ella places the peeled longan on the deck table and, pressing her hand to her lower belly, uses her fingers to search for movement. Surely it's too early. Surely the tiny tug she sometimes feels is just wind, or perhaps food shifting in her stomach.

Beneath the longans is a notebook, covered in tattered brown paper, speckled with grease spots. Ma's cookbook. Ella has to clear her throat, loudly, to dislodge the sadness that catches there. She opens it up, revealing page after page of her grandmother's scrawl, some recipes scratched in Chinese, some in English. The earlier pages are almost indecipherable, recipes originating somewhere along the Pearl River, passed down the Chu family line for over a century. She lifts the notebook, and several slips of paper slide to the table, the first a yellowing playbill of some sort, for a Liberty Theatre, London. Ella doesn't recognise the play or, for that matter, any of the actors, although *Laurence (Sir) Olivier* sounds familiar, and Ella's interested to see, a few lines down, the name *Ruby Wong*. Perhaps a friend of Ma's? Perhaps saved purely for the novelty of a Chinese name on an English playbill. She picks up a newspaper clipping that announces the passing of her grandfather, William 'Bill' Hartley, who died a good ten years before Ella was even born. Apparently her freckles are from him, her small stature from Ma.

Turning over the last piece, she sees it's the old black and white photograph of Ma's family. It used to hang on the wall outside her bedroom, dusty tape binding a loose corner of the timber frame. Sometimes Ma stood gazing up at it, and one day Ella had joined her, but turned tail when she noticed her grandmother's lip tremble. Their mum explained to Ella and Shaun that the photo had been taken in Cairns when the Chinese side of the family still farmed bananas in Innisfail. Eleven children, neatly barbered and wearing starched dresses and suits, are seated cross-legged on the floor. Ella thinks Ma is the one second from the left, in the dark pinafore. An old woman, perhaps Ma's own grandmother, balding and dour, is seated in the heart of the family, her six adult sons standing behind; her five daughters-in-law on either side. None wear Chinese clothing, except one young woman, seated to the right of the picture. She cradles a baby. Ella peers closer to inspect the baby's bonnet, to admire her pretty, dark eyes. And that's when she notices that there's a strange outline around the two figures. Reminds her of the cardboard push-out dolls her cousins had given her one Christmas. Ella traces her finger along the woman's edges, feeling the faint crease of the woman's presence. She's been glued onto the family portrait. There, but not.

The little golden bell above the restaurant's door tinkles as she leaves work. Sent home early yet again. The sky is still blue, but the wind that whistles between the tall, grey buildings has a bite to it. Ella draws her cardigan close about her thin frame as she walks to the bus stop. Sussex Street is mostly deserted, apart from a man sweeping the pavement and a waiter smoking outside the Hong Kong noodle place. A woman walks past at a brisk pace, a surgical mask covering her nose and mouth. Ella wonders if she should wear one too – especially now – but also, she's worried it would be an overreaction. Look foolish in some way. Or racist, even.

She understands why Mr Wang had to send her home early. The virus has scared off most custom and there was only the one couple to serve the whole day. Even then, they only ordered two chicken stir-fries, the cheapest thing on the lunch specials menu. But Ella's also pissed off that Mr Wang has kept bloody Mei, the other waitress, on for the rest of the shift. The smells of the kitchen might leave Ella slightly queasy, but she needs the work. She glares back at the restaurant, its sign – *Double Happiness* – painted in some faux Chinese bamboo script across its façade.

On the bus, Ella manages to find a seat next to the window and, all the way home, she practises the words she could use to complain to Mr Wang about Mei. How Mei springs to action when he enters the restaurant, clearing tables, replacing washed bowls and chopsticks, fawning over him with offers of tea and toothpicks. Yet, as soon as he leaves or goes out back to his office, she returns to her boyfriend – who spends hours parked at a corner table, drinking free glasses of Coke, nibbling on prawn crackers – leaving Ella to pick up the slack. Anger spikes, hums between her ears. And what about when Mei doesn't wash her hands at the beginning of their shift, like she's supposed to? And that time she smoked a cigarette in the ladies' toilet? Indignation rises in Ella's chest, forcing frustrated tears to her eyes.

Perhaps, though, rather than embroiling herself in a shit fight with stupid Mei, Ella should just quit. Find a waitressing job somewhere else with more hours. God knows she needs the money. She draws in her stomach. One way or another, she needs the money. But she also thinks of those months the year before when she couldn't find work; not in a restaurant, not in a shop, not in a warehouse. How her mum had to pay for her phone plan, all her food, the extra ink to print out résumés. At twenty-two! Could she really risk throwing in a job right now? A dull headache taps at the back of her skull. Something like the headache she gets on her period. The bus travels along Belmore Road, passing the Vietnamese restaurant, the bank, Woolworths, the medical centre, reminding her of her follow-up appointment with Dr Chin, and Ella wonders if hormones account for her ragged temper, the ache ticking in her head.

She hops out of the bus at Carr Street and trudges up the hill to her mum's house. Letting herself inside, she drops her bag onto the hall table and turns into the bathroom. She lifts her cardigan and shirt to inspect her belly in the mirror. She can't tell if there is the slightest bump, or if she simply imagines it.

What to do? What to do?

If Ella were really determined, perhaps she could find him – the Irish guy she spent one drunken night with in that Parramatta motel after her mate's twenty-first. All she has to go by, though, is a first name (Kieran), that he grew up near some famous brewery, and that he doesn't like onion or tomato on his kebab.

Sighing loudly, Ella turns on the tap to wash her hands and the splash of water catches a lone ant, sweeping it down the plughole.

Ella lounges back in a deckchair and watches two miner birds bicker between the spiny leaves of the grevillea. A kid over the neighbour's fence insists, 'Well, vampires die if they go out in the sun, and I'm standing out in the sun!' and another child concurs.

Ella slaps at a mosquito that hovers by her shoulder. A motorbike roars past and, if she really listens for it, she can just hear the white noise of the ocean beyond the insistent burring of crickets.

'Bring out the photo album, would you, Ella?' her mum says, as she goes through the box from Uncle Joe on the deck table. 'The pink one, with the lilies on the front.'

It takes Ella a few minutes to find it in the bottom of the mahogany dresser, among all the other albums, the empty frames, the stacks of loose photos yet to be housed. She returns to the deck and hands it to her mother, who slides on her reading glasses.

Her fingers – long, blunt, just like Ella's own – pick their way through the album. She pauses at a photo bleached in light, of two kids standing in the front yard of a house as white as a seagull's breast. They're squinting at the camera, and her mum murmurs, 'That's me and your Uncle Joe.'

Ella nods. She's seen the photo before.

'I had to wear that frock to church and it was as scratchy as all hell.' Her mum smiles. 'Had to wear bloody bloomers under there too. You know what bloomers are?'

'Yep. You told me years ago. Like big pants.'

'Big pilchers, more like.' Her mum shakes her head, flipping over to the next page.

She pauses at the photos taken from one Christmas holiday spent in Innisfail, the year Ella was ten. There's a photo of her mum steadying Shaun, still little, on the back of a grey pony. In the photo she's saying something, laughing, her dark hair cropped in a pixie cut, her arms sinewy and tan. That was how her mum used to look. How she looked before Shaun died. Afterwards, Ella's sixteen-year-old self had been puzzled to see silver strands streak her mother's black hair. But now, watching her mum turn the pages of the album, it occurs to Ella that perhaps she didn't turn grey overnight with grief. Maybe she merely stopped bothering to colour her hair, in the same way as she was finished with mascara and lipstick.

'That's the longan bush,' her mum says, pushing the album across the table. The photograph is square, the colours grainy.

The tree's branches are weighed down with bunches of longan, and a slender Chinese man stands to the side, metal bucket at his feet.

'It's huge,' Ella says, surprised.

'So it should be. It'd be well and truly over a hundred years old by now.'

She picks up the longan that Ella peeled earlier, frowning. 'You shouldn't waste them.'

'Couldn't stomach it.' Even now, just glancing at it makes her feel nauseous, reminding her of the tiny, fleshy thing growing in her belly. She slides Ma's family photo across. 'Look at this.' She taps her finger against the woman glued onto the portrait. 'Why'd they stick her on later?'

Her mum pushes her glasses further up her nose. She pops the longan in her mouth, where it lodges in her cheek as she speaks.

'I can't remember her name. I think the story is she came from China to marry one of my great-uncles, but by then the White Australia policy had kicked in and kept her on the run. My great-uncle was born here so he could stay, but she was shipped back and forth to China to await her visas. For years at a time, I think. She must've missed out on photo day.'

'I wonder how many of these kids were hers. Did she have to cart them back and forth too?'

Her mum leans in, peering close. 'I'm pretty sure they stayed here when they were old enough. Imagine having to leave your kids behind.' She spits the longan seed into the palm of her hand. 'Dragon's eye. That's what the word *longan* means, you know. That's what my po po told me anyway.' She places the gleaming brown seed on the table. 'Reminds me of Shaun's eyes. Remember how dark they were, Ella?'

Ella nods. Her own eyes are hazel, as though the Chinese blood has been steeped just a little too long over the generations. She wonders if the child growing inside her has her pale eyes or her brother's dark ones. She stares down at the family portrait again, at the infant lying in its mother's arms. The baby has the same beetle gaze as Shaun used to have. Ella considers the mother, her slender shoulders, the stoic expression on her face. There are so many ways to lose a child.

She's finally made a decision. She will tell Mr Wang about Mei. Stuff her. If there are any extra hours going at Double Happiness, then Ella should have them.

Before work she heads to the post office and waits in line to send the package her mum has prepared for Uncle Joe. She found some more photos in an old biscuit tin and they had both pored over them, trying to find the glued-in lady.

'I'm sure that's her,' her mum said, pointing to an older woman, seated to the side of a family gathering. Her grey hair is braided, and a toddler sits by her feet. 'I think she was my Great-Auntie Bok. She had seven kids. Seven! You know that relative of mine in Townsville? Henry? The one with the three Alsatians? Auntie Bok was his grandmother.'

As she pulls the package from her tote, Ella thinks that perhaps it would be nice to add to such a large family. Maybe she could name the kid Shaun, after her brother. Or Shauna, if it's a girl.

She waits impatiently for the young Chinese fellow in front of her to be finished. He's placed four small bottles of hand sanitiser on the counter, and Ella's been listening long enough to know that he's trying to send them home to his family in Wuhan.

The post office woman is worried, though. 'I think this gel is flammable, isn't it? I'll have to check if you can send it.'

She goes out the back to ask someone. She returns and rifles through a guidebook of some sort, murmuring back and forth with the young man. 'Hard to say,' she says, eventually. 'We could risk it.'

'What's the risk? If I send them anyway?' he asks.

The woman slides the bottles into a plastic envelope and says, 'They might be discarded somewhere along the way, if they're deemed too dangerous to post.'

The woman has to repeat herself for the young man, and Ella almost rolls her eyes. She feels bad for the guy, but if he faffs around much longer, she'll be late for work. And she wants to be a bit early so she can have that word with Mr Wang about Mei.

Ella sinks into one of the restaurant chairs. Laid off. Sacked. Dismissed. To be fair, Mr Wang had actually said, sadly, 'We need to let you go.' And when her eyes swivelled over to Mei, he added, 'All of you. Yes, the cooks too. I have been losing too much money. Terrible time. Terrible, terrible time.'

She looks around the empty restaurant. It seems as forlorn as she feels, what with its bare tabletops and the glasses stacked in crates on the bar. The cooks stay out the back, and the bell over the front door tinkles as Mr Wang lets himself out, mumbling something about the bank.

'Well, this is fucked.' Mei sits down at the opposite side of the table. She's helped herself to a Tsingtao and prises off the lid. She takes a swig, gazing out on the quiet street through the plate-glass window. A curtain of black hair hangs in her eyelashes as she blinks. Her nostrils flare, so that the tiny ruby nose piercing glints. Ella knows she must take it out every time she visits her Cantonese parents.

She turns back to Ella. 'You look gutted.'

'Well, it's a pain, isn't it?' More than a pain. Perhaps she should try Woolies this time. When she tried Aldi, she got no further than a group interview of eight.

'Yeah, I'm a bit gutted too. This wasn't such a shit place to work.'

Ella watches, irritated, as Mei fishes around in her bag for her cigarettes and lighter. She looks uneasily at the smoke alarms on the ceiling, saying, 'You're not going to have that in here, are you? Mr Wang wouldn't like it.'

Mei laughs, the cigarette clamped between her lips as she lights it. Smoke puffs out of her nostrils, and she says, 'Geez, I hope he doesn't fire me.'

Ella's phone pings with a text reminding her of her doctor's appointment. She's feeling queasy but knows it's nothing to do with the smoke or morning sickness.

Mei fetches another beer from the fridge and brings back two glasses. She has Mr Wang's bottle of whisky tucked under her arm too, the whisky he keeps for special customers.

'Don't worry, Ella. My cousin owns a kebab shop in Miranda. He'll give us work.'

Ella stares at her. 'That'd be great. Do you think he really can?'

'Sure he will. My dad will make him.' She grins.

'Thank you, Mei. That'd be great.' Her eyes follow the smoke that billows around Mei's head. She feels bad, now, about what she was prepared to say to Mr Wang earlier. And wonders, drawing her hard little abdomen in, if Mei's cousin really will give her a job. If he does, she promises herself she will be friendlier with Mei. She tries to smile at her now.

Mei pours two beers and, in each, she adds a generous dollop of whisky. She pushes one across to Ella. 'Least we deserve. What a shit fight.'

Ella doesn't want to go home just yet, to tell her mum the bad news. And there's hours to kill before she sees Dr Chin. She reaches forward and draws her fingertip down the condensation that's formed on the glass. Knows that, should she take a sip, she'll relish the release the alcohol will provide, despite the sick roiling in her stomach.

The Fish Girl

One of these days he would buy himself a house on the hills in Java and marry a pretty little Javanese. They were so small and so gentle and they made no noise, and he would dress her in silk sarongs and give her gold chains to wear round her neck and gold bangles to put on her arms.

'The Four Dutchmen'
W Somerset Maugham

One

I N THE DARKNESS BEFORE DAWN the village men row out in their boats that are shaped like the half-pods from the criollo tree, and in the heat of the day the women scale, clean and smoke the fish the men bring home.

When Junius comes from town in search of cheap labour for the Dutch Resident's kitchen, he calls out to the villagers in their Sunda dialect.

An older, leathery fisherman steps forward. 'My daughter is good with the scaling knife.' His voice grates, as if a fish bone jags his throat.

'How old is she?' Junius asks.

The fisherman stares at him for a few moments and then shakes his head. 'She comes to here,' he says, holding his fingers level with the bottom of his earlobe.

Junius's eyebrow lifts. Although he has only a quarter Dutch blood, he is paler than the crowd of underdressed men before him, and knows how to wear trousers and a necktie. 'Bring her to me. I'll have to look at her first.'

The fisherman disappears in search of his daughter, while the others press the virtues of their family members on the man from town. Two women, still clutching the baskets they are weaving, babies nestled close to their chests in batik *slendangs*, cry out to him, urge him to take their older daughters. A group of men approaches from the beach, tying their sarongs tight about their hips, bare feet shuffling along the sandy earth. Some of them ignore Junius, return to their shacks clustered in neat rows behind the ceremonial hut, but three younger ones stay on, push to the front of the crowd.

Soon the older fisherman returns, followed by a slight girl, her midriff and legs wrapped in a roughly woven sarong. Her straight hair hangs over her face so that only a glimpse of her eyes and nose is visible. Her feet are bare and her shoulders, rounded forward, accentuate her small pubescent breasts.

She is jostled on either side by young men and women, hopeful to gain work in the Dutch quarters. The young men call out to Junius, grinning and joking, but the girl keeps her head bowed.

Junius nods to one lean man and then another, gesturing for them to join him, before stopping in front of the girl. 'Pull your hair back.'

The girl, eyes still trained upon the ground, parts her hair with the backs of her hands, so that the shiny tresses arc like the wings of a black bird.

'What is her name?' Junius asks the fisherman.

'Mina.'

Junius's eyes linger on her high cheekbones and fine mouth and he nods. 'She will do. Have her ready to leave in the morning.'

A sob of dismay rises in the girl's chest but lodges in her throat like a frog in a tree hollow, for she knows better than to cry out. She has never roamed far from the edges of the tiny village, no further than a few metres into the forest that backs on to the beach. Even when the other children disappear deep into the shadowy folds of the casuarina trees to play, she stays behind to help her mother sweep the house or scrape the fish. How will she bear to be so far away from everything she knows?

Following her father the short distance to their home, she keeps her face lowered, away from the gaze of curious villagers. They reach their hut, elevated on short stilts, the walls a medley of bark and timber with a shaggy thatched roof. Her mother is standing on the narrow landing.

'What have you done?' she asks, her chapped fingers clutching at her sarong. Her eyes switch from her husband to her daughter and then back to her husband. 'What have you done?'

The old fisherman simply stares at his wife. His eyes are bloodshot – are always bloodshot – as if the glittering sun has saturated him with its heat. He eventually shrugs past her into the darkness of the hut.

Mina doesn't enter as there is only the one room. She can already hear her mother's voice, soft and plaintive, working at her father, and his low grunts in response. They very rarely exchange harsh words, the last time being two years before when her father wanted Mina to wed. Her mother succeeded in dissuading him then, saying she was too young. Would she succeed this time?

Mina walks down to the beach and contemplates the small triangles of silver fish arrayed on the nets. Her mother has laid them out to dry, but it is becoming dark, so Mina wraps them in spare netting and heaves the lot up to the side of the hut, away from night-time predators. She knows that tomorrow there will be more fish, damp and fleshy, ready to be scaled and gutted.

And that the next day there will be even more. She stares at her feet, at the sand and strands of grass, and for the first time feels a flicker of curiosity. What will be expected of her at the Dutch house? More fish?

Standing at the corner of the hut, next to a cluster of freshly salted sardines strung to the end of a rod, she listens for her parents, but all is quiet now. Her father comes out and sits on the end of the landing and lights a *rokok*, the aura of clove and tobacco smoke rising above his head. A metallic clatter of cooking echoes out from the back, and she joins her mother at the fire. She's frying chilli and fish paste and, despite herself, Mina feels hunger stir in her stomach. She squats down and begins to break apart some salted fish to add to the pot.

'Do I have to go?' she asks.

Her mother wipes the side of her nose with the heel of her hand as if to brush away tears, although she's not crying. She nods. 'Yes.'

'But why? Have I done wrong?'

There are creases between the older woman's brows from when she frowns against the glare of the sun and privation. These lines have become deeper with time, and now resemble keen, inch-long slices in her forehead. She shakes her head, chopping *kangkung* to add to the fish. 'No. No, it's not that, Tak-tak.' Mina knows she's not in trouble when her mother uses her nickname, starfish. Her mother tosses the greens into the pan and stirs them about, and then wipes sweat from her upper lip. 'Your father thinks you will be better off there. You can work, and maybe even send us things sometimes.'

'What things?'

Her mother shrugs. 'Food? Maybe clothing.'

'But how?'

'Your father says you will exchange your hours of work for things we need, like more spice and tobacco.'

'But how will I do this?'

'I am not sure,' her mother answers, shaking her head slowly. 'Your father thinks your Dutch master will allow you to visit us once in a while, so maybe then you could bring us back some goods.'

Mina rests back onto her haunches and sniffs at the salty fish crumbled against her fingers. 'What work will I do there?'

'What you do here, I expect. Cooking, sweeping, washing.' Her strong, bony hand squeezes Mina's knee. 'But you must behave yourself. Remember where you come from. Remember your father and me. Remember one day you must return to us, Tak-tak.' Her voice is quivering now, and Mina feels the force of tears against the back of her eyes. 'And never let anyone see this,' her mother adds, folding back a corner of the girl's sarong.

They stare at the scaly, red rash that covers her inner thighs.

Mina swiftly re-covers her mottled skin, conscious of the fire's heat upon the weeping sores.

The three of them have their meal seated around the fire. They eat the rice and fish from banana leaves with their fingers, and Mina asks, licking the seasoning from her shiny fingertips, 'What will I eat there?'

'Food,' her mother says.

'Yes, but what kind of food? Will it be the same as here?'

Her mother glances at her father, and she knows her mother is trying to gauge how long until he loses his temper and slopes off to smoke. 'I'm not sure, Tak-tak. Shh now.'

And what will she wear? What is the town like? Who will she work with? She asks herself these questions, a tremor of excitement finally mingling with the dread in her stomach, making her feel pleasantly sick like when she eats too much *sirsak*, the sweetness of the custard apple curdling in her stomach.

The evening sun sets as they clear away the pots, food and drying fish, and they retire to their rattan mats in the hut. Mina wonders where she will sleep in the Dutch house. She has only ever seen a white man once. He was tall, as willowy as a kanari sapling, and he wore strange clothes like the man from town. He'd trodden through their village, peering into their huts, as curious as the villagers were as they gazed upon him.

Through a gap in the wall next to where she sleeps, Mina watches the swaying, frayed leaves of the coconut trees on the beach. The waves roll and clap further out to sea, and she hears the familiar hum of the ocean calling to her. Her father snores softly, but she knows her mother is lying awake too.

There is a damp breeze from the water as the sun rises. Mina's father strides onto the beach and glares out at the fishing boats already bobbing on the waves, fidgeting old netting between his hands. Moving back to the landing, he cracks pumpkin seeds between his teeth, making a slight whooshing sound with his lips as he spits the shells to the ground. Her mother stirs coconut milk and palm sugar into Mina's breakfast rice, a sure treat, but Mina is afraid again and almost unable to eat. She forces the meal down, gagging, determined to not waste the food that her mother would never allow herself. Finally, she stands and her mother carefully wraps her own good sarong around her daughter's hips. The patterned batik is still stiff from the wax stamping, the colours earthy, with streaks of ocean blue. Mina tries to protest, for this is her mother's special sarong for ceremonial days, but the older woman clicks her tongue and ignores her. They are both weeping now, as her mother tucks and pats down the edges of the fabric, and tucks a little more, until her father grumbles that it is time to go.

Mina trails behind her father to the centre of the village, wiping snot and tears onto the back of her hand. When her father leaves her with Junius, the man from town, he squeezes her upper arm – reassuring or cautioning, she's not sure. He doesn't look at her. He glances above her head for a few moments, as if contemplating the branches of the mango trees, and then turns and leaves. She watches his sinewy, dark legs from behind and she feels a fissure of hatred for him. Fear slices through her anger. Oh, the gods will have something terrible in store for her for thinking such things.

'I hope you have eaten and drunk well this morning,' says Junius, as he swings up onto his pony. 'It's a long walk to Wijnkoopsbaai.'

There are two brown ponies. One is fat and carries Junius's gear on one side of its saddle and two baskets of fish on the other. Junius's own pony is taller, yet his feet dangle only a foot from the ground as he sways along. Mina falls in behind the two young men – Yati and Ajat. Yati is short, as squat as an eggplant, but Ajat, one of the chief's sons, stands tall, has the broad shoulders and trim waist of a fine fisherman.

They walk slowly from the village. A few friends clap the men on the shoulders, grinning, demanding they bring back some cinnamon or nutmeg. One even calls for them to bring back prospective wives, and he's slapped playfully across the top of the head by his companions. It becomes awkward, for the young men don't know when to stop their cajoling, when to stop following, but soon enough Junius frowns down upon them and they pause under the fragrant kenanga tree that marks the edge of the village. After a few seconds one of the young men left behind calls out to his friends to bring back a *peci* to replace his straw hat, but the ribaldry is done with.

The first part of their journey is pleasant enough as they walk in the shade of row upon row of India rubber trees. The sun is still low and not yet punishing, and the ground is damp and cool. But by midmorning the girl, who is not used to such long periods of trudging, is weary and hot. She sees the glistening perspiration ring the necklines of the young men ahead of her, and her mother's sarong is damp around her waist. The mountainous terrain becomes dusty, the straggle of bushes offering little shade. Her feet are sore, and the tip of her right big toe bleeds from where she jabbed it on a rock. By the time they reach Wijnkoopsbaai, she is wilting, her skin greasy with sweat.

Here the roads are wider, no longer single tracks, arcing a path through a verdant patchwork of tea plantations. Small houses, square and neat with gabled roofs, line the roads next to large plots of rice paddies. Clothing is cast over shrubs to dry, and children and chickens watch them as they walk past. Mina marvels at the never-ending stream of houses.

They come to a crossroad, where the boulevard widens, leading down to the seafront. Oxen laden with baskets plod past white men on horseback. Junius pulls his pony up in front of a gate at the top of the road, and a boy runs out to open the latch. The girl stands on tiptoe but cannot see over the orderly hedges that surround the property.

Mina is the last through, lagging behind the others. She can't resist staring at the creamy orchids or reaching for a fallen *bunga raya*, its happy red petals having narrowly escaped the heavy tread of the ponies. The road is steep, but finally they see the house. It's much larger than even the ceremonial hut back in the village. It is stark white, with timber shutters, columns and wrought-iron balustrades. Even Yati and Ajat are struck speechless by its majesty.

Junius hustles them around to the back of the house. Kneeling in the shade of a frangipani tree are two kitchen maids, dark and slim, grinding seeds in a mortar and pestle. They lean into each other and watch as the young men from the village take water from a pail. The maids each wear plain white kebayas over matching brown and black sarongs, and both have their shiny, black hair pulled into low ponytails. They look so smart that Mina is glad she's wearing her mother's good sarong after all.

Once the soggy baskets of fish are unloaded from the horses, Junius tells her to stay in the courtyard until she is collected, and he leads the village men and ponies away to the stables. Her legs feel heavy so she squats down onto her haunches and watches the servant girls go about their work. They finish with the seeds and start slicing chillies and lemongrass on a wooden board on the ground before them. They talk to each other, but they do not talk to her. One of them rises to lug the heavy baskets up the back stairs to the kitchen verandah, her back arched with the weight of the fish.

An older woman comes from the kitchen to inspect the fish and, noticing Mina, descends the stairs with crab-like steps to allow for the girth of her stomach. She stands in front of the girl and looks her over, like she is a piece of fruit at the market. She makes Mina turn, and even squeezes her upper arms, feeling for muscle tone.

'You will call me Ibu Tana,' the woman says. 'I am the master's head cook. You will work for me in the kitchen, but if you are no good, you will have to be one of the cleaning maids. Do you understand?'

Ibu Tana is shorter than Mina. Her hair, black with wires of grey sprouting at the hairline, is pulled into a severe bun, and her skin is saggy and lumpy. She reminds Mina of a toad.

'Do you understand?' the cook repeats. 'Pray to the gods they didn't send me someone who doesn't speak the language, did they?' she then says, exasperated, to the other kitchen maids.

Mina nods. 'I understand.' Her mother was born in a village on the outskirts of Wijnkoopsbaai where this language of trade was used often. As they knelt in the shallows together, scooping the muck and worm-like innards from the fish, she'd taught Mina many of these words, and told her of bold women like this Ibu Tana.

The cook wraps her steel fingers around Mina's arm again and pulls her to a hut at the back of the courtyard. Inside is the servants' *mandi*, the tub filled with clean water. Ibu Tana grasps the end of Mina's sarong and unravels it from her body, her gnarled fingers rasping the girl's skin. Mina covers the rash on her thighs with her hands, but Ibu Tana pushes her towards the *mandi* and tells her to wash with the sandalwood oil, to change into the servant's sarong and kebaya neatly folded next to the wash bucket. The *mandi* door slams shut behind her.

Mina has never washed like this before, for a modest sunset soak in the sea is considered ample cleansing in the village. She picks up the small bucket by the *mandi* and dips it in the water. Lifting the bucket above her head, she lets the cool water sluice over her body. She repeats this three times, until she is shivering.

Looking around, she can't find anything to dry herself with. Ibu Tana has taken her mother's sarong and all that is left are the servant clothes. She feels a flutter of panic; she doesn't want to keep Ibu Tana waiting. Quickly she wraps the new sarong around her wet hips. It is the same as those worn by the other servant girls. The pattern is far fancier than any she has ever seen before: a shower of black tadpoles in symmetrical russet swirls. The kebaya feels strange as she gingerly pokes her hands into the sleeves and slides the blouse onto her body, for she's not used to the feel of fabric against her back, rubbing against her shoulders and breasts. She's not sure how she'll ever become used to the confinement.

She climbs the back steps to the kitchen slowly but, once there, her trepidation turns to amazement as she gazes around the huge room at the number of stoves and pots. She's never seen an oven built into a fireplace before. There are glass-fronted cabinets, bowls and plates stacked high. One of the kitchen maids is washing crockery in a large tub while the other one stands in front of a bubbling pot of oil. A houseboy pauses in his sweeping and grins at her.

Ibu Tana turns from the oven to look at her. A slow smile curls the side of her mouth. 'The fish girl has brought the smell of the sea with her,' she says. 'You'd better be careful or we'll accidentally fry you up with the crabs.'

The kitchen maids titter when Mina bends her head to sniff her arm, but Ibu Tana shakes her head and tells her to shell the beans.

Ibu Tana tries to teach her to cook other dishes besides fried fish with sambal. The cook grumbles that nobody can live on fried fish alone. Of course, Mina knows this to be untrue. She is aghast at the variety of food the master and his guests insist upon, that even the servants enjoy. Only on very special occasions is a chicken or goat slaughtered in her village. And only the men eat their fill; women and children busily clear the cooking pots, douse the fire, sweep the hearth while waiting for what rice or meat might remain. But in the Dutch house Mina eats well, tastes sauces and sweets she never knew existed. She wishes her mother could try these wonderments and vows to take her some food wrapped in banana leaves when she returns to the village for a visit, even if she has to steal morsels from behind Ibu Tana's back.

One of the first things she learns to cook is *pisang epe*. Ibu Tana teaches her to fry the banana with palm sugar until it is brittle and sweet, how to recognise when to take it from the pan. Mina learns to knead dough for Dutch desserts and Chinese dumplings, how to slice the shallots and garlic so finely that, when fried, they become as wispy as wood shavings.

Once the day's cooking has been done and all the dishes washed and sorted, Mina stands on the kitchen balcony and breathes in the traces of spice left on her fingertips – the peppery coriander, the tang of the lime leaves. She smells the night air, searching for the salt of the sea on the evening breeze. She closes her eyes and strains to hear the ocean's whisper, which is occasionally disrupted by a dog barking or the night call of an owl. It's in these closing moments of each night, when she feels the ocean's presence, that Mina remembers who she is. But the memory has weight, sinks in her chest like a pebble in the sea. She misses her mother. She misses the silence of plaiting the netting with her, she misses their rhythm of scaling the fish. She misses falling asleep beside her mother's soft breathing, while the ocean whispers to her through the gap in the wall.

Each night at the Dutch house the kitchen maids sleep on bamboo mats on the kitchen floor. If the room is stuffy from the day's cooking and the others are already quietly snoring, Mina drags her mat outside onto the verandah and braves the mosquitos by hiding under her mother's sarong. The morning after she had arrived at the master's house she was horrified to see the sarong cast on the ground, bunches of washed spinach arranged in rows upon it. She was too scared to say anything. All day she waited and watched between the tasks Ibu Tana had set for her. She waited until the kitchen maids cleared away the greens, their bare, flat feet treading across the sarong as they went. Then Mina flicked the sarong into her grasp, rolled it into a ball, hid it away under a bush until nightfall. That first night when she brought it out from its hiding place, when she lay with the sarong across her mat, her skin cringed, waiting for Ibu Tana's sharp words, a clip to the ear. But nothing happened. Maybe they didn't notice. Maybe they didn't care.

Although she works alongside the other two kitchen maids in the small, hot kitchen every day, they are locked together in their own dialect and their own history, for they are sisters come all the way from Aceh. The houseboy is friendlier, younger, so young he still doesn't have any down on his cheeks, or across his upper lip. His name is Pepen and he's small with a thin face and ears that stick out from his head. He has been with the master for so long he can hardly remember his parents and doesn't know what village he is from. All he has left from that time is a small kris, fastened to his waist, its wavy, sharp blade sheathed in leather.

The first story Pepen ever tells her, while they roast cacao beans over the fire, is how he watched a man in the market have a fit, how the man just collapsed to the ground and shivered, how his spit frothed like waves on a windy day.

'And there was this terrible smell. It seemed to seep from his skin, a frightened smell, a rotten smell,' he says. 'And he swallowed his tongue.' Pepen blinks a few times, and his large ears become red.

Pepen's job is to sweep the floors and polish the timber, fill the *mandis* and bring in wood for the fires. Sometimes, when Ibu Tana gets irritated and shoves her aside, Mina helps Pepen with his chores. One morning she follows him into the dining room, for she'd spilt the cooking fat, been banished from the kitchen. The main section of the house is vast and airy. Palm fronds nod in the dulcet breeze that drifts through the open doors, and the heavy furniture from the master's homeland seems to overwhelm the delicate teak pieces.

She's sweeping the floor, the spidery straw of the broom wafting ash and dust against her ankles when she notices Ajat, one of the young men who'd accompanied her from the fishing village, standing in the doorway.

'What are you doing?' She doesn't know him very well. Growing up, her shyness had bound her close to her mother and home, and she'd always been extra bashful of Ajat, the son of the head fisherman. But she yearns to feel the language of their village upon her tongue, wants to feel she is still a part of something.

'Waiting for Master,' he says. His skin is as smooth as polished ebony, dark and tight, and his wiry hair is tucked into a batik headwrap. 'I've brought his horse.'

He doesn't offer any more information, just stands patiently on his right foot, the other one tucked against his right ankle.

Mina resumes her sweeping but feels his eyes upon her and becomes self-conscious, all elbows and shuffling feet. She doesn't notice the master of the house enter the room upon a cloud of tobacco smoke.

'Be more careful, girl,' he snaps at her, as he squashes the cigarette beneath his shoe. He watches Mina for a few moments through his pale crow's eyes and then says, his tone less harsh, 'You're making more mess than there was before.' He walks onto the verandah and leans over the rail to the pond. Bringing up the phlegm in his throat, he hocks into its green depths.

Mina sees Ajat's mouth twitch as she sweeps the ash towards the corner of the room. She's forgotten to bring the dustpan with her and is unsure what to do with the debris. Conscious of Ajat's gaze, she tucks the broom under her arm and returns to the back of the house in search of Pepen.

'What do you mean he wants the fish girl to serve?' demands Ibu Tana. 'She can barely hold a pot without spilling *lodeh* down her front.'

It's true. The girl fingers the yellowish, stiff soup stain that has dried upon her kebaya. She thinks she will never become used to the cook's abrupt ways. It's as though her hands aren't her own when Ibu Tana is near and her heart jitters high in her throat. Sometimes when Ibu Tana scolds, a crystalline blind spot nudges at the corner of her vision.

Pepen shrugs. 'The master said he wants her to wait table from now on. He said when she's not working for you during the day, she is to help me in the house.'

Ibu Tana stares at the girl for a moment, her mouth twisted to the side, eyes narrowed. 'Well, you'd better change your kebaya.'

213

She reaches out, pinching the fabric between her fingers, catching the tiniest bit of flesh.

Later that day Mina returns a spittoon to the sitting room. She pauses, hearing Ibu Tana's voice, high-pitched. She hides behind the doorway, for she doesn't want to anger the cook.

'She has leprosy, I tell you,' Ibu Tana is saying. 'I've seen it. It's disgusting.'

Penyakit kusta. Leprosy. The girl's hand twitches at her sarong and she feels her cheeks burn red. Was Ibu Tana talking about her? Please don't let it be so. Her family had taken much care over the years to hide the offensive flesh. Who knew what the other village families would have done to her if they thought she could contaminate them too? And her father had traded much fish and shells for herbs to alleviate the itchiness, the pain. But somehow she'd been careless enough for Ibu Tana to notice.

'Rubbish.' The master's voice is low and clipped. 'It would be obvious if she had this sickness.'

'But she does,' the cook insists. 'I have seen it myself upon her legs. What if she passes it to all of us? What then? It would not be good if it is known that this sickness is in the house. Who will visit you then?'

'That is my concern, not yours.' Mina hears him strike a match to light his cigarette. 'Bring her to me.'

It doesn't occur to the girl to run; she has been brought up to be obedient, after all. Ibu Tana almost collides with her as she bustles around the corner and grabs her by the arm. 'Were you listening, you sly thing?'

The girl nods. Her face is hot as she's dragged to the master, worse than on the day her father gave her to Junius. She won't look up at him, just stares at his richly polished brogues.

'Show me your legs, girl,' he says. His tone is abrupt, but softens when he repeats, 'Show me your legs. There's nothing to be scared of. Ibu Tana is here. We just want to be certain you are not sickly.'

Her breath won't come as she slowly parts her sarong at the front. Averting her face to the left, Mina squeezes her eyes shut and can almost feel her skin bloom fresh red welts under the others' gaze.

'That is nothing more than a rash, you foolish woman,' the master says eventually.

'You won't send her away?' asks Ibu Tana.

The girl's eyes lift to meet the master's. She would walk into the sea rather than disgrace her father. Her mother.

'Of course not.'

Mina can't sleep listening to Ibu Tana's cranky snore. Any wariness she felt for the woman has been replaced with a sullen dislike, as unyielding as the twin shells of a fresh clam. Just the memory of her words to the master pulses heat through the girl's body, making the sores on her thighs flare and sting. She wants to rake her fingernails through the welts, really dig at the itch, but knows the lacerating damage is not worth the momentary relief.

If she were at home her mother would soak cabbage leaves, drape them over the sores. She would mash papaya, chew betel nut, smear the paste across the rash. But here, in Ibu Tana's kitchen, the girl lies in agony, too embarrassed to tend to the sores. If she were home in her village she would wade into the water, let its salt balm the pain. The warm water would lap at her legs, dissipate the burn.

Mina longs to hear the ocean but cannot over the others' sleeping breaths. Tiptoeing onto the verandah, she can only hear the lowest murmur from the sea. She wants it to be louder, loud enough to drown out the high pitch of pain that hums through her body. She steals down the steps, across the master's land, until she reaches the gate. It's locked, so she scrambles through the hedges, the branches snagging her kebaya, scratching her arms, until she reaches the road. The clammy sea breeze draws her forth, and she's not afraid when there's a rustle in the bushes and a gecko clucks from inside a tree trunk, for her need to be in the ocean clamours through her body. She ignores the rocks and prickles that pierce the soft soles of her feet, the burrs that cling to the bottom of her sarong.

Thin reeds whip her shins as she runs onto the beach, the sand still warm from the heat of the day. The full moon shines across the slate surface of the sea. The waves rush up the wet sand towards her, their frothy white fingers greedily beckoning to her as they retreat. She sheds her sarong and clambers into the cool water. Sinks to her knees. Feels a flash of pain as the water licks at the sores on her thighs, but then, the relief. A sigh catches in her throat as she leans back, digging her palms into the sand behind her. She lengthens her legs, and the salt water lolls against her tortured skin. Her whole body gently rolls back and forth with the rhythm of the sea.

She stands and steps a few feet further into the water. She's cautious because she's never learned to swim. Too many of their village men and children had drowned for Mina to be careless. But the sea pulls her further until the chill water reaches her hips. The current is strong, tugging at her body so that she sways on the spot, and her feet seep into the sand. The sea's roar, hollow, familiar, rushes through her, talks to her, matches its cadence to hers. It reaches around her, velvet soft, draws her in, draws her further until the water is at her waist. Its arms are so soft, softer than the white underbelly of the stingray, and she can hear it whispering to her. *Putri*. Princess. *Putri*. Its arms are dark and long, gently sucking, kissing at her damaged skin, until the agony of flesh melts away, leaving a faint tingle in its place.

Mina shivers, for a breeze has picked up. She backs out of the water and, once on the beach again, drops into a low curtsy, murmurs her thanks to Nyai Loro Kidul, apologises that she didn't bring a flower or shell as an offering. She feels heavy, restful. She's so relaxed she could fall asleep on the sand, but knows that the Ocean Queen cannot protect her there, so she slips back to the hot kitchen, back to her bamboo mat.

They were the greatest friends, all four of them; they were like schoolboys together, playing absurd little pranks with one another.

'The Four Dutchmen'
W Somerset Maugham

Two

MINA WONDERS IF ENVY, as redolent as soured durian, makes Ibu Tana hiss at her through her remaining teeth. For the girl has become a favourite of the master's. She has freedoms the older woman has never experienced. When she isn't in the kitchen being bossed around by the head cook, she can be found in the cool, relaxed world of the main house. Maybe, too, Ibu Tana resents how the master calls for Mina with the word *mooi*, which means 'beautiful' in his language.

Mina helps Pepen return some bedding to the spare room and catches a glimpse of herself in the mirror. She's seen the shape of her thighs, her buttocks, when reflected in the puddle upon the *mandi* floor. She's seen the shadow of herself in the still water of the well, in the windowpanes of the master's house. But never like this. Her fingers trace her full bottom lip. She leans in close to the mirror so she can search out the flecks in the brown irises, the curl in her lashes. She smiles. So this is *mooi*. She doesn't linger long at the mirror for Pepen is grinning at her.

'The master's sister stayed in this room when she visited from Belanda,' he says, sweeping under the mahogany four-poster bed.

He straightens and the grin slips from his face. 'She was bitten by a mosquito and her foot swelled up so she couldn't put her shoes on for many days. Her doctor – one of their doctors, they would not see the medicine man Ibu Tana sends for – wanted to saw her foot off but the master wouldn't let him.' He shrugs. 'Luckily she got her feet back into her slippers and she returned home to Belanda. The master was very sad.'

Back in the kitchen Mina squeezes the juice from a grapefruit, wondering how the master can stand the sour fruit. She thinks of the sweet, green mandarins that grow near her village, and kisses her tongue against the roof of her mouth until she can almost taste their juice.

'Fish girl,' says Ibu Tana, shoving a piece of clothing over Mina's shoulder. 'The master wants you to fetch goods from the produce store. You're to change into this.'

The girl holds the kebaya up before herself. The front panels of the silk blouse reach her ankles; the cloth's rosy lustre is like nothing she has ever seen before. She's confused as to what she's supposed to do, but Ibu Tana has already gone. She looks to the kitchen maids who pretend to ignore her, even though they peer at her from under their heavy brows as they fry and chop the evening's meal.

The kebaya is heavy on her shoulders as she waits on the kitchen verandah for further instructions. Its fabric is thick. It blocks the sea breeze. But it's gorgeous, and she can't help running her palms down her sides, her work-roughened skin catching on the silk.

She's pleasantly surprised when Ajat guides the pony and cart to the back steps. She's glad that he will see her in her finery.

'Come along,' he calls to her. 'I'm to take you to the store.'

'But I don't know what we need to get,' she protests, looking through the kitchen door in vain for Ibu Tana.

'I have the list,' Ajat says. 'I'm to help load the goods; you're to make sure that sneaky Chinaman doesn't swindle the master.'

She struggles to climb the steep steps of the buggy due to the tightness of her sarong. Once there Ajat shifts over on the bench seat to make room for her. She takes the chalkboard from him, stares at the calligraphy scrawled across its surface.

'We can't read this.'

Ajat grins. 'The Chinaman doesn't know that.'

They're quiet on the short drive to the produce store. Her arm rubs against his as they sway along the dirt road and she watches for finches in the trees, on the curiously shaped roofs of the Dutch houses. Sometimes she glances down at Ajat's fingers, dark and tapered, controlling the reins. She peers at the vein that ropes up from the heel of his hand and across his forearm. He doesn't smell of the sea anymore. His scent is sweeter, of sweat and horse. His knee bumps against hers once in a while.

They trundle down the road towards the beach and she leans forward, yearning for a touch of the salt water on her toes.

Ajat presses her back. 'No swimming today,' he says. 'Junius needs the cart again soon.'

He steers the buggy alongside a square building. Mina stares at the sloped red roof. At the peak of each eave is a golden creature, scrolled and lizard-like.

'Dragons,' a voice says from behind. 'They are called dragons. They guard my store.'

The Chinese merchant holds his hand up to her, takes the chalkboard, looks it over. He's shorter than Ajat, but much more stout. His head is the shape of a pumpkin, and his sparse black hair is slicked to his pate with perspiration. He grunts at the list and gestures for them to follow him into the back of the store.

The space is filled with such an assortment of produce Mina can only stare. Bolts of fabric, sacks of rice and tapioca, greens, fruit and dried sea cucumber among chests of crockery, baskets of silk slippers, fans and seeds. She doesn't recognise many of the goods with their strange scents, awkward shapes. There are two young women behind a counter. They resemble the Chinese merchant: wide faces, shiny black hair. They wear heavy smocks with long sleeves and pretty buttons. Gold bangles jangle up and down their arms, and jade earrings dangle from their ears. One is trying to catch a striped gourami from the aquarium behind her, although the fish sluggishly bobs away from her net. The other woman stares back until Mina drops her gaze and returns to the hot yard.

Ajat helps the merchant's men fill the cart with sacks of food. Lastly, they heft up a wooden barrel.

'Beer,' says Ajat. 'Junius says that the master doesn't drink it, but he has guests coming tonight who drink a lot.'

The afternoon sun has lost its heat and myna birds argue among the branches, dropping shreds of leaf onto the patio. Mina is crouched down grinding dried coriander seeds in the stone mortar. The crushed coriander resembles silt, she thinks, as she dips the tip of her finger into it, rubs its chalkiness between her finger and thumb. She touches her fingers to her nose, against the surface between her nostrils, so she can smell its sharp fragrance. Pepen half-heartedly sweeps away the fallen leaves of the persimmon trees nearby while telling her of the cargo tramp that arrives in port most months, and how the four huge Dutchmen who work on the vessel have dinner in the master's house.

'These men are great friends, but no-one can tell them apart. We just call them "the four Dutchmen",' Pepen says, as he chews on the pink flesh of a fallen persimmon. 'Tonight they are bringing a friend. I heard Master say he's famous. A famous storyteller. From far away.' He spits a seed out onto the ground. 'I'd like to be a storyteller. I tell good stories, huh, Mina?'

Mina has helped wait table for several nights now, but she has only had to serve the master, seated alone at the head of the table. The quietness of the dining room is usually punctuated by the rustle of her sarong, the clinking of china and cutlery, the buzz of the cicadas hiding in the nocturnal garden. But tonight the whole house reverberates with the presence of the Dutchmen. The floors vibrate as they stomp by, the walls echo with their loud voices. The master plays music on his gramophone, and when Mina enters the living area with a plate of *lumpia*, the men are bellowing along with its heavy tune and strange words.

She lowers her gaze as they take the spring rolls from the proffered plate. Suddenly they are quiet and, glancing up, she sees they are staring at her, smiling, curious, as their yellow teeth sink into the *lumpia*'s crispy skin. She backs out of the room, and the din picks up again.

Pepen helps her lay the table with platters of chicken, salads in peanut sauce, savoury pastries and pickled fruits. Pepen keeps the visitors' glasses of beer filled to the brim. And he was right. Mina finds it hard to tell the difference between the big, pink men from the cargo tramp. But their friend, the storyteller, is taller, slim. His hair is black and his moustache is as shiny as a polished whelk.

He has the look of a garuda hawk, and when he speaks his voice is hesitant, deliberate, until he drinks more of his clear draught that has the pungency of the substance Pepen cleans the windows with.

It's not long before Mina becomes aware that one of the Dutchmen, the fattest of the four, watches her as covetously as he'd pondered the syrupy coconut pancakes on the dessert platter. Somehow he finds out that she is the one who cooks the konro, so he makes a point of eating only the rib dish, the gravy slicking his lips. While the others pour more and more food into their wide mouths, and shout and joke with each other over a card game, the fat man continues to watch her. He wipes sweat from between his chins and smiles so that his blue eyes crinkle almost shut. His friends tease and nudge him and even though they speak in their own language she can tell they are taunting him about her. The garuda man's dark eyes peer at her as he scribbles in a little black notebook, and the master laughs too, but not as loudly. When no-one else is watching, she sees him frown.

The following morning the master calls her away from the kitchen where Ibu Tana is teaching her to cook yellow chicken. Mina's hands are stained with turmeric and the freshly sliced garlic stings the tiny fissures in her coarsened fingertips. Wiping her hands down her sarong, she finds the master seated on the verandah next to the fat Dutchman, who is even pinker than the night before. He's wiping the back of his neck with a red bandana. The master explains that the man, who he calls Captain Brees, wants to practise Malay with her. He says this will be beneficial for her too, as she can learn some Dutch. The master's pale eyes are blank. She cannot tell if he is pleased with her or not. He tells her to stay in his gardens, not to go beyond the gates.

She leads the way down the front stairs, and the timber steps shudder as the captain lumbers along behind her. She can't look at him, can't smile, feels her insides shrink in his presence. Her head is hot like when Ibu Tana opens the door of the ravenous oven and it whooshes its fiery breath around her ears. The captain clears his throat but doesn't say anything. He wipes at the back of his neck again, mops at the perspiration dripping down his temples, across his red cheeks. Stroking the brazen, cerise petals of the orchids between his thumb and finger, she notices his chubby fingers tremble a little and she wonders if he feels as shy as she does.

He points up high at the jagged palm leaves.

'*Daun kelapa*,' she says, and then remains silent until he points out a hibiscus. '*Bunga raya*.'

'*Bunga raya*,' he repeats.

But his pronunciation is so strange and funny to her ear, she is soon giggling at him, covering her mouth with a cupped hand as she has been taught by her mother, and he laughs with her, so that his whole body shudders up and down with each gasp. Once their lesson is finished he presents her with a small rattan box. It's painted in a wash of jade green with a pattern of pink dots, and inside she finds sweet-smelling frangipani flowers. She's never owned anything so pretty. He says something to her that she can't understand, smiles, pats her arm.

The master sees the captain off, and Mina returns to the kitchen. While Ibu Tana is engrossed in counting the fifteen eggs to go into the *lapas legit* cake, Mina hides the rattan box at the back of the shelf that holds her bedding. Not until everyone is asleep later that evening does she take the box out and, hiding it under her kebaya, she carries it all the way down to the beach. She lifts the lid and places it carefully on the sand. The frangipani fragrance escapes on the sea air. This time she wades with confident steps into the waves, the box of flowers clamped against her chest. The water is as black as squid ink, as warm as tears. She hums the tune her mother used to murmur to her, *kerning naning kerning naning*, nonsense words, yet the melody so soothing. She holds her hand in front of herself, rotating it at the wrist as she sings, watching the moonlight glimmer across her milky fingernails. She calls for the Ocean Queen. Only when she feels Nyai Loro Kidul's strong, smooth pull, feels the soft arms suckle at her damaged thighs, does Mina scatter the flowers upon the sparkling black water.

A kingfisher cackles high in the branches, ruffling its turquoise wings, watching for stray pieces of meat. The afternoon sunlight dapples Mina's skin as she stands in the shade of a banyan tree. She has never been among so many people. They are gathered in a clearing near the beach; men, women and children load tables with platters of rice, curries and sweetmeats.

Ibu Tana shoves a basket of *bacang* in her hands and nods to the nearest table. 'Make yourself useful. Stop staring and help us carry the food the master has provided.'

Mina places the basket on a table next to a bowl of rambutan. Pepen squeezes her elbow. 'That's the elder who is putting on the feast.'

The *priyayi*, an old Javanese man, slight and as bent as a knob of ginger, quietly surveys the food. He is accosted by several people who take his hand in theirs, bow their heads low. Mina already knows from Pepen that everybody in town, every single villager, from the ragged field worker to the elegant batik artist, has been invited to celebrate the town elder's successful tea harvest. Only the very meanest of the Dutch masters have neglected to give their workers the night off.

By the time the stage is erected and the *gamelan* band is assembled, it is dark enough to light the lanterns, which lend a flickering glow to the festivities. The *priyayi*'s servants encourage everyone to eat, heaping mounds of food on swatches of banana leaf. Mostly the guests sit cross-legged on the ground to watch the performance, except for the *priyayi* and his family, resplendent in rich velvets and jewels, who are seated at a table with a white tablecloth. Mina skirts the pretty dancing girls and admires the sprigs of jasmine that speckle their coiffed hair and the flecks of gold in the green satin of their costumes. But it is the *wayang* puppets, hanging from the side of the stage, that draw her close. She has never seen anything like them before.

The miniature, glossy people are gorgeous and grotesque, each one different. This one has a red face, angry black eyes, white rabbit teeth. This one is a warrior, with a tin sword inserted in its stick hand. The princess wears a striped sarong and a golden, peaked headdress. The prince has a crown, and his black eyebrows are bold, his nostrils coiled. Mina lifts her hand, wants to feel his sharp nose.

'You'd better not touch it,' Ajat says, grinning. He nods towards the puppeteer. 'The *dhalang* has his eyes on you.'

Mina smiles back at Ajat but drops her eyes. Every time she sees him now, whether it's fleetingly in the master's yard when she takes food to the stablehands, or on their swift trips to the Chinese store, she feels as if a band tightens around her chest.

'Let's get away from here,' he says. 'I can't stand how they look at us like we're children.'

She follows his gaze to where a Dutch family has joined the

priyayi at his long table. A pallid man watches the dancers, and his thin lips smile as if observing an infant stumble over its first steps. His wife surveys the villagers with a benign air and puzzles over the proffered food, while their three young daughters droop with boredom.

'Come with me.'

Mina follows Ajat from the quivering circle of light, through the bushes to the edge of the beach. A murmur of music and voices drifts through the branches as they settle under a banyan tree.

'The *priyayi*'s servant gave me these to taste,' Ajat says, pressing a small package into her hands. The food is wrapped in smooth, neat rectangles of banana leaf. 'He called them *lemper*.'

She presses the green wrapping to her nose. It's fragrant, more interesting than the watery smell of the triangular beef *bacang* Ibu Tana has taught her to make. When she peels away one end, the moist rice leaves a residue on the banana leaf, on her fingertips. She licks the coconut milk from her skin and bites into the *lemper*. The chicken is sweet; the shredded coconut catches between her teeth.

'Delicious.'

Ajat presses his mouth to hers, seals in the sweetness, the wonder. He softly takes her lower lip between his lips, runs the tip of his tongue along hers. The band around her chest tightens until she can barely breathe. Falling back, Mina scrapes the heel of her hand against the tree trunk. The full moon shines on Ajat's cheekbones, lights his teeth.

'Do you want to return to the feast?' he asks.

She nods slowly, touches the tips of her fingers against her mouth. She wants to reach her hand out, feel for his lips too. Leaning against the tree, she pulls herself into a standing position. Her legs are weak, can barely hold her, like the time she had the fever.

By the time they find the others, the lamps are guttering, transforming the villagers into shadow puppets. It's not until they are all walking home to the master's house that Mina realises she still clutches the *lemper* wrapping in her fist.

The next morning Mina waits in the kitchen courtyard, dressed in her good kebaya. But it is not Ajat in the buggy today, it is Yati, the other boy from her village. She scrambles up onto the bench next to him. 'Where's Ajat?'

Yati makes a grunting noise. 'His father summoned him back to the village.'

'For how long?'

Yati's face is chubby, has a fat, flat nose. 'What do you want to know for?'

She shrugs, watches a greenfinch hop to a lower branch of the persimmon tree. 'I'm just surprised he's not here, that's all.'

The buggy rolls down the master's long drive, turns onto the main thoroughfare. Mina leans her knees to the side of the buggy, away from Yati.

'Ajat might never come back. Who knows?' the boy says, lightly slapping the reins against the pony's back. 'His father wasn't happy about him coming here anyway. Said he could only stay a year at the most.'

Dismay flushes Mina's skin. Ajat may never come back. Her heart already misses him, but she also feels a pinch of jealousy. If only she too could go back home. Go back to the people she knows, the ones she loves. If only she could return home with him – with Ajat. But he is the chief's son. He is worth something to the village. He will not be traded. She has been exchanged for rice, tobacco, maybe even a live chicken or goat. There will be no need to summon her home.

Yati pulls the buggy to a stop at the back of the Chinese store. 'Ibu Tana said you know what to do.'

She stares into his face, then glances away, has to gather her scattered thoughts as though they are wisps of papery garlic skin caught on the breeze.

Entering the dim shop, she smells the spices, familiar to her now, and the white smoke that rises from the incense stick in front of the crimson and gold Chinese altar. She closes her eyes for a moment, remembers she needs four cans of butter – the red tins that feature a picture of a grazing cow, not the ones with the blue and white label. And black cotton to mend Pepen's trousers. How her mother would marvel at Ibu Tana's sharp little needle – but thinking of her mother scorches Mina's chest.

Today there is only one girl serving, the shorter one, who has a thick fringe of hair across her broad forehead.

'May I have eight potatoes, please,' asks Mina, placing the cans of butter on the counter. She wonders if her voice sounds as tight as her chest feels. 'And a pound of flour?'

As the girl shovels potatoes into the bag and weighs them, Mina thinks of Ajat's smooth skin, his strong hands. She wonders if she will ever see them again.

She looks down at the bag of potatoes the Chinese girl pushes across to her. She's given her the wrong type, the sweeter kind. The girl is already measuring out the flour, and Mina knows that if she asks her to exchange the potatoes she will become grumpy, but if she takes them home, Ibu Tana will scream at her. Sweat moistens her underarms.

'You swim with the sea dragon at night-time,' the Chinese girl says to her, softly. Her dark, almond eyes peer at Mina as she shovels another spoonful of flour into the container.

Mina's face slackens. She glances around the store. They're alone. 'What do you mean?'

'You've been seen.' The girl plonks the container down, tilts her head. Her black fringe is oily with sweat, hangs in straight, narrow strips like the teeth of a comb.

Mina shakes her head slowly. 'No.' All thoughts of home, of Ajat, of her mother, skittle away. 'Who says?'

'Gok. He guards the store during the night. He said he's seen you creep down to the beach, that you swim with a dragon.'

Perspiration prickles Mina's upper lip, but she forces a smile to her mouth. 'No. No, that is not true.'

'But you do swim there at night-time?' the girl persists.

Mina tries for a friendly, casual tone. 'Only the once. It was a very hot night.'

'I knew it,' the girl says, her thick lips widening into a smirk. 'He probably saw a dolphin or a mackerel or something, the idiot.'

'Yes, yes,' says Mina, light-headed with relief. 'That reminds me. I also need to buy a fish. Whole. To bake.'

The Chinese girl picks up the fish net and climbs her little ladder. Swishing the net back and forth she eventually scoops out a grey fish, as waxy and sharp as flint. She slaps it down on a wooden board, holds it still with her left hand.

'You best watch out,' she says to Mina. 'Horrible things could happen to you if men like Gok know you're wandering around alone at night.' Taking a knife, its blade keen and narrow, she positions it above the fish's head. 'But it'll be even worse for you if the local people think you're a witch.' She pierces the squirming fish above the gills, slices down through its throat until it's decapitated.

The sky has darkened, and cool drops of rain splatter her arms, her head, as they fill the cart with the goods. The sun has taken on the silver of the moon, the clouds are as leaden as her thoughts. Mina has lost her friend, Ajat, and she misses her mother. She is so heavy with sadness she can barely haul herself up into the buggy. She thinks of how she will also have to give up her evening visits to the sea, to the Ocean Queen.

The rash on her thighs rubs against her sarong as the buggy trundles home and the raindrops become plump and heavy, until the downpour drenches her hair, soaks through her kebaya.

Seven weeks pass and Ajat still does not return from the village. It rains every day. The driveway and roads are reduced to mud, and the master's lawn grows so tall it looks like a rice paddy. When she can escape her chores, Mina steps through his gardens, lets her feet sink into the cool rainwater, the mire of dark soil and grass. The earth is so drenched she sometimes sees worms wriggle blindly across the ground. She lifts her face to the sky, closes her eyes, and tries to feel each raindrop, each dash against her cheek, her forehead. It is in these moments, against the lit backdrop of her eyelids, that she pictures her mother by the fire, the black birthmark under her thumbnail as she guts the fish.

The only relief she feels from her loneliness is on days like today, when the cheerful captain visits her. In her time in the master's house she has learned many Dutch words, but the captain still likes to visit her for their lessons. The master has told her to wait on the verandah, to sit on one of his cane chairs. She has seen the captain twice since that first language lesson, and each time he has presented her with a new gift from his travels. The batik from Malacca, with pink flowers and blue butterflies, she folded up tightly and hid away in her rattan box. She was going to wear it one day for Ajat, but now she thinks she might give it to her mother. The second time the captain visited her, he gave her a whole jackfruit from Batavia. She hid it in a coal bag under the house and it had taken her and Pepen two days to feast on its sweet, pungent seeds.

She hears Captain Brees long before she sees him: his bellows to the master from his buggy, his stomps up the front staircase, the creaking of the floorboards under his tread. Taking a seat next to hers, he beams at her as he wipes his brow. He is so bulky that triangles of fat push through the pattern of the cane chair.

He hands Mina a sheaf of paper, a little like the newspaper the master reads. But rather than just lines of black figures there are pictures awash in colour.

'*Tijdschrift*,' he says loudly.

She inspects the paper, how it is folded down the middle, how there are portraits of fair women on most of the pages. Tall women, who lean and taper like the dedalu tree. '*Tij-sift*,' she says.

He laughs and shouts something at her, makes her repeat the word. She turns the pages, studies the long gowns, of dull green and blue. The fabric is plain, without the elaborate designs that decorate the very best batik. She rests her finger on an olive frock, says the word *pakaian*. He copies her, then tells her the word in his language, which she already knows, but she obediently repeats the word. Turning the page, she studies their hats. '*Topi*,' she murmurs. They are much the same as those worn by the local Dutch ladies – short brimmed with a sprig of flowers on the side – but she is curious as to why one of the women has a dead lemur flopped over her arm. When she points, raises her eyebrows, the captain chuckles and speaks too swiftly for her. His words roll from his mouth like he is eating something hot, like he is choking on it. He embraces himself and pretends to tremble. Mina nods. She doesn't understand.

They peruse the magazine together, trading words, until she turns the last page. They smile at each other. He pats the pockets of his jacket, then his shirt, until finally he pulls forth a small basket, the size of a dumpling, from his breast pocket. He hands it to her.

Mina lifts the top and resting on a cloud of cotton lies a sparkling sliver of gold. Nobody in her village owns gold. She has never even touched it before. She'd only ever seen it jingle on the arms and ears of the Chinese merchant's daughters.

She carefully picks up the slender chain and even in the shadows of the verandah it glimmers. A bell encased in a tiny, golden ball tinkles as the chain sways, and Captain Brees laughs. She folds the chain over her wrist but it is too long, so the captain takes it from her, gestures to her feet. Lifting her left leg slightly, she watches as he leans down, his belly between his thighs, grunting with the exertion. He clasps the chain around her ankle, manages to fasten the tiny hook with his meaty fingers.

Mina thanks him profusely and holds her prayer hands to her forehead. When he takes his leave, she does not stand up. She feels too self-conscious, like the anklet has tethered her to the floor. But, of course, some time after he has said goodbye to the master, she has to move. She has to resume shredding the coconut for the master's curry.

The anklet feels very strange, nestled against the top of her foot.

She cannot stop marvelling at it, fascinated with how special she has become. Every few steps, she stops to gaze down upon it, and is sure the strangeness of it makes her walk differently, more stiffly.

Mina creeps past the kitchen staff and slips into the back room. She takes out her rattan box and retrieves the piece of banana leaf that once wrapped the *lemper* she shared with Ajat. She presses the shiny leaf to her nose, inhales the coconut fragrance, and feels giddy, wobbly, like when she stands up in her father's fishing boat. That kiss. That kiss had opened up something in her. Smouldered through her limbs, heated her belly. She felt like she was bursting through her skin, like the lush, buttery flesh that peeks through the spiky crevices of an overripe durian. Placing the leaf back alongside the sarong from Malacca, she gazes down at the gold chain around her ankle. She decides she will keep it on, after all. She will not hide it.

When Ibu Tana sees the anklet she glares at Mina, but for some reason she leaves her alone. Mina doesn't understand it, but Ibu Tana no longer shouts at her or pushes her around. She doesn't yell when Mina brings the wrong produce back from the store, or when she overcooks the pork. In fact, Ibu Tana rarely speaks to her. She uses Pepen to relay her messages.

'Ibu Tana wants you to take some fruit to the master's friend,' says Pepen.

Mina looks up from the peanuts she is shelling. Pops one in her mouth. 'Why do I have to go? Can't she just send Yati?'

'The master wants you to cook some *bubur* while you are there,' says Pepen. 'They're all sick. Even the servant.'

Mina pulls a face but places the basket of peanuts on the kitchen bench. 'Where is it?' She ties two cups of rice into a square of linen.

'Far away. You're going in the cart.' He takes a plucked chicken from the pantry, holds it out to her. 'Ibu Tana said to take this. She'll have another one killed for dinner.'

Mina walks down the kitchen steps carrying two baskets of food, and waits for the buggy. It hasn't rained for three days, and the sun, frangipani yellow, gently seeks out moisture from under the fallen leaves.

She looks up at the rumble of the cart's wheels, and wonders if it is a trick of the sun's haze and her secret thoughts that she sees Ajat seated on the driver's bench. But it is him. He's grinning down at her.

It's as if a canary is trilling high notes in her chest as she climbs onto the bench beside him. Its feathers prick and flutter, almost smother her.

'You're back,' she says. His full lips, his white teeth.

'Yes.' Ajat clicks his tongue to urge the pony onward.

'How is the village?' His chest is broader than she remembers. Bronzed.

He shrugs. 'The same. I had to go back and help my father. He wanted to plan some things.'

She's quick to realise what he means. A future. Ajat's future in the village. Something she would do anything to be a part of.

'And my mother? Did you see her? Or my father?'

He nods. 'Yes. Your mother has sent some smoked fish for you. She is sure you must be missing it.'

They smile at each other. She is so happy and so sad she could cry. But she won't. She hugs the feeling to herself and tells him what he has missed at the master's house: how Ibu Tana caught one of the gardeners pissing on the slices of mango left out in the sunlight to dry, the geese who wandered into the gardens and bit

Pepen, the master's yen for juice made from custard fruit.

Suddenly she remembers the anklet, feels the weight of it. The buggy bumps over a rock and she can hear the faintest tinkle from its bell. She looks up at Ajat, at his fine, angular jaw and his ear, as neat as a seashell. She won't tell him of the captain's gifts.

The master's friend lives on the outskirts of town. The small hillside house has the sloped roof of the local *kampung* homes and is perched on stilts. A servant girl opens the door, ushers her in. Ajat is not far behind with the baskets of meat and fruit. There's a rancid smell to the house, of unwashed sheets and the seepage of illness. They tiptoe past one of the bedrooms, glimpse a man, as naked and pink as a swine, feverishly tossing in his bed. Mina looks away, holds her breath until they reach the back of the house where the kitchen is. The stovetop is simple, a grate over a fireplace, not much better than her mother's cooking arrangement in the village.

Ajat leaves the baskets on the table, returns to the pony. There's only the one tiny window in the kitchen and, peering through its grimy glass, Mina can't see where he is waiting. She fidgets impatiently at every little chore she has to do that long day, from boiling the rice to dismembering the chicken. First, though, she has to wash the dishes, encrusted in ancient food scraps, because the dratted servant, the only one in this sorry household, pretends to be ill, moaning as she rests her head in her arms. But Mina doesn't believe her, thinks her skin looks cool, her eyes clear, so she pinches her on the elbow, tells her to fetch some water, slice the pineapple. While the servant girl is gone from the room, Mina crouches down, unhooks the gold chain from her ankle. She wraps it in the linen that held the rice, screws it up, shoves it at the bottom of the fruit basket.

Finally, the rice in the *bubur* is soft, porridge-like, ready to ladle into bowls. Mina tells the servant girl that once it is cool she is to serve small mouthfuls to her master. She then escapes into the fresh air. She swings the baskets as she walks to the buggy, and smiles up at Ajat.

'That was a horrible place.' He grimaces as she joins him in the buggy.

She nods, widens her eyes. 'Horrible.' She catches a length of her hair to her nose, sniffs it. 'I hope I don't smell of it.'

Ajat takes her hair from her hands, smells it. 'Mmm. Still nice.'

His face is close to hers, and she feels shy as she remembers the last time they were alone. That night by the beach. She withdraws slightly, is quiet as the pony pulls them down the mountainside towards home. The ocean is spread out before them, framed by the curving coastline and a canopy of jagged banana fronds and coconut palms. The sun's glare bleeds into the horizon, has the shimmer of a coral trout. Ajat guides the buggy into a clearing and points at a low-set table.

'Let's watch the sunset from here. It won't take too long.'

She kneels, while he sits cross-legged. He places two pieces of fruit on the table. Both are round, smaller than apples, and encased in a hard skin darker than the master's mahogany blanket box.

'Mangosteen,' Ajat says. 'Have you ever tried one?'

She shakes her head. The Dutchmen had brought the master a box of them, and they filled a large bowl in the dining room, but not knowing what they were, she had yet to taste one. 'Did you take them from the basket of fruit?'

'Yes, but don't worry, Mina,' he says. 'They won't miss them. The master will never know.'

Mina hopes he's right. She presses its leathery skin. There is a cap of four fat leaves on its top and a tiny, barky flower pressed into its base. 'How do I eat it?'

Ajat picks up the other one, squeezes and twists until the mangosteen lifts open, revealing five creamy white segments of fruit. He offers it to her, gestures for her to eat. She sniffs, but there is no fragrance. She pokes her fingertip in but can't peel a segment free, so she holds it to her mouth, flickers her tongue against its flesh. It's sweet, fresh, so she digs her tongue in, prises a piece of the mangosteen into her mouth, and its juice dribbles down her chin. The flesh is softer than a rambutan's and encases a pulpy pip. She eats another piece, savouring the sour flavour that peeps through the sticky sweetness. Offering the last few segments to Ajat, she watches as he slurps up the fruit.

'There were five sections in this mangosteen,' he says. 'How many do you think are in this one?' He holds up the remaining fruit.

She's puzzled. It looks like it might be slightly smaller than the one they've eaten. 'Four?'

'Four?' His lips curl into a grin. 'Should we wager on it? I think there might be seven sections.'

'Okay.' She smiles back. 'But I've changed my mind. I think there are six.'

'But what shall we bet?'

Mina frowns. 'What do you mean?'

'Well, we have to bet something. If I win, then I get something, and if you win, then you get something.' His eyes seem darker than usual.

'Like what?'

Ajat looks to the sky for a moment. 'If I'm right, and there

241

are seven pieces of fruit inside this mangosteen, then you have to meet me under the ebony tree tonight after everyone has gone to bed.'

Mina draws her hands to herself, presses them into her lap. 'You're mad.'

He laughs. 'No. And anyway, I have to give you the fish from your mother. So, if there are seven pieces you have to meet me. But if there are only six pieces, then you don't have to meet me. How's that?'

She's unsure, so she says nothing, watches as he twists open the mangosteen. He places one half in front of her. Her eyes count the plump segments. An empty roar is in her head like when she presses the opening of a cowrie shell to her ear, but she still manages to hear Ajat murmur, 'Seven.'

Mina can barely swallow her dinner that night. She scrapes the rice and chicken to the side of her plate, hides it under a cabbage leaf. All the evening noises – the clink of cutlery against china, the swishing of water in the washing bucket – clamour in her ears, irritate her senses, like an itchy blanket has been thrown about her shoulders that she wants to twitch away. She wishes they'd hurry up and go to bed. It's only when she notices Pepen wiping out the basket she'd used that day that she remembers her gold chain is still poked down into its recesses. She taps his hand aside, pulls out the twist of linen. She goes into the storeroom, Pepen following, and as she lifts the lid of her rattan box and slides the chain into it, he tells her a long story about the time the tooth doctor came and yanked a blackened molar from the master's mouth. He describes the splash of blood in the dish, and the rotten stench that was like the sediment of the stables on a wet day. He even mimics the master's moan, deep and drawn-out, eyes squeezed shut.

Mina elbows him out of the way and gathers the eggs and vegetables she'll need for the morning. She rolls her eyes to the ceiling when Ibu Tana gives the other kitchen maids extra silver to shine.

Finally, they settle on their mats. Mina lies rigid, eyes pressed shut, and waits for their breathing to even out, slow down. Only when she hears the maids' faint snoring and a juddering fart leave Ibu Tana's lumpy stomach does she quietly lift her mat and pull it out onto the verandah. If anyone wakes, she will tell them she's moving outside where it's cooler.

The sky is luminous grey, the moon as slight as a pin bone. She gazes out across the shadows of the garden, to the very back where she knows the stables are. But it is too dark; no lights glimmer through the shroud of trees. Taking three cautious steps down the stairs, she cranes around to look at the silhouette of the ebony tree in the furthest corner of the garden. Ajat had pointed it out to her when he dropped her off – the tallest tree, the one past the chicken coops. She runs down the last few stairs lightly, flits across the grass, until she reaches the soka shrubs at the bottom of the garden. She hesitates, peering into the gloom that the moonlight cannot reach.

Ajat catches her around the waist. She has to cover her mouth with her hand to stop from squealing, from calling out loud, but the laughter that racks her body vibrates against his chest. He holds her close. Waits for her to calm. He makes soothing sounds against her ear, like she is one of the ponies. But she is trembling, wonders if she can ever be still again.

He leads her towards the tree's black trunk, hands her a straw bag. She loosens its tie, can already smell the smoked catfish her mother has sent her. Reaching in, she breaks off a little of the papaya leaf that encases the fish, nibbles on it, hopes its bitterness will steady her heartbeat. She offers the bag to him. 'Take some.' But he shakes his head, leans forward, folds her lips in his.

She sways against him, feels her knees weaken. He smells of the ocean again, of salt, of sandalwood. Her head falls back, heavy, and she stares at the glowing sky, at the glittering stars. She wants to stay like this, let the contentment seep into her bones. She only rights herself when he steps back, drops his hands to his waist.

Unravelling his sarong, he lets it fall from his hips and even though it is so dark that his body is a shadow, she looks away. He spreads the sarong on the ground, says, 'Lie down, Mina.'

She sits, waits for him to join her. He kneels down, wipes the hair from her face and his lips find hers again. He gently pushes her back. He hovers over her and his hand slides under her sarong. His fingertips trail along the inside of her thigh, but she holds his hand away from the rash. It hasn't flared in weeks, maybe because of the ointment the master gave her, of coconut oil and something else that has the odour of a goat's hide. She's afraid Ajat might feel the coarse skin, might sense it, and then he won't like her anymore. But he perseveres, and the sweep of his hand becomes soothing, as if she might melt away like butter in a frypan.

He lowers himself on top of her, pressing her into the ground. Twigs and grass prickle against her back through the thin fabric of the sarong. He's as hard as a pestle as he nudges between her legs, snuffles against her throat. She grips his shoulders as he pushes against her. Finally, he stabs into her, groaning, and it hurts, like she is being scaled, as he inches further inside. She presses the heels of her palms against her closed eyelids. She is his now, they are one. She wants to stay suspended in this moment because it feels good, she feels sated, but it's painful too. Opening her eyes, she is momentarily blinded by the pressure her palms have put on them, only sees gleaming light, but soon realises the glare is concentrated to one area, a few metres to their left.

The master holds a lantern aloft. 'Get off her,' he says, his voice guttural. His face is waxen, as rigid as his words.

Pepen stands just behind, both hands clamped across his mouth.

The captain was always losing his head over
one brazen hussy after another ...

'The Four Dutchmen'
W Somerset Maugham

Three

'I AM SORRY, MINA,' SAYS PEPEN. His big ears burn red, his eyes have the glaze of tears.

Mina turns her shoulder to him. She never wants to see his silly face again.

She's hiding in the small back room, leaning against the shelf that holds her things. She can hear Ibu Tana bang a frypan onto the stovetop, crack three breakfast eggs into it.

Pepen twists his face around so he's in her line of sight, but she closes her eyes.

'I saw him grab you in the dark,' Pepen whispers. He glances over his shoulder, falls silent as one of the kitchen maids passes the doorway. 'I thought he was going to hurt you.'

She shrugs his hand from her arm. 'Just go away, Pepen.'

He stands next to her and sniffles. When she hears him leave she opens her eyes.

Mina grips the shelf, watches her fingertips turn white, then bumps her forehead twice against the back of her hands. Does Ibu Tana know? Embarrassment curls through her stomach, breathes heat into her face. She thinks of the dry blood on her inner thighs, the leaden feeling between her legs. And she's sore, feels scalded like when she burnt the side of her thumb on the baking tray.

'Where is that fish girl when you need her?' Ibu Tana says from the kitchen.

Mina straightens up. As she approaches the cook, she squares her shoulders and wills her face to be as still as the teak Balinese mask that hangs in the master's sitting room.

There's the usual irritation on Ibu Tana's face, but that is all. 'Take the *perkedel* to the master before they get cold,' she snaps, pushing a platter towards her.

Mina steps closer to the table but doesn't pick up the platter. 'I don't feel well today. Can you get Pepen to do it?'

'No.' She slices through a papaya. 'That stupid boy has disappeared, so you will just have to get on with it.'

Mina's heartbeat drums loudly in her chest as she thinks of meeting with the master again. He will send her home. And, one way or another, the dishonour of it will kill her. She wants to see Ajat first. She must return to the village on his arm before the master has the chance to send her home in disgrace.

She takes up the platter, treads softly towards the dining room and peeps around the door. The room is empty. The master calls out from the verandah, and she flinches. The patties slide across the plate. But he's shouting to one of the gardeners, not to her. She slips the platter onto the table, steps quickly back to the kitchen.

She has to return to the dining room twice more, with a basket of bread rolls and a pot of coffee, but it is not until her third trip with a bowl of fruit that she finds the master at the table. She comes to a halt in the doorway, studies how he pours the coffee, stirs in the sticky, sweet milk. She moves forward, places the bowl on the table as quietly as she can. Should she apologise? Should she cry? Worse – should she tell him she did not understand what had happened the night before?

The master flips open his newspaper, and his pale eyes flick across the pages. Apart from twisting slightly in his chair so that his back is to her, he shows no interest in Mina's presence.

It's not until late in the morning that she can escape her kitchen chores. While Ibu Tana is preoccupied with paying the vendor for the stove wood, Mina leaves the mortar full of crushed peanuts on the table and trips down the stairs, runs across the grass to the stables. She needs to talk to Ajat. She needs him to help her before the master changes his mind, tells everyone of her shame.

She rushes from one shed to the other, but they are empty of both ponies and men. The manure on the floor of the second shed is still fresh. Straw is strewn across the dirt. Mina walks behind the sheds, gazes across the fence into the neighbouring field, but all she can see are two water buffalo, ankle deep in the mud of the rice paddy, grazing on reeds.

'Are you looking for someone?' Yati comes up behind her, carrying a shovel.

'I'm looking for Ajat,' she says.

'He left at dawn.'

'Left?' she repeats, her voice rising in panic. 'Left for where?'

'He went home. To the village.' Yati shakes his head and enters the shed where he scrapes up clumps of manure.

Mina follows him, cups her hands over her nose and mouth in shock. 'Did the master send him away?'

Yati looks puzzled. 'No. He was only here for the one night. He's getting married. He came to town to swap two baskets of fish for oxen meat and nutmeg for the wedding banquet.'

The words pound over her like an icy wave. She almost staggers.

Turning back to the house, she holds her hands before her as if she is blind, conscious of every twig and dry leaf that catches under her toes. Parrots shriek high in the palms; the sunlight is too bright. Her fingertips tingle as she reaches forward.

Pausing, she looks back over her shoulder. 'Who will he marry?'

'Hamida.'

Hamida. An older girl from their village. Bossy, loud.

Mina wonders if Hamida has also felt the grass prickle her back through the thin fabric of Ajat's sarong. She thinks not.

The other servants peek at Mina as she peels the bananas for the *pisang epe*. She knows her eyes are red, as puffy as a pastel. She'd wept in the servants' bathroom through the lunch hour into the afternoon. When others were in need of the *mandi*, she'd cried out that she had terrible cramps, that she could not move.

'I must have rubbed some sort of nettle in my eyes when I was picking the lemongrass,' she grumbles to them, dipping the banana in the batter.

Yati's words pulse through her. When the hot oil splutters and stings the back of her hand, she rubs the spot with her thumb. Ajat's getting married. As she tosses food scraps to the chickens, watches them peck at the grains of rice, quarrel over spinach stalks. Wedding feast. Meat and spices for the wedding feast. She lights the candles on the dining-room table and they barely flicker in the still, humid air. Hamida. Tall and buxom. Lives in the village with her widowed mother. Mina passes her finger through a candle's tiny flame several times, then allows it to hover there for a moment, waits for the flame's bite. Hamida. Ajat.

Anger sears her chest, molten as simmering chilli sambal. By the end of the evening the rash on her thighs flares, and she drags her fingernails over the papery skin, glad of the streak of pain that momentarily masks her misery.

She shuts herself in the *mandi* again, smothers the rash in the ointment. Sobbing with relief, she stares at the white cream smeared across her legs, as it douses the pain. She clutches the bottle to her chest and scoops out a glob with her fingers, forces it into her mouth, to the back of her tongue. She swallows, feels the ointment's slow glide down her throat, can taste where the gamey oil of the ointment pastes the insides of her mouth. She waits. She wants the cream to cool the fury in her chest, like it has calmed the sores on her thighs. But it rises in her throat. Clamping her hand to her mouth, she lurches outside, vomits into the undergrowth beneath the persimmon trees, where it glows against the fallen leaves.

Wiping watering eyes with the back of her hand, Mina crawls up the patio stairs to the kitchen. She doesn't care how much noise she makes as she steps over the sleeping kitchen staff and reaches for her rattan box. The gold chain tinkles as she lifts it from between the folds of the batik and clasps it back around her ankle.

Ibu Tana kneads the dough into the timber tabletop. 'The master doesn't want you tending table anymore.'

Mina searches the cook's face for malice, but there's only a frowning curiosity in her beady eyes. Mina shrugs, keeps chopping the spring onions, but wonders if a blush eddies across her chest, creeps its sneaky fingers up her neck.

'I don't know what's been happening around here lately, but you and Pepen better get organised or else I'll have to hire a new kitchen maid,' she warns Mina, shoving the tray of bread in the oven. 'The stupid boy forgot to wipe the mud from the master's shoes last night and the fishcakes you cooked this morning were almost inedible.'

When Mina thinks of how the master and Pepen caught them under the ebony tree, she wants to curl up into herself like a scaly anteater. For days, Pepen has been cringing around her, trying to lure her back into friendship by taking on some of her chores. He told her stories of dark men who wore turbans and purple scarves from far away who had visited the master, of the time a rabid monkey chased Junius out of the forest. She was too distracted to pay him attention, though. It was only when he gave her his precious kris to cut back the chilli bush, and said, 'You should keep it. You need it more than me,' that he came back into focus. His constricted voice, the way he blinked into the distance, belied the nonchalance of his words. She squeezed his thin hand, smiled, and returned the dagger to him.

But still, a hardness suffuses her chest, burdens her shoulders, makes her feel heavy. It is only late one night, when she lies on her mat and remembers the time her mother fed her a clove syrup for a sick stomach, of how she stroked the tears back from Mina's face with the flat of her free hand, that the hardness in Mina thaws, and a tear trickles down the side of her face, teeters over her right ear. She squashes the tear into her skin with her fingers, rises from the bedding and walks out to the verandah.

In vain, her eyes search beyond the other houses and palm trees for a glimpse of the sea. She will run away. She will flee to the water's edge, and the Ocean Queen will tell her what to do. And if something happens to her – if that sly guard sees her, or if a villager thinks she's a witch – who cares, after all?

In the kitchen, one of the maids turns over, says something in her sleep. Mina decides that tomorrow she will pack her few possessions. She will escape.

'Mina, the master wants you. On the verandah,' says Pepen. Mina is surprised, but as she brushes past Pepen he catches her arm. 'He's with the captain.'

She steps lightly through the house, can almost feel her heavy mood dissipate as the morning mists lift from the mountaintop. Finally, someone who will be pleased to see her.

The two men stand at the top of the front stairs. The master scrutinises his fingernails as she approaches, but the captain seems nervous. Sweat drips down his reddened cheeks.

'The captain has asked my permission for you to accompany him on his next voyage,' the master says swiftly in Malay. He smiles, but his pale eyes are cold. 'I have told him that you may.'

Disbelief pricks the skin on the back of her neck. The master is giving her away. Alarm makes her insides shrink, but the lonely rage that has kept her company for weeks keeps her gaze steady.

The captain looks from the master to her. Although he can't quite understand the master's words, there's a hopeful smile on his fat face as he nods at her.

Mina's smile to the captain is fixed as she leads him down the stairs towards a garden setting by the coffea shrubs.

She kneels on the grass next to his garden chair and he beckons to her, then lifts her onto his lap. His huge belly is surprisingly firm. She teeters on his legs, holding her hands tightly together, crossing her ankles. He calls her *schatje*, his treasure, as he struggles to retrieve a small booklet from his breast pocket. Taking out two photographs, he shows her the first one, a portrait of the place from which these large Dutchmen come. The master has many such photos and paintings in his bedroom and sitting room. In this picture, there is a road of flattened stones and a very long house. She traces her finger along it, says, 'Big house,' and the captain laughs and explains to her that it is actually a row of connected, narrow dwellings. And everything is grey. Even the light looks grey. The captain points to one of the houses and then points to himself. She nods and peers at the picture, but there isn't much else to see.

The next photo is of two women: his mother and sister, he tells her. She studies this photo more closely. These women do not look like Captain Brees at all. They are very thin and wear dark gowns that are buttoned high on their necks and flow low to the floor. Their hands are folded before them and their ashen faces are grim. The captain tells her he will take her to this grey place, where the rain falls white and solid and the women cover their whole bodies from the cold air and stares of men. He says they will visit Singapore and eat *rijsttafel* at the Van Dorth Hotel and shop for her first pair of shoes. As he says this, he picks up Mina's foot, so small and brown in his large, meaty hand, and chuckles at the gold anklet. He asks her again if she will go away with him when they leave port. Mina thinks of the master's house, of how only Pepen will speak to her. And she thinks of how she can't get home to the fishing village. She presses her prayer hands to her forehead and thanks the captain. She nods yes.

When she hears that Mina will leave with the captain in the morning, Ibu Tana places the heavy knife onto the tabletop and presses her eyes shut. 'Ah,' she exhales. 'Now I understand why the master no longer prefers you.' She looks Mina up and down. 'What have you been up to, you shrew?'

Mina is helping Pepen fold the tablecloths. She avoids eye contact as she smooths the creases from the fabric. 'Nothing. The captain's just a very kind man.'

A snort whistles from Ibu Tana's nostrils. 'He won't marry you, you know. You will be nothing better than a *pelacur.*'

Mina's head rears back as she glares at the old cook – that toady, terrible woman. *Pelacur?* Mina wasn't like one of those poor, shunned women who eked out a dreary existence down by the wharf. She didn't wander the dirt roads heavy with child, bereft of a future. But she knows exactly what the captain wants of her, whether they marry or not. She thinks of the darkness of that night, of her body sinking into the ground under the weight of Ajat. Of how she thought that meant they were one, that they would be interwoven forever. She's almost thankful this is no longer a mystery to her. Almost.

'You don't know what the captain will do.' Mina's words are as inflexible as a cleaver. 'Whatever it is, it will be better than living here with you.'

She drops the tablecloth into a basket and, ignoring the leg of goat Ibu Tana has laid out on the kitchen table for her to dice, makes her way down to the stables.

'Yati, when you are next in the village, can you tell my parents I've gone away to be married?'

Yati straightens up from where he's scraping the pony's hoof. 'Who are you marrying?'

'It doesn't matter. Just tell them I will be fine. I am happy.'

She holds her chin high, but her smile falters as she thinks of what she will miss. She wishes she could have a wedding at home, with fragrant *sedap malam* petals entwined in her hair, and the sacred, embroidered matrimonial batik swathed around her hips and shoulder. Her mother would cook her favourite snapper *pepes* sprinkled with salted anchovies and treacly sweet soy sauce. And her father would not fish that day. He would sit with Mina's husband on a rattan rug and sip rice wine.

'I will see them soon,' she says as she moves back towards the house.

Mina thinks of how one day, when she is a fine and rich lady with a dark gown buttoned high on her neck, she will return from the grey place and buy her parents a proper house. They will leave their thatched hut and endless fish behind.

But not yet. She feels a dip in her stomach like she's falling from the tallest palm tree. She may not see her parents for a long time. Impossible to return now, with nothing, to a village where Ajat is married to Hamida. She will have to wait, as long as it takes for the spiny stems of her heart to soften, until she can return with a full basket. Mina leans against a tree, rolls her forehead gently against the prickly bark. She takes a deep breath. She will need to be very strong. She will need to be like one of the *dhalang*'s *wayang* puppets, as hard as lacquer, as enduring.

The clouds are low the next morning when the captain comes to collect her. He and the master laugh loudly as they stroll through the gardens, but as the cart draws away, the master frowns.

Mina holds her rattan box in her lap. She lifts the lid so she can peek at the pheasant feather, sleek and the colour of ochre, that Pepen had pressed into her hand as a parting gift. His eyelashes were wet and a translucent trail of snot reached his upper lip as they walked down the back stairs. He rushed to finish telling her the story of the Javanese prince who constructed a thousand temples in only one night for his princess. 'That is love, true love, isn't it, Mina?'

She doesn't say goodbye to Ibu Tana who stands at the stove with her back to Mina, or to the kitchen maids, kneeling on the patio, grinding spices like the very first time she'd seen them that day she arrived with Junius. She doesn't take one last look at the persimmon trees, or the ebony tree looming in the corner of the garden, and she doesn't breathe in the scent of the coffea flowers.

All through the East Indies they knew that the supercargo and the chief engineer had executed justice on the trollop who had caused the death of the two men they loved.

'The Four Dutchmen'
W Somerset Maugham

Four

MINA CLAMBERS UP THE GANGWAY of the tramp behind the captain. The vessel sways with the waves but not as fiercely as her father's small fishing boat when he guides it out to sea. Several sailors dash back and forth, readying the cargo and tramp for departure, while the captain's three friends are gathered together on the quarter-deck, shouting orders. They look serious. These must be their work faces, Mina decides. She smiles shyly at them, for these are the men who, on their noisy card nights at the master's, had tried to cajole her into sipping beer and teased her with songs of love. But as the captain introduces them – Bulle, the chief officer, darker than the others; Haas, the supercargo, who has a thin moustache; and the engineer, Jonckheer, the tallest – they continue to scowl, continue with their work. As she passes, the engineer turns his head and spits on the deck.

The captain shows her his cabin, a poky space just big enough for a narrow bed against the outboard wall, with a desk tucked into the nearest corner. He bids her to sit on the mattress, places her rattan box in the small bookshelf that occupies the other corner of the cabin. Above the desk is a portrait of a couple; she thinks maybe it is another picture of the captain's mother. The woman stands just in front of a man who has the captain's thinning fair hair, his thick, gingery eyebrows.

The captain gestures to the upper deck. 'I work now.' He holds his hands in front of himself, palms flat to her. 'You wait.' He backs out, closes the door softly.

Mina kneels up on the lumpy mattress and peers out the porthole. The water is as blue as the hood of the fig bird, and she can just see the damp sand of the beach. It's not long before the drone of the tramp's engine pulsates through her body. She feels both the pull of the ocean as they edge their way from port but also a painful tug back towards what she knows. The sun has not reached its highest point, so her mother must still be slicing open the fish from the morning catch. Her father probably squats nearby, smoking. But there is no-one here to wave her off, no-one here who will miss her. She hops down from the bed and inspects the captain's books to take her mind off the fading landscape of home.

Mina keeps mostly to the cabin during the first few days of the voyage. When the captain has finished his day's work and eaten with the other crew members, he joins her there. He shows her his collection of atlases; the coloured lands that have been discovered and named, and those that are still waiting to have their mark upon them. He draws a line from where they have just left, to the port in Nieuw Guinea where they will next dock.

He brings her fruit and rice dishes, fresh from the crew's *rijsttafel*. He laughs when she eats with her hand. He gives her a heavy silver spoon and shows her how to dip its tapered end into the curry. The spoon is so large, she only covers a third of it with *nasi goreng*, and when she licks the rice from its surface, the silver leaves a metallic aftertaste in her mouth.

He flourishes a mangosteen in front of her. Mina stiffens, remembers her wager with Ajat. Ajat and Hamida.

'Look, *schatje*, see the brown flower at this end of the fruit?' His sausage finger daintily points it out for her. 'Count its petals. One-two-three-four-five.' He twists open the mangosteen, reveals five portions. His face lights up. 'Five,' he cries. But his brow lowers when he sees Mina's face tighten. 'You don't like my trick? It is no witchery, Mina. Everyone knows that if you count the petals you can tell how many pieces are inside.'

She pretends to laugh, claps her hands, but she won't eat any of the fruit.

Two evenings later Mina carries a jug of fresh water from the galley. The light from the saloon spills onto the deck. She knows supper time is almost finished, that the captain will be in his cabin soon, but she's curious to see where the men eat their meals, what they do when they're not working around the tramp.

As she draws close to the open doorway, she slides her back to the wall and steals closer to sneak a look into the saloon. She knows to stay hidden. Mostly the crew ignore her, although on the third day of the voyage Haas and Jonckheer had complained to the captain of her presence on the upper deck, called her 'that Malay girl'. And yesterday she'd heard Jonckheer mutter 'hussy' just before he hawked onto the deck floor. When she'd later asked the captain what he meant, the captain had stomped away, and she heard him shouting at the engineer down in the hold.

In the saloon, there's a long table, laden with the half-finished dishes of their *rijsttafel*. Several of the crew crowd one end of the table, talking, smoking over their empty plates. Their voices are raised to counter the scratchy music that blares from the gramophone in the corner of the room. They joke and peg screwed-up pieces of paper at each other as they continue with their gaming. At a separate table, a square table for four, the captain is seated with the chief officer, the supercargo and the engineer.

The captain stands, waves his hands as he smiles at the others, but they gesture for him to sit, call for him to take up his cards.

Bulle, the dark one, pours more beer into the glass in front of the captain. 'Stay, you old rascal, stay.'

'At least finish a game of *klaverjas*, for God's sake,' says Haas. His face is flushed, annoyed. He gulps down a whole tumbler of beer, and his head rolls as he pours more into his cup.

'No, no,' protests the captain, backing away from the table. 'I must check on my Mina.'

Bulle throws his cards on the table, takes a swig of his beer, but Haas's chair scrapes as he pushes himself to his feet, the table rattles as he slams his fist down on it. The room falls quiet, except for the gramophone that continues to scratch away.

'You are making a fool of yourself, you stupid man!' Haas shouts at the captain. He's unsteady on his feet as he tries to poke the captain in the chest. 'You should never have brought a woman on board. Never. This is no place ...'

Mina grips the jug to her belly and runs back to the captain's cabin. When the captain joins her, several minutes later, he looks glum. His brow is heavy, his fleshy jowls droop. He tells her how the others, his three friends, are annoyed with him. He contorts his face into a grimace to show their anger. They don't like him spending so much time with her, spoiling their fun, keeping him from late nights of beer and cards.

Mina rests her hand on his thick arm, feels the texture of the short, curly hairs that cover his skin.

He smiles sadly at her with his cod-blue eyes, embraces her close into his body. 'I just want to be with you.'

Early in the morning Mina climbs onto the upper deck so she can feel the sun on her shoulders. She glances around warily for Haas and Jonckheer, but has chosen this early hour because she knows from the habits of the captain that these Dutch sailors like to sleep off the excesses of the evening.

Mina takes a seat on a stool and opens up the small magazine she has brought from the captain's cabin. It's full of writing that she cannot read, but she likes the strips of curious pictures, drawings of people and animals on funny adventures. But the wind whips the pages back and forth. She closes it, holding it shut in her lap, and watches the dark water peak and glint. After a few minutes, she senses a shadow to her right. The chief officer, Bulle, stands a few metres away, arms crossed, staring at her. His lip lifts, like when a dog snarls, but she thinks it's a smile, so she smiles back, doesn't want to provoke him.

The day before, on her way to the galley with her used dishes, they had met each other in the narrow corridor. Instead of waiting, the chief officer pressed against her as he shuffled past. He was stinky; the stench of onion seeped from his cavernous armpits, the pong of damp fishing nets wafted from his shoes. In her head, Mina calls him Bau-Bau Bulle: smelly.

But now Mina's smile snags as his eyes roam slowly over her body, down her shoulders, across her outstretched legs. She turns away, lets her hair fan across half her face, tries to pretend he is not there.

~

It's late afternoon when they dock somewhere on the Nieuw Guinea coast, and the captain goes ashore with four other crewmen in order to deal with the local traders. He leaves Mina with Johan, the cook in charge of the galley.

Johan admires how deftly she fills the *pastels* with egg and noodles, how neatly she curls the edges of the pastry.

'You are well trained,' he says, beaming at her. He speaks mostly in Dutch, but adds Malay words if he sees she doesn't understand. 'You must have had a good teacher.'

Mina grimaces and tells him of how Ibu Tana flicked water into her face if she didn't concentrate, and how red her knuckles could get when the cook swatted them with the ladle.

'My sweet, you're lucky you were not trained in Belanda.'

She looks across the table at him. 'You've been there?' She's keen to know of this place. She wants to know what to expect.

'Of course. I was born there,' he says, stirring the peanut sauce. 'My father was a Dutchman, but my mother was a little Indo woman from Makassar.'

Johan's skin has the sheen of amber, is lighter than hers, but his eyes are dark, almost as black as a coffee bean.

'From now on you must help me every day with the *rijsttafel* for the sailors,' he says. 'I'll teach you how to roast duck in banana leaves and how to make a *speculaas* cake so delicious the crew will weep for home.'

The sun has set by the time Mina leaves the galley. The spices from the beef *rendang* infuse her hair, and her fingers are stained with coppery cinnamon. She leans over the side of the tramp, smells burning copra, can see smoke rise from among the coconut palms. The sky is the dull grey of a mackerel that has been dead for days.

She makes her way to the captain's cabin. She wants to wash before he returns. The only light in the darkened corridor comes from an open cabin: Bau-Bau's. She doesn't want him to see her, so she tries to squeeze past in the shadows, but as he's taking a swig from a bottle of dark liquor, he glimpses her from the corner of his eye.

He snarl-smiles at her. Beckons. 'Come. Come,' he says. 'You like books. Look, I have many books.'

She doesn't want to appear rude, so she peers into his room from the corridor. He gestures towards three green leather-bound books that are stacked on a wooden crate.

'Come in, come in,' he says, taking her elbow. 'You can see them in here.'

Alcohol is heavy on his breath. He stumbles back a step, pulling her with him. She doesn't resist. Bau-Bau doesn't grumble about her like Haas and Jonckheer do. She wants to appease him, humour him, thinks that maybe he will be her friend, like Johan.

He leans against the door as it clicks shut.

Mina learns that, really, he hates her as much – more – than the others do.

It is too late by the time the captain finds them. He knocks and pokes his head around the door, and the smile that lifts his heavy cheeks freezes. His eyes switch from the chief officer, naked and slick with perspiration, to Mina, who is huddled into the corner of the cabin, a sheet wrapped around her body. He gobbles at words that will not come and lumbers from the room, staggers down the corridor.

When he returns, it is with his pistol, which he waves at Bulle, who's tying a sarong around his thick stomach.

Bulle sneers, takes another slug from his bottle. His words slur as he says, 'You would shoot me for a hussy such as this?'

The captain becomes red in the face, much redder than when he's laughing, takes a step back, and shoots the chief officer in the chest. He clasps the pistol to his own forehead as he watches the life gurgle and shudder its way from the chief officer's body.

Then his wild eyes find Mina, and she realises she is screaming and screaming. He aims the pistol at her.

She shields her head with her hands, crouches lower into the floor. 'No, no. Please. I didn't mean for it to happen. I didn't mean for it to happen.' But she's speaking in Malay; can't gather words together that he might comprehend.

The captain's hand wavers, and he lurches from the room.

Several moments later the sound of another shot crashes through the silence.

Haas and Jonckheer stumble into the cabin, and their bulk fills the confined space. They fall to their knees, bellow over the body of their friend. They lift the chief officer like he's a small child, cradle him onto the bed.

They leave the cabin and a few moments later Mina hears them crying out again, further down the corridor. Mina's not sure how long she cowers in that corner. She presses her forehead into the wall, away from where Bau-Bau lies, away from where his right hand hangs limp over the edge of the bed. She wants to crawl across the floor, escape into the corridor, but she's unsure of what she will find there. Where is the captain?

The engine of the tramp stutters to life, and she feels the

magnetic pull of the ocean as they leave port. If only she were at home with her mother, lying on her mat, listening to the waves and her mother's gentle breathing. If only Ajat had taken her – taken her home, taken her as a wife.

When Haas and Jonckheer return she immediately knows from the hatred that skews their faces that they have not come back for Bau-Bau; they have come back for her.

She tries to slip past Haas, almost reaches the doorway, but he grabs her by the hair. He braces her to his side as he unclasps his belt, loosens his trousers. Mina tries to push away from him, so breathless she cannot scream, and he slaps her hard across the face, so hard she falls to the floor.

There's a ringing in her ears when he drags her close, shoves himself into her. Her joints strain to fit his girth. She can smell the garlic on his breath, can see spinach caught between his front teeth. She covers her face with her hands, shrinks away from another blow to the head from his raised hand. She thinks this is how it will be for her now, and when the supercargo finishes, she waits for Jonckheer to thrust his way into the other's leavings. But he stays by the door, turns his head, spits on the floor.

Haas presses relentless fingers around Mina's throat, tries to push the life from her. She peels at his fingers, feels her eyes bulge with the force, tries to wriggle out of his hold.

Jonckheer takes Haas by the shoulder, says he has a better idea.

A feral stench of fear coats Mina's skin, reminds her of a tethered goat just before its throat is cut. They try to pick her up, but she screeches, digs her nails into their pink skin. Jonckheer punches her in the stomach, and she retches as he stuffs one of Bau-Bau's briny socks into her mouth, securing it with a bandana. They tie her hands and feet with rope, haul her up onto the upper deck. As they pass the galley, she sees Johan's black eyes peeping through a crack in the door. She squeals for him through her gag as he disappears back into the galley, and the door gently closes.

It's pitiful how weak she is compared with the two men. She flaps on the deck like a fish. When she hears Haas call her a Malay trollop, her chest fills with so much hatred she's sure the power of it will help her break free of her restraints. She wants to hurt these men, to sink her heel into their scrotums, to stomp on their fleshy throats. She yearns to kill them, these fat devil men. She wants to kill them.

But she can't.

When they lift her, she writhes in their strong hold, she bucks her legs, but they easily hoist her onto the side of the tramp and roll her into the dark sea.

The first shock of the cold ocean smites the fury from her. She falls through the water, as swiftly as a coin. Blackness smothers her, surrounds her in tiny bubbles. The blurred lights of the tramp waver and dim as she sinks. She panics, inhales salty water through her nostrils. A blank pressure builds inside her head. She feels she might burst.

Putri …

Her descent slows. Specks of seaweed and silt swirl around her head, punctuate the murky depths.

Putri … Princess …

The Ocean Queen whispers to her, wraps her warm arms around Mina's constricted body. Loosens the folds. Nyai Loro Kidul promises her much, buoys her descent.

Mina's limbs relax and the tramp is nothing but a glowing spot in the distance.

The silken water draws Mina further down into nothingness.

Until she is finally back in the sunlight, scaling fish with her mother.

Acknowledgements

I have written these stories over several years now and there are many wonderful people to thank. Special thank you to my publisher, Aviva Tuffield, who has been so supportive and a great champion of me and my work. Thank you to everyone at UQP, especially Cathy Vallance and Vanessa Pellatt, for helping me shape this book. I am very grateful to the *Griffith Review* team, particularly Ashley Hay and John Tague, for originally publishing *Annah the Javanese*, and to Seizure Viva la Novella and Alice Grundy for publishing *The Fish Girl*.

I have been lucky to belong to some stellar writers' groups and to be surrounded by great writers who have helped me develop these pieces. Thank you to Emma Doolan, Kathy George, Andrea Baldwin, Lesley Hawkes, Trudie Murrell, Janaka Malwatta, Jonathan Hadwen, Catherine Baskerville, Chloe Callistemon and Rohan Jayasinghe. To Laura Elvery – you are forever inspiring and I am sure many of these stories would not have been written had I not met you in our PhD years. Thank you.

Versions of the following stories have appeared online and in print. 'Annah the Javanese' in *Griffith Review* 66: The Light

Ascending; 'Invitation' in *Meanjin*, Spring, 2018; 'Hardflip', *Australian Book Review*, online; 'Hazel', *The Saturday Paper*, 29 August 2020; 'Dignity' in *Best Summer Stories*, 2018; 'Growth', in *Best Australian Stories*, 2017 & *Review of Australian Fiction*, Volume 21, 2017; 'Cinta Ku', in *We Stand in that Place*, 2020; 'So Many Ways', in Kill Your Darlings, *New Australian Fiction*, 2020; *The Fish Girl*, Seizure Viva la Novella, 2017. Huge thank you to the editors of these publications and to the Australia Council for the Arts for their generous support. Also, I am incredibly grateful to W. H. Chong for the stunning cover artwork.

Thank you to Mum and Papa and to all my extended family. Your rich lives and thoughts inspire so much to be found in my stories. Particular thanks to Tina and Vinnie; Liam and Damien; Samantha Paxton, for fast becoming my muse; and to Dave and Jett, for the correct skateboarding terms and feats. All my love to my children, Bianca, Jett and Mae. I am so proud of you.

UQP Quentin Bryce Award 2022

The Burnished Sun
Mirandi Riwoe

About the UQP Quentin Bryce Award

The Honourable Dame Quentin Bryce AD CVO is an alumna of the University of Queensland, where she completed a Bachelor of Arts and a Bachelor of Laws before becoming one of the first women admitted to the Queensland Bar. In 1968 Quentin Bryce became the first woman appointed as a faculty member of the University of Queensland's Law School. From 2003 to 2008 she served as the twenty-fourth Governor of Queensland, and from 2008 to 2014 she was the twenty-fifth Governor General of Australia, the first woman to hold the office.

In addition to her professional roles, Quentin Bryce has always been a strong supporter of the arts and Australia's cultural life and is an ambassador for many related organisations, including the Stella Prize and the Indigenous Literacy Foundation. Across many decades she has championed the University of Queensland Press (UQP), its books and authors.

To honour and celebrate her impressive career and legacy, the University of Queensland and UQP have jointly established the UQP Quentin Bryce Award. The award recognises one book on UQP's list each year that celebrates women's lives and/or promotes gender equality.